VIATICUM

Viaticum

A Novel

Natelle Fitzgerald

CANADA

Library and Archives Canada Cataloguing in Publication

Title: Viaticum : a novel / Natelle Fitzgerald.
Names: Fitzgerald, Natelle, 1977– author.

Identifiers: Canadiana 20190154756 | ISBN 9781988098876 (softcover)

Classification: LCC PS8611.I8913 V53 2019 | DDC C813/.6—dc23

Printed and bound in Canada on 100% recycled paper.

Now Or Never Publishing
901, 163 Street
Surrey, British Columbia
Canada V4A 9T8

nonpublishing.com
Fighting Words.

We gratefully acknowledge the support of the Canada Council for the Arts
and the British Columbia Arts Council for our publishing program.

For my husband, Pierre.

Viaticum: 1. Holy Communion given to one dying or in danger of death.
2. Supplies or money for a journey.

Prologue

Tall, gaunt, silent, his head bent forward in an attitude of prayer, Matt Campbell sat beside the dying man and imagined a calm, clear pool of water. He pictured the pale, round stones on the bottom; he imagined a soothing coolness across his own brow. If he could only make his own mind still enough, his own thoughts clear enough, he believed or hoped or wished that the dying man, from whatever shadow realm he now wandered, might perceive his presence by the bedside and know, in some way, on some level, that he was not alone. It was all there was left to do.

Hours passed. A square of sunlight crept across the grey flagstones then up onto the bed, warming the intricate reds and yellows of the batik quilt that Sasha had brought back from Indonesia; then it stretched across, the carnations on the nightstand suddenly numinous, the light in the room turning gold then deepening, like autumn, like evening; then, just when it seemed that twilight had finally descended, a last gasp of daylight pierced the far window and flared with strange and sudden brilliance on a small, framed photograph that was half-hidden by the flowers.

Look at us. See us. The light was piercing, urgent. Matt leaned forward and picked the picture up off the nightstand. For weeks, he'd avoided looking at it; it felt too intimate, too private, too deep. Now, he studied the faces there, running his fingers gently over the glass.

The picture showed a slim young woman with dark hair cut in straight bangs across her forehead; a little boy of about four or five sat on her lap, his smile so gleeful Matt could almost hear a gurgle of childish laughter just looking at him. This was the man's wife and son, he assumed, and yet there'd been no sign of them, no mention of their absence. It made him sad. He kept hoping they'd show, but they didn't.

Instead, it was the man's ageing parents that stayed with him at the hospice. A few of his co-workers had visited also: big, strapping oil-workers who'd driven all the way from North Dakota on their week off, who'd swaggered in full of brave humor and good intentions, then grown awkward and self-conscious when they saw their friend so whittled away by cancer. Why did it tear his heart so badly to see these big, strong men acting so unsure? Matt had made a point to be extra kind to them, to let them know that the quiet halls, the artwork, the beautiful healing space that Sasha had taken such exquisite care to create, was for them also, lumbering and imperfect as they were.

They were like him, he thought, how he used to be.

He sighed, then gently placed the picture back on the nightstand, careful to arrange it exactly as it had been, but the light, its urgency, was gone. Was he wrong to have read some meaning into it? Some demand? He was allowing this death to get to him, he knew. It was the man's age, the nature of his disease, taking Matt back to things best left alone. Matt shook his head, hoping to clear it. Again, he closed his eyes. Again, he tried to picture the pool.

Suddenly, the man's breathing began to change. It was a subtle difference, an airiness, a frailty, something indescribable; yet Matt recognized it right away. He'd heard it before. The man's breath hiccupped, then caught, then hiccupped again. It was time. He went out to the hall and called Sasha, then went to find the parents.

They weren't in the reading room or at reception, so he continued out through the main entrance, then across the lawn, past the pond, the walking trail, the quiet benches tucked under the trees. Down the hill, the lights of Saltery Bay twinkled along the edge of the harbor; the water in the bay was still milky and full of light, the dark shapes of the hills rising sharply all around it. He paused for a moment, looking down. The town had the same smallness, the same slowness as when he'd arrived here years ago; yet how different it appeared to him now! The first time he'd set foot on the island it had been foggy; the town an orange smear in the darkness, like a fire burning under a cloud. It had seemed so sinister to him then, jealous of its lies, its secrets. He shivered. He did not like to think about that time in his life, but this death, this relatively young man . . . it haunted him. Crossing his arms over his chest and pulling his sweater tight around him, he hurried on.

At the back of the property where the lawn butted up against the forest, he came to a tiny chapel. The building was already cloaked in shadow, barely visible except for a small flickering in the stained-glass windows. He breathed a sigh of relief. The parents were inside. He'd found them. He took a deep breath, then paused before entering. No matter how much people prepared, no matter how long they'd been expecting it, news of death's imminent arrival always came as a shock. He stood for a moment, wishing the parents peace; then slowly, quietly, he opened the chapel door.

They were seated in the front pew, leaning against one another, maybe sleeping. Light from a tiered rack of candles washed over them, lapping up against the arched beams of the ceiling, glittering on the icons on the altar: Jesus on the cross, a smiling Buddha, a cosmic Ganesh, amongst the many others Sasha had collected in her travels. Death is the one thing we all share, she'd told him once, the only universal, and then, out of nowhere, another memory, not in Sasha's voice, not in his own but a whisper, like someone leaning close and whispering in his ear: *everybody dies* . . . and suddenly the candles became the city lights streaking by and his face began to prickle with shame.

When he shook himself free, he found that the parents had turned in their seats and were staring at him: the woman, tiny and frail with fading hair and fading skin, the ghost of a great beauty in the cut of her cheeks; the man a mirror of what the son must have been: tall, broad-shouldered, stoic. Matt cleared his throat. "It's time," he said as softly as he could. "You should come and be with him now. Please, follow me."

He led them gently, oh so gently, across the lawn, then back to the room where they knelt, one on each side of the bed, holding their dying son's hands. The mother whispered softly but Matt couldn't make out her words. The father said, "I love you, I love you," in a strangled voice then was silent. Matt turned on the lamp. He stood quietly next to the door.

Soon, Sasha arrived, cold colouring her cheeks, clinging to her sweater. As a palliative nurse and the hospice owner, she always came at the end, in case there were complications. She nodded to Matt as she entered the room and he took his leave.

He went back outside and crossed to the far side of the property, passed the maintenance shed to where a small trailer stood half-hidden amongst a tangle of black berry and alder. A wave of relief swept over him: he was home.

When the door was shut safely behind him, he crumpled. All the tension he'd been holding inside left him in a great whoosh of air. He held his head in his hands, leaning forward with his elbows on his knees. The parents, the suffering, the sadness . . . It never got easier. Sasha kept reassuring him that his reactions were normal, that it meant he was still human, but sometimes he thought he couldn't stand to see another death; he'd drunk so much grief working here; he'd breathed it, infused it in his pores . . . When would it be enough? he wondered. Would it ever be enough? He didn't know.

Shaking, he sat down on the edge of the bed and turned on the lamp. The light revealed a small and bare room. There was a bed, a dresser, a nightstand, not much else. Everything else he needed he used at the hospice: the kitchen, the laundry, the shower. Sasha teased him about it. She said he was either the eternal bachelor or a saint. But he liked the simplicity, needed it. The bareness in the trailer calmed him somehow. It made him feel like life was manageable, contained, not squirming out from underneath like it could do, like it had done once before.

He took several slow, deep breaths, then opened the top drawer of the nightstand. With infinite care, he took out a small mirror with a brass stand, a plain linen cloth and a candle. He set them down, then stood, walked over to the window and opened it. Cold rushed in and quickly filled the room. He breathed deeply, feeling the cold on his face, holding it in his lungs, then he sat back down on the bed. He lit the candle, pausing as the flame flickered then steadied itself. Next, he stood the mirror upright on the stand, catching a glimpse of his own fingers, his own grizzled face with its silver stubble, its hollow cheeks and sad grey eyes in the glass, then slowly, deliberately, he covered the mirror with the cloth.

There.

He didn't actually believe that souls could bounce back, that departing souls might mistake a mirror for a window and get trapped on Earth to spend the rest of eternity flapping around like a wounded bird. It was an arcane belief, medieval even, and yet the ritual calmed him; it made him feel neat, quiet inside. It helped him remember why he'd come here, why he'd stayed. He could still picture her down to the smallest line on her face. She had given him a gift. He would not forget it. He bent his head against his chest and whispered "Annika, Annika, Annika."

PART ONE

CHAPTER ONE

The clean, bright waiting room filled Annika Torrey with dread. Everything was different now. Everything had changed. Sometime in the past three years, she did not know when, Dr. Zagar's once familiar waiting area had been renovated: the old oriental rugs replaced by a blonde parquet floor; the eclectic collection of armchairs she'd once found so cozy exchanged for molded rows of blue plastic seating. In the corner, there was a new children's play area stocked with blocks and crayons and colouring books, while a rack on the wall showcased trendy magazines. The new décor was clean and modern; yet Annika sensed a dagger of blame in its brightness, like a long-lost friend who proclaims their joy at your return while the wrinkles round their eyes and their half-grown children in the hall whisper of time lost, of years gone by, of missed opportunities that can never be retrieved.

She pressed her hands together in front of her and found that they were shaking. Her foot twitched on the floor. There were two others waiting also: a young, athletic-looking man in grey sweats, one long leg held straight out in front of him, his sweat pants bulking around a white cast that was visible at the foot; and an elderly woman bundled into a puffy, green parka, her tiny shriveled face trembling constantly as if the infirmity came from deep within her. Neither met Annika's eyes.

Even as she sat waiting, Annika could feel the strange hardness sitting like a stone inside her belly. It was not a pain, exactly, but a hardness, a stubborn knot in the v of her ribs that wouldn't go away. For months, she'd convinced herself it was only a cramp until one awful morning, two weeks earlier, she'd looked in the mirror to find the person looking back was almost unrecogniz-able: a thin haggard waif with crispy hair, like a witch . . . Why didn't I come sooner? she moaned inwardly, a fresh wave of anx-iety swelling inside her. She did not want to think about why the doctor needed to speak with her in person. She did not want to think about what any of it might mean.

Desperate for distraction, she studied the posters on the wall. There were three of them, all the same size, arranged neatly in a row: a picture of an elderly couple on bicycles, smiling and fit; a young man in a lamp lit room staring sadly into space; and the cross-section of a woman's breast like a pink-volcano. Below the pictures were slogans in blue and teal and magenta lettering: Choices Homecare, Depression Hurts, Breast Health Awareness Starts With You. She closed her eyes.

Before the renovation, there'd been a large framed print, a black and white drawing that used to hang where the posters were now, and she found herself wishing it was still there. It used to comfort her; she wasn't sure why.

The drawing had depicted a scene in a country home: a young woman lying on a bed amidst tangled sheets, her eyes closed; a man and woman, her parents one assumed, were look-ing on; the man standing, his wide rough features creased with worry; the woman seated in front of him on a plain hard chair; his hand resting on her shoulder, her face buried in her hands. In the foreground of this tableau, a well-dressed man with an intel-lectual air about him was seated at a table, his brow furrowed as he rubbed his beard in concentration? Frustration? It was difficult to say. Underneath the picture had been two words in simple black font: The Doctor.

Years earlier, when Annika and her ex-husband Hamish used to come to Dr. Zagar's office together, he'd said, "What an awful picture. What a terrible message to send," and she'd kept silent, unable to admit her fascination with the drawing or the fact that she'd studied its every detail. Was the girl alive? Would the doc-tor save her? What was wrong with her? The tangled fabric, the dark shadows, the worry in the faces . . . It had made her own worries feel less strange, like they were part of some larger human drama, one that had been going on long before her and would go on long after. It had made her feel less alone. Still, she'd kept her opinions to herself. Hamish wouldn't have understood. He'd have argued that darkness and grief were inappropriate to a doctor's office; he'd have said that death was not a suitable preoccupation for someone in the hopeful stage of trying to conceive a baby, and then things would have broken down along their usual fault lines: Hamish the reasonable and Annika the crazy, not that it made any difference now.

Hamish had moved on and the picture had been taken down.

Suddenly, the door to the inner office swung open and a heavy-set man with a greying mustache and ball cap came out and began walking away, head down and shoulders hunched, his body curved inwards as if ushering away an awful secret.

"Annika Torrey?"

Annika looked up. The pretty, blonde secretary was standing in the doorway to the inner office, holding a clipboard, her face pleasant and inscrutable. Annika stood. "Right this way, please," the secretary said. Annika followed her wordlessly through a door into an interior warren of doors and hallways that remained untouched by the renovations.

The secretary opened the door to an examining room. "Have a seat. Dr. Zagar will be right with you," she said, then she closed the door and Annika was alone.

The room was Spartan. Bare. There was an examining table. An eyechart. A small window high on the wall that let in a pale white square of late October sun. Annika could hear a man's voice rumbling through the wall but couldn't make out what he was saying.

When she'd gone to the cancer clinic for the tests, the technicians kept leaving her alone like this in rooms. They'd been friendly and professional and tried to make her feel comfortable but then they'd leave, and she'd be alone, as if illness had already singled her out, had already marked her. In the white room with the tube she'd been able to see them through the window. Their voices had come over an intercom and told her what to do.

There'd been a red light and a green light and even though she was used to being alone, seeing them there on the other side had filled her with terror and she'd had to fight the urge to spring up and pound against the glass for it felt like her aloneness, secret for so long, had finally taken on walls and locked her in.

Now the door opened and Dr. Zagar came in, a severe little woman with short salt and pepper hair and wire-framed glasses. She sat on the stool with her legs spread wide, her grey trousers climbing up her skinny shins so there was a flash of bony white above the severe line of her black socks. She looked down at the chart, then at Annika, then down at the chart again.

Annika held her breath.

"The results came back from oncology and I wanted to discuss them with you in person," the little doctor began. She took off her glasses and put them on the table. She looked Annika in the eyes.

And Annika knew.

Sound drained from the world. It bled slowly from the too bright little room until there was a strange blankness, a kind of vacuum of sound.

"I'm afraid that the growth is in fact a cancer, and that it's quite advanced." The doctor's voice came from far away. Annika heard it and did not hear it both at the same time. "It's a stage four malignancy on top of the pancreas."

Annika blinked. The room seemed too bright, overexposed, every detail of it pierced through with awareness and heightened somehow: a cob web in the corner of the window, a crinkle in the paper on the examining table that lifted and fell in an unfelt draft, the wrinkles around the doctor's eyes.

October was a hard light, she thought. It found people out and pierced right through them. One time, when she was young, she'd swept up a nest of field mice from under the grain bin by accident and the little babies had scattered over the boards. They'd been naked and translucent and curled like leaves and the hard white light from the window had pierced right through their bodies so she could see their little hearts fluttering inside then her father had come in as she tried to gather them up and said, it's too late, you can't put them back now, your smell is on them, what's done is done, and so she'd gone out behind the barn and crushed them with a stone.

Dr. Zagar's mouth moved and words came out. Treatment. Care. Possibility. Annika thought about the mice and how nothing could ever go back to the way it was and how she had to crush them even though she hadn't wanted to.

A hand waved in front of her eyes. "Annika? Annika? Do you understand what I'm saying?"

She blinked. It was too bright. The silence roared all around her.

"Can you acknowledge that you hear me? I need to know that you understand."

Annika looked into the Doctor's face and there was a horrible blank feeling and then it snapped to, a kind of knowing, as if the hard light pierced right through the doctor as well, illuminating the most intimate details of her life. For years, Annika had assumed that Dr. Zagar was a lesbian until Hamish, whose parents travelled in the doctor's circle, informed her that the androgynous German was in fact married to a man and had two children.

Annika had never been able to picture what this other woman's life was like, yet now here it was, all at once, right there and so very obvious: Dr. Zagar driving home eating nuts and yoghurt in the car, ordering her kids around as she made dinner, having a glass of wine with a weedy academic husband, going to bed and waking up and coming to work again and going home again. Oh yes, it was right in front of her face, the traffic and the turkey at Thanksgiving and the ageing parents and the phone calls across the ocean. A life full of motion and people and tasks, in the hard light, right there.

"Do you understand what I'm saying?"

And why is it that one life fills up as another empties? Why is it that one is brimming and bursting at the seams while another winds down and shrinks to a desk and a couch in a tiny apartment, that one goes forward, ever forward into the loud, busy bluster of the world and another is sucked back into a bubble of silence as bright and unforgiving as the pale October sun? "Why?"

"Excuse me?"

"Why?" Annika repeated. Her own voice came from far away. It seemed important that this question be answered although she wasn't entirely sure what she was asking.

"Well, it's hard to say why, exactly," the doctor began slowly. "In terms of what causes it at the cellular level, it's the mutation of a proto-onco gene which is the gene responsible for cell division; the mutation causes uncontrolled cell-division, so you get a tumor." Her voice gained confidence as she entered the certainties of science.

"As to the why the gene mutates in the first place . . . there could be a whole host of reasons."

Annika blinked in the hard-white light.

"Genetics play a part, certainly. Environment. Certain chemicals. Carcinogens. And then there are the lifestyle culprits: drinking, smoking, stress. But at the end of the day it's impossible to say, exactly, because our genes are mutating all the time. If people were to live long enough, eventually we'd all die of cancer. At the end of the day, it's a game of probability. Chance."

Chance. Genes. Small, scattering things. Like baby mice, like the seeds across the floor . . . *Behold the sower went out to sow . . .* in her mind she could see the hard light in that old Church with its plain windows. Why did she think of it now? Other Churches had stained glass windows that were beautiful and ornate and threw patterns of colour into the aisles but in Rose Prairie the windows had been bare, and the sun used to come in hard on Sunday mornings and make all the faces ugly *and some fell beside the road, and the birds came and ate them up . . .* She shook her head. Stop, she thought. Stop.

"Just breathing oxygen introduces free radicals into the blood. Highly reactive molecules that cause all kinds of chemical reactions. I sometimes tell people, the number one cause of cancer, is life." Dr. Zagar barked a short dry laugh, then stopped.

And others fell among the thorns and the thorns came up and choked them out . . . It was as if the preacher's voice was still there, twenty years later, alive inside her brain. Why did it come to her now? She didn't believe those things anymore. She'd left that life behind.

Again, she shook her head. She took a deep breath and squared her shoulders. Focus, she told herself. She looked the doctor in the eyes. "So, what are you saying? I need to know how long." Her voice came out surprisingly clear and business-like.

"There are options we can explore but..."

"Please."

Dr. Zagar looked down at the floor, nodded her head slowly then looked back up. "Well, treatment options at this point are quite limited. It's difficult to predict exact time frames, but this is a very aggressive form. I would say six months to a year, no more. I'm truly sorry."

Annika nodded. She didn't feel much of anything, only this strange whirl of unrelated thoughts and the brightness. She forced herself to sit up straight and nod as Dr. Zagar went on about possibilities, about what to expect. The little doctor was very good at her job, compassionate yet direct. In a far-off part of her mind, Annika recognized this. She admired it. *One day, I would like to thank her*, she thought. *One day, if I get the chance.*

"People often need time to think, and I want to respect that, but if I may give you some advice, I wouldn't wait too long to come up with a plan," the doctor said.

"Yes. I understand." Annika stood to leave but her knees buckled underneath her, and she had to grab the counter for support. The touch of the doctor's hand on her back was dry and light and hollow, like a bird.

"Sit, please. You've had a shock. Is there anyone you'd like me to call?"

"Excuse me?"

"A friend? A family member? Someone to drive you home?"

"Who?"

"Do you have any family here?"

She shook her head. "No, no they're all still in Montana. We're not close."

"I could call Hamish for you."

She blinked. *Did she not know?* "Hamish and I aren't . . ." she said slowly.

"Yes, I know but surely he would . . ."

She frowned. Surely he wouldn't. He'd told her that she couldn't even call since he'd moved in with his new woman. He'd told her it was like ripping a Band-Aid. He'd called it letting go. "No, I'll be okay," she said. "I'll be fine."

She closed her eyes, took a deep breath and stood again, determined not to waver. She clenched her guts and steeled herself like she'd learned to do when she'd worked fighting forest fires many years earlier. A person made choices and bore the consequences. A person could suffer most anything if they tried. She believed this. She thanked the Doctor firmly and walked out into the bright and brittle air.

CHAPTER TWO

Standing alone beside the buffet in the Sheraton's Ball Room A, Matt Campbell popped chilled prawns into his mouth one after another and listened to the bright, busy chatter of his colleagues as it rose up on the tinkling air all around him. He wasn't quite sure what he was listening for: a honk of exaggeration, a squeak of untruth, a rush, a nervousness, something, anything really, that might indicate someone else felt the same way he did; yet the voices rose and fell so effortlessly, the laughter expanded so seamlessly into the twinkling lights and overall buzz of excitement, he was almost convinced that his colleagues' optimism was genuine. As his eyes shifted from one glowing face to another, he felt his own failures wake up inside him, squirming around like a dirty secret.

It wasn't quite noon yet and already the atmosphere seemed more like a cocktail party than an industry conference. Throughout the wide, elegant room, realtors from across the Northwest, nearly identical in their dark business attire, were gathering in groups of three or four, drinks in hand, chatting excitedly to one another; others had seated themselves around the small tables on outskirts of the room and were leaning towards one another, deep in conversation, while teams of black-clad servers went back and forth, weaving through the crowd, clearing glassware and re-stocking the buffet, a lavish spread of cold meats and cheese boards and bowls of fruit with great clusters of purple grapes overflowing onto the dazzling white tablecloth *just so*.

It was all so grandiose, so excessive . . . Was he wrong to read a note of desperation into it? But then, looking at the faces . . . they seemed so keen, so sure of themselves . . . He reached for another prawn, but his hand was intercepted. Startled, he whirled around to find himself staring down into the impossibly white smile of Sandy Tagliatti, the year's keynote speaker.

"Matt Campbell," she said, staring meaningfully into his eyes. "How ARE you?" She had a way of making her every word vibrate with knowing and possibility, as if even this simple question were an invitation to conspire.

"Busy," he heard himself say, "I'm super busy." He was still holding one of the wet, papery shrimp tails and didn't know where to put it. A prickle of heat began at his collar. He was a blusher, a mad blusher, and he hated it.

Fortunately for him, Sandy Tagliatti wasn't the shaking type. Seattle's top sales agent four years running, the pert forty-something dynamo with her bright eyes and flowing red mane knew a thing or two about cultivating intimacy and the fact that they both worked Seattle North put them on terms far more intimate than a handshake, apparently. She leaned in so close he could feel her breast brush against his arm. Lightly, but there. "I KNOW what you mean," she said, shaking her head as if he'd just offered some profound insight. "I'm just RUN, absolutely RUN off my feet these days. All these rumors . . . I wish someone would tell MY clients there's a downturn."

He laughed. She laughed. Her face was all feature: big lips and big eyes and big hair like one of those Claymation princesses from his son Jacob's cartoons.

As their laughter petered off, Matt was aware that it was his turn to speak, to say something witty or charming in return, but he paused, still distracted by the shrimp tails in his hand. He saw Sandy Tagliatti's smile dim ever so slightly. Her eyes flickered away, scoping out another more beneficial conversation, perhaps. "I saw your talk this morning," he recovered. "It was great. I mean, it inspired me."

She stood, head cocked to one side, the breast still touching his arm, the smile fixed on her face. "I felt like I could relate to the part about overcoming your personal darkness. Being your own worst enemy and all of that," he fumbled on, each word digging him deeper in a direction that felt at once too personal and yet oddly clichéd; her wide, fixed smile goading him into ever more explanation. "I mean, I've been through some things myself and can understand that feeling, like you've screwed up and not being able to get out of it . . ." he stammered, then trailed off.

Her talk, billed on the schedule as '*How To Be A Top Sales Agent,*' had turned out to be more like an AA meeting or one of those religious revival things he'd seen on TV. There'd been no props, no PowerPoint, just her, Sandy Tagliatti, wide-eyed and sincere at the front of the room, talking about her life. It would have made a good movie: a small-town girl pregnant at 19; an abusive marriage to the local cop; a desperate flight in the middle of the night with three small children in the backseat; a series of dead end jobs that barely paid the bills; several years battling depression; then the great turnaround, the grand redemption after she'd taken her real estate course. Now, at forty-five, Sandy Tagliatti owned her own house. She owned a cottage on the Oregon coast. Her children were all in University, their tuition paid for. Selling Real Estate had saved her life, she'd whispered fiercely to the crowded room, her eyes brimming with tears. "You just have to work hard, you have to beat that pavement till it bleeds then beat it some more," she'd said at which point everyone had started murmuring and nodding in agreement, while he'd sat with his arms crossed and his face on fire, acutely aware, suddenly, of all the time he'd wasted in the past months: the coffee shops, the driving around, the phone that never rang.

The blush expanded across his face. He could feel it blossoming over his cheeks like a dirty algal bloom. "You know, the part where you were running from your husband, when you were in the car, wondering what you were going to do . . ." he continued then trailed off.

Sandy Tagliatti blinked once then patted his arm, "I'm SO glad you enjoyed it, Matt," she said, then turned to gaze out over the buffet. She shook her head as if in amazement. "What a spread! I think it gets better every year." She smiled, then he smiled, then she turned, and he watched her bustle off, her perky little rear-end practically shrink-wrapped into an impossible pencil skirt, her high-heels clicking on the floor. A cluster of smiling realtors opened up to receive her and shortly he heard great peals of laughter rise up in the air.

He looked around again, desperate for a familiar face, for some friendly group he might hide in, and his eyes alighted on the bar.

The bar was set into the wall in the far corner of the room, a kind of twinkling alcove with the glassware racked up above and the bottles on lighted tiers behind, their browns, blues and greens glowing softly like the stained-glass windows of a Church. In front of the bottles, a strapping young bartender presided, his features stoic, his dark hair glistening in the twinkling light. A long line of would-be drinkers snaked out in front of him, so the young man was busy; his hands were a blur of motion; yet there remained a stillness about him, an aura of calm. Even from across the room Matt recognized it, having been a bartender himself most of his adult life. He knew the feeling, that feeling of being in perfect control, of knowing exactly where everything was, knowing that your hands knew exactly what to do without thinking. He watched the young man working and envied him the solitude of his position; he envied him the neatness, the sureness of that type of knowing.

Watching, he could practically feel the cool, simple weight of a glass in his own hands. He could feel the bottles, the ice scoop, the calm . . . he let his mind go, imagining himself in the young man's place and just like that, the desire for a drink bullied its way to consciousness, as if it were always just there, waiting behind a door in his mind, waiting for some small crack in his resolve. A drink! How he wanted, how he needed a drink! That burn, that lovely tingling heat in the back of the throat and then the loosening, the smoothing out of all the tangledness inside . . .

He shook his head abruptly and turned away. He'd made promises, rules for himself to follow when it came to the drinking; they had to do with his wife and his son and the kind of man he wanted to be, and though they were privately held, though he'd never made a great drama of his renunciation, his rules were still important to him. They meant something. Sometimes he felt like they were all that was holding him together.

He took a deep breath, squared his shoulders and drew himself up tall. No matter how bad things seemed, he wasn't going to go down that road again. Not yet. He steeled himself, trying to muster what remained of his willpower to the task of networking, then, just at that moment, a scraggly looking young man pulled up next to him at the buffet.

Matt wiped his hand on his pants. He pocketed the tails. He was about to introduce himself, then hesitated, frowning slightly.

There was something strange about the man. His brown suit stood out amongst the blacks and greys of the other conference attendees; it didn't quite fit him right, either, sagging over his lanky frame, gathering in sad puckers at the knees and elbows. He seemed much younger than the others and his face had a wild look; his bulging eyes darting nervously from person to person; his hair strangely dull and dusty looking, a kind of matte blond that was dead to the lights. An antique looking leather satchel was slung over his shoulder.

Matt began to turn away, then stopped himself. Was he simply making excuses again? Procrastinating? It was impossible to tell who was worth knowing in this business with so many second chancers and hard-luck stories walking around, he reminded himself. Christ look at me, he thought. He held out his hand. "Hi there. I'm Matt Campbell. We haven't met yet."

The young man started. He looked at Matt's hand then at Matt. The lanyard around his neck was all twisted up so that Matt couldn't read the name tag. They stood facing one another for a long moment, then, after what seemed an eternity, the young man held out a strangely weather-beaten hand.

Matt gripped it. He caught a glimpse of blue ink at the wrist, barbed wire or thorns, something twisted and prickly tattooed just out of sight but chose to ignore it. "Quite the spread, isn't it?" he offered. "I think it gets better every year."

The man's feral eyes peered at him incredulously from a sallow face darkened by stubble, then a strange expression spread over his gaunt features, like the dawning of a malevolent awareness. "Oh yes, it's very nice indeed, Mr. Campbell," he said. "I particularly enjoy these little croissant type things. Aren't they just fabulous? Don't mind if I do, actually." Then, in a motion that seemed more animal than human, the man unslung the satchel from his neck, flipped open the flap and held it against the edge of the table.

It took Matt a moment to understand what was happening. He watched dumbfounded as the man grabbed an entire tray of sandwiches, croissants filled with roast beef and ham and cheese, and dumped them into the satchel's gaping mouth. Cherry tomatoes bounced on the floor and rolled away. Matt blinked. The lanyard had untwisted now so he could read the card; the writing was different from the neatly-typed name tags being handed out at the front. In a handwritten scrawl the card read: Uncle Buck.

Quickly, Uncle Buck hefted the satchel back over his shoulder. He fixed Matt with his glittering eyes and whispered, "It's a house of cards, man. It's all a fucking house of cards," with that same malicious awareness, then his eyes darted about again, settling briefly on the main entrance where several of the black-clad servers were speaking urgently to a burly oriental man with a buzz cut and head-set. "Gotta run," Uncle Buck concluded, winking at Matt before taking off, weaving in and out of the dark clusters of happy realtors as the burly manager straight-lined the buffet, arcing and ducking and coming in behind the tables until he at last made the entrance and was gone into a slip of grey light that came in from the lobby.

Then the manager was there, standing next to Matt, red-faced and huffing. "Did you see him? Did you see where he went?"

Matt pointed to the door, feeling ashamed and absurd all at once. "He got out. I saw him go."

The manager shook his head. There were beads of sweat on his scalp, clinging between the thin spiky hairs. Two dark, wet patches were forming under the arms of his burgundy shirt. "Poachers," he said grimly, talking to Matt but looking towards the door. "This group of street punks. One of them gets a suit and then they're in here after a free lunch . . ." He looked at Matt directly now, his face suddenly open and searching, like a small child looking for approval. "It's impossible to police the door every second with this many people, you know what I mean?"

Matt said he did know and that it must be tough and that they were doing a great job, then he watched the manager lumber off, just a kid really, despite his position, just a regular guy who was worried, like the rest of them, that he was doing everything wrong.

Matt stood, alone again, still beside the buffet, pondering this latest humiliation, his own inaction, his lack of social acuity, all of it. He felt deflated, the false glimmer of determination with which he'd begun the day utterly gone. He took one last look around the ballroom, then walked out through the main doors and into the lobby.

He intended to go home. He went down to the parking garage, got in his car and drove out into the downtown core where the canyons between the buildings were already filling with shadow, then he continued northwards, away from the city, the towering glass of the skyscrapers behind him glazed dull grey in the colourless October afternoon. Already, his thoughts were reaching towards Jen and Jacob, reaching like a drowning man for home, for the simplicity of warmth, for Jacob's sidelong press against him when he read him bedtime stories; for Jen, Jen in the early morning before she remembered her grievances against him, sliding across the cool sheets to press her sleepy, warm body into his back. Yes, he intended to go home to his family.

He exited onto the viaduct, a great concrete tentacle that curled down under the Interstate before it ramped back up onto the other side and in the roaring gloom under the highway he saw sleeping bags and shopping bags and pillows tucked in the crook where the concrete retaining wall met the road above. Uncle Buck was suddenly in his mind again. A house of cards. A house of fucking cards, he'd whispered. Matt couldn't get it out of his head.

Now he merged up onto the Interstate and joined the lines of traffic that were snaking northwards, the red taillights ahead of him sparking along the grey ribbon of the road, the whole procession stopping and starting mindlessly like one of those Chinese dragons in the New Year's Parade he'd gone to with Jacob. Eventually, the traffic loosened, and he passed the lake, its moody surface scuffed by the wind, then he exited the highway and after a series of stoplights and turns, he was back in his own subdivision: Sandy Hills.

Usually he felt a twinge of pride when he entered Sandy Hills, yet on this day the great brick sign with its nostalgic cursive lettering irritated him. It was too big, too pretentious somehow. There were no hills in Sandy Hills, no sand, just a series of empty lots still for sale and street upon street of sprawling brick and beige houses.

He slowed the car to a crawl. Most of the houses were empty at this hour and their darkened windows took up his reflection, passing it from house to house, like a secret. Suddenly he wasn't sure if he even wanted to go home. Not yet. He felt strange, guilty somehow, though he hadn't really done anything.

The car growled along, creeping slowly past the same houses he drove by every day; yet somehow it all seemed strange to him, as if he were seeing it for the first time. Now, as he drove, the signs began to jump out at him. They'd been there before, but somehow, he'd failed to notice how many of them there actually were. FOR SALE in bold red. REDUCED in screaming fluorescence and now here was one that was different, one that had changed overnight: FORECLOSED in solemn black, the seal of doom.

At the conference, they kept saying that Seattle would be saved by foreign investment, that what was happening in the rest of the country couldn't happen here, yet he no longer felt persuaded. The fact was, his listings simply weren't moving. Maybe he wasn't productive all the time, maybe he wasn't Sandy Togliatti, but there were only so many cold calls he could make, only so many open houses he could host. And the signs. He wasn't imagining the signs. They were everywhere.

He pulled over to the side of the road. He foresaw a fight with Jen if he went back now. She'd wonder why he was home early and then what would he say? That he'd just left the conference? That he'd felt too anxious and ashamed? That he'd been humiliated by a street kid stealing sandwiches? He didn't know what he'd say. He sat with the engine idling, staring at his own house up the street, its steeply angled roof slashed onto the darkening clouds above. It was strange to look at it from this perspective. He felt removed from it somehow, like a spy on his own life, and as he sat there looking at the house with its brick entranceway, its great bay windows dominating the front, its curving flagstone drive and double car garage and all the bells and whistles that were meant to increase the resale value but were, in fact, exactly the same as every other house on the street, as he sat there looking at it, his face began to burn.

His plan had been to flip it. Do some renos, then make a chunk of cash on the turnover. He knew people who made their living that way, colleagues who'd made 60, 70 grand, a 100 even on the resale of their homes. He'd been confident then, still vain enough to believe his initial success at the real estate game had something to do with talent. It made him squirm to think of it now . . . how they'd encouraged him, his mother and Jen's parents congratulating him as if he'd surmounted some great pinnacle of adulthood and was finally taking responsibility, treating the whole purchase like it was some sort of cathartic surrender to the obligations of manhood or fatherhood or husbandhood or what the fuck ever, he didn't even know.

Suddenly, he jammed his foot down on the gas and cut the wheel so that his tires screamed against the pale dead asphalt. Fuck it, he said. The car accelerated recklessly, and he made the loop of the cul-de-sac without braking, his stomach lurching as the car was sucked sideways. Part of him wanted Jen to look out the window and see him . . . part of him wanted some housewife to report him to the neighbourhood watch, to come out on the porch and yell at him so he could get out of the car and tell her exactly what he thought of it all, what he actually felt for once. Fuck it, he said again, then pretended he didn't know where he was going.

When he got to the mall his rage had subsided and he felt kind of sad but didn't consider turning back. He could feel the anticipation of the burn already tingling in his toes as he stepped out into the parking lot. Somehow it didn't feel like he was making a choice. It felt as if the choice had already been made some time ago and this was just the fact of it making itself known, the sad simple fact of it sliding to its consequence.

He remembered the day after Jacob was born. He'd left the hospital early in the morning when Jen and their newborn son were still asleep, and he'd gone down to the shoreline where he sat on a log looking out at the sparkling waters of Puget Sound. The sun had come up over the hill and its warm, yellow light crept down the sides of the buildings behind him then out onto the sand and into the water, so he could see the rocks and the sand underneath. It was a warm spring morning and he'd been full of wonder at the strength of the new, unexpected love in his chest for his son, for Jen despite their troubles, for the day, the shapes of the islands blue on blue out in the Juan de Fuca Strait, the white of the boats, the gleaming, brilliant city. Everything had seemed so exquisitely beautiful and new that tears had sprung to his eyes and he'd found himself whispering please, please, please though he didn't know why or to whom, then he'd sat on the log and made promises, he'd made rules for himself to follow so that the feeling of that day might stay with him always. He hadn't touched a drink since.

He thought about this even as he entered the mall. He walked through the anonymous twilight of the tiled avenue, passed winking storefronts and other shoppers to a bar called the Elephant Castle, remembering the rules and the promises with a kind of sadness and regret.

The bar was dark and quiet, tucked away from the prying eyes of the day, from the rush and the busy, everyone so god-damn busy.

I'm a grown man, he reminded himself and it's only a drink.

He took a seat at the bar and ordered a whisky from a tired looking bartender, a man his own age with heavy circles under his eyes. He watched the bartender's hands on the glasses, the ice scoop, the bottle. He could feel the cold in his own hands as he watched, and this calmed him.

The bartender slid the drink wordlessly across. Matt nodded and was glad for the man's silence.

He brought the glass up to his lips and sucked the whisky over his teeth then held the burn, the blessed, blessed burn against the roof of his mouth where it prickled and spread like sunshine through the trees and he thought that he might get there, to that brightness in between, then his phone rang, and he answered it.

"Matty? Matty Campbell? Is it really you?"

He froze. He stared down into his drink as if it had spoken. Its slick golden glow winked back, and he wondered briefly if he'd somehow conjured it for if whisky had a voice, if surreptitious afternoon boozing had a voice, this would surely be it. He closed his eyes and for some reason he found himself thinking of his father, the old man sitting outside the RV with the ice cubes clicking in his glass, he thought of a great river carved deep into the surface of the Earth, an ancient river winding silently through the desert, its surface brown and opaque and unfathomable. Then he shook himself free and said, "Ken! Well holy shit. I can't believe you're calling. What's it been now? Twenty years?"

CHAPTER THREE

The morning after her diagnosis, Annika woke at the regular time, ate her breakfast and got ready to go to work. She put on her coat, locked her door, then walked down the hall and out into the parking lot where the morning sky was just beginning to pale. The spindly birch trees that lined the lot were silhouetted against the sky's brightening, their naked limbs begging upwards, their fallen leaves scattered across the cold, grey pavement like yellow teardrops, strangely delicate as they lifted and swirled in the unsettled air. In a few weeks they'd be lumped in rotting piles along the curb, she knew, wet mats that smelled of worms and decay, but the winter rains hadn't started yet. It had been warm and sunny for most of autumn and then suddenly cold, the weather changing almost overnight, the way a person can change, just like that.

Annika shivered and hugged her coat close around her. People here talked as if the lack of snow made Seattle winters gentle but there was an unpredictability to the West Coast, a changeability from day to day that struck her as brutal. She would have preferred the long, slow turn of the seasons followed by snowfall and steady cold the way she remembered things as a child.

She made her way across the lot then let herself into her little hatchback, piled her purse and lunch onto the passenger seat, then turned on the heat. Cold bled up from the steering wheel and into her fingers as she sat watching a thin spider web of frost melt away from the windshield. Her hands on the wheel looked old, thin and corded with the veins protruding. They looked like someone else's hands.

When the frost was gone, she backed the car out and exited onto the street where each turn brought her into a greater flow

of traffic. It was only 8:00 but it was already busy on the
Interstate, all four lanes rushing, the red tail lights on the road
ahead moving not as separate points but in waves, like sheets of
rainwater running down asphalt. Everyone was on their way to
work, just as before. There were times when the morning rush
made Annika feel like she was part of something larger, that she
was part of the life of the city, but mostly it still felt strange to
her, having spent the majority of her life driving dirt roads and
two-lane highways.

After twenty minutes on the Interstate, she took the
Northlands exit to where traffic narrowed, then stopped, then
flowed into the main avenue of the industrial park, a warren of
flat, low buildings with wide empty lots in front of them. She
passed a Safeway and a Walgreens and an Office Supply store,
then she turned again into a maze of non-descript businesses and
storage rental units.

Lifeline Insurance was a low, modern looking building with
a front wall of mirrored glass that reflected an anonymous landscape of manicured shrubs and grey asphalt. Annika parked her
car, gathered her things and got out. She stood still for a moment,
feeling the cold air against her skin; it had an acrid taste, like
blood and winter.

She shook her head and started across the parking lot, her
shoes clipping smartly on the pavement as she walked.
Sometimes, when she walked in heels, she found herself looking
over her shoulder to see who was behind her only to realize that
the sound, that hollow, polished sound, was her own footfall.
Now, as she listened to the click of her cheap, too-tight shoes,
she felt her anger stir against Hamish. Above her, a swollen
underbelly of cloud was darkening by the minute and she
thought bitterly that Hamish had stolen the sky; he had taken the
sky and the wind and the sun away from her and there were
nights that no one knew about, dreary, rainy nights when she lay
curled on the floor of her apartment whispering you thief, you
thief, you thief even though she knew in her logical mind that it
didn't make sense. Hamish hadn't forced her to move to Seattle,
she reminded herself. He hadn't forced her to do anything.

She stopped at the front door of the building, breathing deeply until her anger stilled inside her, then she opened the door and clipped along the foyer, letting herself into the main office where a group of her co-workers were standing by the coffee station. Susan said, "Hello, Annika," and John said, "Good morning, Annika," and Ray said, "Annika Bo Bannika, what's shakin'?" and she smiled and said hello and commented on the cold. She felt strange, distant. Everything seemed vivid and portentous yet untouchable also, like she was a deep-sea diver trapped in a glass bubble, looking out at her own life. She couldn't decipher if this strangeness was the illness or her fear. She hoped, she wanted it to be fear.

The office was a long, rectangular room that was divided into smaller sections by moveable partitions that reached only partway to the ceiling so when people were standing you could see the tops of their heads; when they were walking you could see the heads gliding along. Annika made her way to her desk at the far end of the room, the grey light from the windows on one side, the island of cubicles on the other. Already the air was full of sounds: tapping fingers, the whirring of the copier, the buzz of fluorescent lights.

When she arrived at her cubicle, she hung up her coat, put her lunch on the desk then turned on her computer. She put on her headset, checked the messages on the phone, then answered all the email enquiries that had piled up overnight. Once she'd dealt with the backlog, she began to process new applications, entering data from the mail-in forms into the database where it could be further vetted by claims.

Throughout the day, Annika fielded calls from clients who had questions about their life insurance policies. The majority of them wanted to know what would happen if. What if they died in a storm or a flood or an Earthquake? Would they be covered? What if they were attacked by an animal? Or a terrorist? What about a car accident where it was their fault? Suicide? What if their husband died and hadn't made out his will yet?

She'd always just followed protocol, quoting verbatim the FAQ sheet without much thought to the lives or the fears behind the questions, for she'd only ever considered the job as temporary. It had simply been a way to get some work experience in the city, then, after that, a way to save money after the divorce so she could get back on her feet again. Yet on this day, the questions felt different, full of foreboding and personal somehow. Annika could hear the fear and the need behind them and she found herself wanting to explain that she didn't actually know the answers, that the future was uncertain and that life was full of cruel surprises. Instead she said, yes, you're covered or no, you're not or for an extra $15 a month I can add coverage for surfing, or no, we don't actually cover medical.

Shortly after lunch, an elderly woman called. "So how does it work?" the woman slurred. Annika could hear her labored breathing as if the woman were sitting right there beside her, whispering in her ear. She could smell the loneliness and liquor through the telephone.

"Pardon? I'm not sure what you mean."

"How does it work? What will happen when I die?" Not if. The woman didn't ask if the way most people did. She said when.

Annika looked out the gap in the partitions to the parking lot and the restless stream of cars beyond it. "Your policy will go to the beneficiary you named in your will," she said. There was an ugliness, a meanness in the woman's voice that frightened her.

"But how will they know?"

"Ma'am?"

"What if I drop dead and no one is around? How will any of them know I'm dead? No one comes to visit anymore."

"Well, do you have . . . a partner? A spouse, maybe? Someone that takes care of you? A neighbour that looks in on you, maybe?"

There was more labored breathing and an awful quiet like a great dark country behind it. "I suppose they'll hire a nurse. I suppose they'll stick me in a home or something like that." There was a long pause. "But what if I don't want to name anyone? What if I want to just let them fight over it? It would serve some of them right."

As the words came through the phone, Annika felt them sink into the very core of her, hard and ugly yet familiar somehow, terrifyingly familiar. After she hung up, she sat looking out the gap at the greyness. She could feel the hardness, the lump at the top of her stomach, sitting inside her like a poison stone.

"Ha! Caught you spacing!"

Annika looked up to find her co-worker Beverly's dark rimmed eyes peering overtop the partition. "Oh hi!" she recovered quickly. The sounds of the room came rushing in, the quick scurrying of fingers over keyboards like mice feet on the floorboards late at night. How long had she been sitting there? She didn't know. "I was thinking, that's all," she said lamely.

Beverly came around and leaned her narrow haunch against the side of the partition. She wore slim, black pants and a dark blouse, her hair slicked back in a high, tight bun like a ballet dancer's. Beverly looked down and studied her own fingernails. They were painted a deep burgundy, almost black. "Ugh," she said, "Al and I are fighting again. It's really bad this time."

For reasons Annika couldn't understand, Beverly had identified her as a confidante, coming around to her desk at break times to share stories about her tumultuous marriage. Annika was flattered, in a way, for she didn't have many female friends. She made a point to keep track of Beverly's stories, to ask questions that showed she'd been listening, yet suddenly she found her memory uncharacteristically blank. She had absolutely no recollection of what they'd talked about last. "What are you fighting about?" she tried.

Beverly tossed her head then scanned the tops of the cubicles for gliding heads. "Come out with me," she half-whispered. "You're not doing anything. Come out with me for a smoke."

Annika got up and followed wordlessly. She didn't know if she wanted to go or did not want to but felt she should. Beverly marched ahead with her black coat undone and her arms swinging.

They took the fire exit out to the side of the building, then stationed themselves on the walkway in front of the wheel chair ramp, a concrete path that ran up between two planters, each holding a single row of manicured cedar shrubs that never seemed to get any bigger.

Beverly leaned against one of the planters and took out a pack of cigarettes, cupping her thin manicured hands around the cherry as she lit it, then she snapped the cap back down on her lighter, flicking it quick like a switchblade, her wedding ring sparking in the grey afternoon. She narrowed her eyes at the parking lot. "He's going to suffocate me," she said. "He keeps harping on me about how irresponsible I am." She brought the cigarette to her lips and sucked in, holding her breath for a moment before letting out a long, thin line of smoke.

Annika propped herself up so she was sitting on the edge of the planter and let her hand wander among the cool, rough edges of the bark mulch. She liked Beverly even though she often didn't know what to say. The younger woman reminded her of a colt with her flashing eyes and big dramatic gestures and long and restless legs.

"He's on my case about the smoking. And about the coffee, too. He says I need to get my priorities straight." She let out another long stream of smoke. "He keeps telling me I'm selfish."

"It's your choice, not his," Annika offered. "And people do far, far worse things to each other than smoke and drink too much coffee."

Beverly moved closer so that her arm was touching Annika's. "I told you that we're trying though, right? That we went to this clinic?"

"The clinic?" Why couldn't she remember? It bothered her that she couldn't remember.

Beverly made her eyes wide. "The fertility clinic," she said in a low, meaningful voice, her smoky breath warm on Annika's face.

"Oh. Oh yes. I remember now." Yet Annika didn't. She had no recollection of any earlier conversation about fertility or clinics. Of all things, she should remember that, she thought, with the disappointments and humiliations of her own experience still so fresh in her mind, not to mention the giant debt her and Hamish had incurred trying to make a baby. "How did it go? At the clinic?" she asked, trying for a brightness she didn't feel.

Beverly moved even closer and now Annika felt the other woman's warm thigh pressed up against her own.

"Well, it was weird. I can't tell this to anyone else. Everyone tells me I'm being over-sensitive and that I should just accept it, that a certain amount of poking and prodding is necessary and worth it in the end. Al's super excited about being a Dad; it's all he talks about but I just . . . It really freaked me out to be honest. The clinic. I don't even know that I want to go back there. It was kind of spa-like and science-y at the same time. Do you know what I mean?"

Annika did know. She thought Beverly described it very well, that weird contrast that had unsettled her so deeply: soft music and hopeful serenity in one room, your feet up in stirrups and a hard light shining into the most secret parts of you in the next.

Beverly's hand touched her arm, light and unsure. Her wide, pretty eyes weren't mean or flashing now but questioning, searching Annika's face and Annika was aware that there was an invitation here for closeness, that an intimacy she'd once longed for and dreamed about was being offered, yet she felt trapped somehow by her own sense of strangeness, as if the secret of her illness was blocking any words of comfort she might offer.

When Annika was young she used to imagine what it would be like to have female friends. On the farm there'd been only her and her brother and the neighbouring families, the Christian ones they were allowed to associate with, had only boys. Even at Church there'd been few girls Annika's age and so she'd grown up fantasizing about the whispery, secret world of women. In high school, she'd sometimes catch the town girls clustered in the washroom, looking lithe and dangerous in their tight jeans and desert boots, whispering together with wide eyes and glossy lips, breathless as the secrets passed between them, then Annika would clomp in in her sturdy, sensible shoes and long rustling skirt and whatever it was, whatever magical fleeting thing that passed between them would suddenly stop and they'd turn and stare at her with mean, glittering eyes.

Annika looked into Beverly's hopeful face. "What was it like?" she asked, hating the stiffness in her own voice.

Beverly held her cigarette out to the side. She tapped the ash onto the concrete with a burgundy nail. "Well," she continued. "When I got there I thought it was going to be alright. The waiting room was nice. Zen-like. There were these leather seats and this giant picture of cherry blossoms on the wall and a fountain with those fish in it. What are they called? The Japanese ones?"

"Koi. They're called koi," Annika heard herself say. She did not know how she knew they were called koi only that she did. Had Hamish told her? Someone at work? Her own words seemed to swim away, rippling between the curls of smoke that rose and melded together in front of her eyes. She shook her head. She felt sick, she realized suddenly. She didn't feel well at all.

"Koi," Beverly repeated. "I always call them carp but I guess a carp is ugly. I guess a carp is grey. Anyway, there were these koi swimming around in there and these pale coloured stones on the bottom. Then the doctor came out and it got totally weird. First of all, she looked like a plastic surgery experiment gone seriously awry. Pretty, but like a robot, you know? And then she starts talking about egg harvesting and injecting embryos in this bright, positive voice, staring at me the whole time with these big, earnest eyes and acting like the whole thing is totally normal. I mean, it was like walking into a creepy sci-fi movie. And I know that the smoking is bad for me, I just . . . I don't even know what I want to do. Everyone's like you're in your thirties now, time to decide but I don't actually know. I feel like I don't know anything. Is that weird, to not know?"

There was a pleading in Beverly's voice that Annika recognized and she wanted to make it go away, she wanted to say the things she herself had once longed to hear. "If I can give you some advice, Beverly, I wouldn't get too caught up in it," she began slowly. "Things don't always work out like you plan and it's a whole lot of time and worry and expense that you'll never get back. Hamish and I went to one of those clinics for a while and it didn't work . . ." She trailed off as Beverly's eyes grew wide and incredulous.

"You and Hamish tried to have a baby? I didn't know that."

Immediately, Annika regretted saying anything; she felt a wave of emotion building inside, rushing dangerously towards this one small disclosure, all her secrets and worries and loneliness scrambling over one another to be relieved. "Well, Hamish wanted to have kids," she back tracked, trying to sound casual yet feeling her voice thicken with every word. "I was never quite as sure about any of it as he was. I felt the same as you, that I didn't know. That life was day by day. I guess what I really wanted was for him . . ." she almost said '*to love me*' but it was too late, the wave of emotion was coming; it was in her chest, now in her throat and she could not speak.

She felt Beverly's hand touch her back, unsurely, softly, the hand coming and going as if it didn't quite know what to do. "Annika? Annika?"

There was such a thing as too much loneliness, Annika knew. It was a physical need, just like hunger or thirst, equally powerful if denied long enough; beyond a certain threshold of loneliness, it no longer mattered what you thought or did not think; what you believed or did not believe; whether a person was worthy of your affection or deserving of your trust or wanted any of the same things in life at all, after a certain point there was simply the fact of your own loneliness, willing to do anything, to try anything, that it might be relieved.

A sob escaped from Annika's throat. She could feel the hardness at the top of her belly throbbing each time she breathed in. She gasped, desperate to get control of herself.

"Annika?" Beverly's voice came. "I'm so, so sorry. I wouldn't have brought it up if I knew."

With a great effort, Annika straightened. The blood came rushing to her head. The world narrowed then widened again and she thought she might pass out but then the feeling passed. She took Beverly's hand in her own and squeezed it. Beverly looked at her, surprised. "It's nothing you said. I'm not upset about that," she managed, smiling weakly. "Hamish and I . . . that's old news now. I'm really just not feeling well. I think I must be coming down with the flu or something. Come on. Let's go back inside."

Beverly helped Annika back to her desk where Annika sat for several hours trying to decide what to do. Before she left, she took a long look around, aware it was unlikely she'd be returning.

It was already dark out when Annika drove home. She felt weak, hollowed out inside by her grief, by illness, by fear. She took the slower road along the water where she could see clusters of lights along the coastline: Port Orchard, Bremerton, Kingston, floating up from the blackness as if they'd become unanchored and were drifting away, the Western edge of the continent breaking up and drifting away like sea ice.

It was strange, she thought, how the lights at night always reminded her of Rose Prairie. Seattle couldn't be more different, she couldn't have come further away from her childhood home without dropping into the sea, yet the lights at night always made her think of it, that tiny hamlet floating up from the darkened prairie when you crested the rise and took the long, straight country road to town.

I could go back there, she thought.

It surprised her. That she would even think it, even briefly after so many years away was foolish, preposterous even, yet as she drove she found herself imagining how it might be: the fields shifting in the Prairie wind, the cattle moving off under a wide arc of blue, the old house with its narrow doors and knocking footsteps and the plain white curtains full of light. What would they do? she wondered. What would her parents say if she were to show up now? They would be old now, old and wrinkled; perhaps they'd be softer, more forgiving . . . she shook her head. Unexpected tears blurred the lights as they floated up from the water.

Eventually her route took her away from the water and into town where the buildings pressed closer and closer to one another and came forward to the curb, square and flat-faced and ugly. She turned onto Eddy St. and drove passed the pawn shops, the Good Hope Employment Centre, the South end Diner where all the old people went on Sundays. There was a woman on the sidewalk staggering in high-heeled shoes and an old man guarding the cherry of a cigarette in the entrance of the Eddy St. Tavern.

She drove a little further then pulled into the small lot in front of her building where she sat in the darkened car a moment before getting out. Walking slowly in her too-tight work shoes, she crossed the pavement and let herself into the dim, brown foyer with all the names on a list outside the inner door, swiped her card, then climbed the stairs and walked down the narrow hall passed the other doors, the other lives she smelled and heard but did not know. At last, she let herself into her apartment.

She didn't even bother turn on the light, she simply lay down on the futon, still in her work clothes. She folded her hands across her chest and lay flat on her back, closing her eyes as she tried to shut out the murmur of voices and televisions that came through the walls, the groaning of the old pipes in the ceiling above her, the fact that it was only seven o'clock and there was another long, lonely evening ahead of her.

She could feel the hardness in her belly plain as day now, a deadly lump in the V of her ribs. Each time she breathed in she felt the flow of her breath part around it, her living breath tracing its shape, a dark, blank place like a question inside, like Who? What? Where? Insisting on an answer.

She did not know what to do. The mere idea of the hospital, of being poked and prodded again, of being stuck in that dead airless space with doctors and nurses who knew nothing of her, filled her with dread and the thought of dying here, of simply letting time run out in this ugly apartment was no better. That her life might actually end here, in this waiting place, in this wet and dreary city she'd intended to leave behind, seemed too awful, too unfair to even contemplate.

Again, she found herself thinking of her childhood home. She thought about the wideness of the landscape and the smell of the Earth and the deep, deep quiet at night and the stars . . . And again, she stopped herself, an image of her father coming into her mind: her father, who, upon seeing her strong and fit and healthy, upon seeing her happy and independent for the first time in her life, had turned his head away in disappointment.

It still staggered her, each time she thought about her parents: that they could be so rigid, that their love could end over something as seemingly meaningless as a summer job, that an impulse decision made by a lonely teenaged girl could cause a lifetime of estrangement.

But that was how it was. That was how they were and she had stepped outside their love in a way she hadn't understood; what to her had been a job, a chance to meet other kids her age, was to them a rebuke, an insult to everything they'd ever stood for: their otherwise obedient daughter taking off to work like a man, in a man's world, at a man's job, living in co-ed dorms, staying in hotels on her nights off . . . Yes, she'd gone and embraced the very thing they'd pitted themselves against their whole lives; she understood this now; and yet, the crazy thing was, at the time, she hadn't felt like a rebel, just lonely, just excited.

When the forest service recruiter at her high school job fair had told her that he liked to hire farm kids because they worked hard, her heart had leapt with excitement. She'd filled out the application on the spot. Growing up, she used to see the firefighters outside the coin laundry on their days off and they'd always seemed magical to her, these groups of tanned young people standing outside the white crew vans, laughing together in such a free and easy way. There'd been women too, girls not much older than herself, that used to sit on the curb in the sunshine, all in a row, talking to one another as they waited for their clothes to dry. They'd looked so close to one another, almost like sisters. Sometimes they'd catch her watching them and smile and she'd smile back, a shy little Christian girl twisting in her sturdy shoes on the hot pavement.

Yes, she'd known her parents would be angry when the Forest service man called to tell her she'd got the job, yet she'd never imagined they would actually disown her. Oh, the fights it had caused! They'd even sent her older brother, Jonathan, to fetch her during training and she'd had to refuse him in front of everyone. She could still remember her sinking dread as he'd come across the lot, his glaring white shirt cutting straight across the dusty training ground, the sudden silence as the other recruits stopped to watch, then his face in her face all twisted up with righteous fire when she'd refused him. "You've made your choice, Annika," he'd hissed into her ear, "Don't think you can come crawling back when it all falls apart. I can see you've made your choice."

And now she was here.

She lay awake for a long time going over these things in her mind. The choices. The consequences. The genes and the seeds. She was no closer to an answer. Finally, she fell into a fitful sleep, her dreams punctuated by the entrances and exits of all the people in her life, its many stages, a strange trajectory of places and jobs and ways of being. It was in this state of half-dreaming that an idea suddenly came to her.

It was a strange memory to have stored away, a second-hand conversation she'd caught one time in the staff room, years before. She'd been making coffee and had overheard her manager, Tiffany, talking to another woman from the claims department about something called a viatical settlement: the practice of selling a life insurance policy to a third party for part of its value up front; the investor receiving the full benefit when the seller dies. "It *is* legal in Washington," Tiffany had said with a kind of sad, what is the world coming to indignation. "And Lifeline is a licensed provider, whether you agree with it or not. As long as those premiums are paid, we have to pay it out."

"But it's awful, though!" The other woman had protested, "Why would someone consent to it at all? I mean, there have to be other ways," and then the two of them, both mothers with small children and husbands and houses and extended families that came to visit every second weekend, had launched into a tight-lipped condemnation of the practice and Annika remembered that she'd felt annoyed at them; she'd been going through the divorce at the time and felt she knew something of it.

Now, she opened her eyes and stared at the darkened ceiling. Perhaps she was not quite as hard up for money as she'd originally thought. Perhaps there was a way she could get out of Seattle and find some peace, some quiet, some sky, at least for a little while, before the end. The one good thing about her job at Lifeline, she thought with bitter irony, was that they offered a hell of a generous life insurance policy to their staff.

CHAPTER FOUR

Matt Campbell was drunk; he was drunk; it was one in the morning and he wanted to go home, yet he couldn't seem to extricate himself from Ken's back-slapping, hard-drinking resurrection of old times. He handed the bartender the last of his money, closed his eyes and prayed for someone to save him.

At first, he'd been glad to see Ken. They'd met for dinner at a downtown pub and it had felt all warm and brotherly; there'd been rounds of drinks and hugging and stories, but he'd let it go on too long, a series of bars and close-talk and taxi-cabs that was starting to blur together: Ken with his crackling intensity and ice blue eyes; Ken with his Machiavellian liver pouring booze down his gullet like it was water, getting brighter and quicker and more energetic as the night wore on, while he, Matt, just grew dumber and meaner, lumbering along behind his old friend like a compliant thug, like Ken the brains and Matty the brawn, as if the past 20 years had never even happened.

"You all right, bud?"

Matt opened his eyes. The bartender was looking at him in a sharp, quizzical way, holding a full pitcher of beer just out of reach, as if he hadn't quite decided whether to cut Matt off or not. Matt straightened himself out and smiled with the corners of his mouth in a way he hoped looked world-weary rather than wasted. "Long day at the office," he offered.

The bartender studied him a moment longer, then finally released the pitcher. "Take it easy, bud," he said, eyeing him critically.

Pitcher in hand, Matt turned towards the main part of the bar. It was one of these gritty working class places like the ones he and Ken used to frequent back in River City, the kind with rough timbers up above and sports on TV and a lurid little corner housing a couple of VLTs, some hollow-faced local planted on a stool in front of them as if he'd always just been there, probably wearing a diaper so as not to lose his machine; the kind of place where the girls all wore plaid shirts and tight jeans and made a big show of how much they didn't give a fuck but still wore mascara glopped onto their raccoon eyes.

I *need* to get out of here, Matt told himself as he started across, weaving through the tables of hunched over drinkers, trying not to spill. He passed the pool tables and made his way over to where Ken was holding court, regaling three of these sexy lumberjack girls with the sort of fascinating bullshit that makes twenty-year-olds twinkle and giggle and cross and re-cross their legs. It felt surreal: Ken the runt, the scrappy little wiseass of Matt's youth, had morphed into some kind of fancy Seattle investment broker, the very picture of urban chic in his dark under-stated clothes, silver stubble and pointy Euro-style shoes.

"Here he is! Matty Matt! Seattle's finest!" Ken hollered, reaching over to slap Matt on the back as he sat down, a solid blow that rattled memories Matt had long put away: the street where they'd both lived, its rows of dirty townhouses with yellow lights in their windows and shouting through their walls; Matt half expected to get a whiff of cigarette smoke and cheap whisky, to smell the faint sour smell of the pulp-mill in Ken's clothes, but it wasn't there. Ken smelled clean and fresh, like new leather and aftershave. Ken gave him another solid whack. "I was just about to tell the ladies here how I sleuthed you out!"

Matt leaned forward and began filling the girls' glasses. "Yeah, how about that? How did you find me?" he asked absently, his mind already preoccupied with his exit.

"It was totally random. Serendipitous, even . . . is that the word? Serendipity?" Ken went on, lowering his voice so that the girls had to lean closer, their eyes widening, their cleavage deepening, that dark crevice between the mounds of young flesh pulling Matt's attention despite his best efforts to ignore it: a lacy bra strap cutting in, a girlish pendant falling forward and rocking slow . . . It made Matt think suddenly of Jen; it made him miss her achingly, despairingly. He fished his phone out of his pants pocket and looked at the screen but she hadn't called him. She hadn't even texted. Not once. Why won't you ever call me? he wanted to scream but he already knew why: she was too stubborn; she was pretending not to care, sitting at home and hating him for the fact that he was here in the first place.

Beside him, Ken was rattling on, warming to his subject: "So, I'm rushing home to get to this BBQ after work and decide to pop into the grocery store in Northview, which is not where I usually shop . . ."

Northview! Matt's attention came crashing back. The grocery store in Northview! He set his phone back on the table and took a deep, long drink. He knew exactly where this story was going. Already, he could see the teasing in his old friend's eyes.

"It's super-busy and I get in line at the checkout," Ken continued. "When it's my turn, I slap my pork roast down on the conveyor, then this lady whirls around and gives me a look like how dare you put that dirty animal carcass near my organic arugula sprouts or whatever she had on there . . ."

A blush began to prickle at the back of Matt's neck. He drained his glass, then reached for the pitcher again.

Ken glanced over at him with an evil twinkle in his eye and kept right on going, "one of these self-righteous skeleton types who walk around with a yoga mat and get all precious about the micro-fauna in their guts, the kind that examine their own stools and . . ."

"Stools?" one of the girls, the chubby one who kept pulling the tails of her shirt back down over her muffin top, interrupted and then the tall skinny one with wild blonde hair said, "He means their shit," in a thick Aussie accent and the three of them dissolved into a giggling heap.

They were so young! Again, Matt looked down at his phone. Please, please, please, he thought but the phone remained silent, inert. Jen wouldn't call; she wouldn't save him.

Ken waved his hand for silence and the girls stopped their giggling. "So, this woman picks up the divider from the metal runnel alongside the conveyor and sets it down real deliberate-like and I'm standing there, prepping to say something really nasty when I get this creepy feeling, like someone is watching me. I look around and no, no one is paying me any attention. The conveyor is moving forward and forward and then I notice the divider. There's a photo on it, an ad for real estate. I squint; I look a bit closer and then I'm like holy shit! It's Matty! There he is, River City's very own prodigal son, staring at me from a grocery store divider!"

"Like one of those plastic bars you put in between?" the fat girl asked, wrinkling her nose.

Matt closed his eyes. He hated the ads, hated the fact that he'd put them there in the first place. Jen had convinced him it was a good idea, and his mother and her parents, egging him on . . . The photographer he'd hired had told him to wear a sweater instead of a suit; she'd told him to project warmth from his eyes and he'd tried to do so, thinking about Jen and Jacob with a hand over his heart, but the sweater had been itchy, too-tight and too hot and the man in the photos looked squint-eyed and flushed, like he didn't quite fit, like he was lying somehow.

Now the third girl, a waif-like creature with a toque pushed back on her forehead and her eyebrows plucked into a mask of perpetual surprise, said earnestly, "People are so immune to advertising now you have to be original. You have to find a captive audience."

"A stroke of genius," Ken concurred magnanimously but Matt could see the old mischief in his face; he could see Ken's evil awareness taking it all in: his embarrassment, the way he'd downed his beer, the way the girls annoyed him, and he felt a wave of anger rising up inside, a frustration so deep and pervasive, it scared him, how strong the feeling was.

He stood suddenly, knocking the table with his shin so the beer sloshed over the rims of the glasses. "It was cheaper than taking out an ad on the bus," he snarled, then wondered what his own face looked like just then because the girls were staring up at him with big wide eyes. They looked terrified.

"I need some air," he grumbled by way of apology, then made his way outside where he stood next to the service entrance in the red glow of an exit sign. A cold drizzle prickled on his skin and he stood, gulping at the wet, black air, trying to drink its coolness, to soothe the great beast of his anger still tearing him up inside.

Help me. Please help me, he thought. He dialed Jen.

"Hello?" She was awake.

"Jen," he breathed, cupping the phone against his face. The sound of her voice filled him with relief. His wife. His son. He wanted to be reminded. "It's me. I'm at a bar."

She didn't say anything. Then: "Do you need a ride or something?"

"No, no. I just wanted to talk to you, that's all. I know I should have called but I . . ."

"So, you're waking me up at one in the morning to tell me that you're at a bar?" she asked, her voice sharp and clipped, each word a slamming door.

"I thought you might care where I was," he tried, switching gears and trying to sound light. "I am your husband, after all. Maybe you remember me? The father of your child?"

She said nothing. There was a time when she might have bantered back, a time when she'd been sharp-tongued and witty and dark but that was years ago, before Jacob was born. He waited. He could hear Sweet Home Alabama pounding through the wall.

"Look, I know I should have called earlier," he tried again, "But I got talking to Ken and we had a few drinks and well, I just . . . I wish I was home with you and Jacob right now. I miss you guys," he said and meant it—he did!

"Well, whoever she is, she must be pretty special for you to get loaded on a Thursday night, just out of the blue," she said coldly.

"Why do you do this?" he exploded, then lowered his voice to an angry hiss. "Why do you always have to assume the fucking worst?"

"You tell me why, *Matty Matt*," she sniped and it literally made him writhe in frustration because there was no reason for it; he'd always been loyal; he'd changed his whole fucking life around to make it work with her, and yet, *somehow*, because he was that much older, because—GOD FORBID—they'd hooked up at a bar, because he had a penis and some waitress from another life had called him Matty Matt, *somehow* this made him guilty. Of everything. He was guilty no matter what he did. Here he was, hiding in the fucking alley.

Suddenly the door burst open and a young couple all tangled up in each other practically fell over into the alley before they steadied themselves, the guy pushing the girl up against the dumpster where she wrapped her legs around his waist and started grinding her hips into him. Then she looked up and saw Matt. "EEEeek! There's someone here!" she squealed and they both started laughing then scampered off hand in hand into the night.

Matt put his hand over the phone but it was too late. "Who was that?" Jen cried, her indifference immediately dissolving to panic. "I hear voices. Who's there with you?" she pleaded, and even though it pissed him off, he felt his heart break under his anger because he knew that her panic was real and that it had something to do with him. She'd been like this ever since Jacob was born: impossibly fragile, insecure. Nothing he ever did made it better.

"Who is there with you?" she pleaded.

"There's no one."

"I heard a woman, Matt! You're lying."

"I love you, Jen but I can't do this right now. I have to go." There was no point in arguing when she was like this.

"Tell me who she is."

"I'm going."

He hung up and stood there in the cold.

People always said you were supposed to ask for help. On TV, they were always on about it, about how you should call a friend instead of taking that drink, or talk to a health care professional if you were feeling blue or stressed out but what the fuck? He'd tried all that after Jacob was born, so he already knew what they'd tell him. They'd say he was lucky, that he had a good job and a beautiful family and that he should just do this and just do that in these muted self-righteous tones and they'd be right, it would all be true, it would all be absolutely fucking true and he'd say yes, you are right, I am so lucky, I'm so fucking privileged and blessed and then he'd go away and nothing would actually change. His wife would still hate him; his debts would still be there; he'd still be drunk in a fucking alley with a rage he didn't understand. He looked up at the black, prickling night and thought: no, I am alone.

Suddenly, a warm, firm hand gripped his shoulder. "Brother," Ken's voice said softly, next to his ear. "How are you doing? Are you sure you're alright?" And in that instant, all his pent-up frustration, all his loneliness and tangledness and screwed-upness came rushing towards the warm weight of his old friend's hand and he thought he might fall down in the street and weep.

In the cab, on the way home, Matt confessed. He told Ken everything: about his debts, about his marriage, about how he was afraid to lose his house. It felt good to confess. No one in his Seattle life knew him in the way that Ken knew him. They'd grown up together, heard the yelling from one another's houses and used to walk the streets late at night when it was bad at home, talking about girls and sports and politics and religion but mostly about getting away. Of all the people Matt knew, Ken was the only one who understood how very close they'd both come to not making it. Matt could still remember the moment he'd known he had to get out of there: the two of them were in the parking lot outside the River City bar after another pointless bar fight, the jaundiced underbelly of steam from the mill looming over them like a giant pillar, rising and swirling like some condemning God as they spat blood into the snowbank, saying fuck this and fuck that, the same two who'd once talked for hours saying fuck over and over like it was the only word they knew.

Yes, Matt thought, Ken understood him in a way few people could, and now here they both were in Seattle, this shiny West Coast city where everything was new, where everyone was reinvented.

He leaned his head against the window and watched the rainy streets streak by, the lights smeared in broad strokes across the windshield.

Ken said, "You know Matty, I might be able to help you out. I've got a line on a pretty sweet investment deal if you're interested. It's a big payout, low risk, basically a sure thing."

"Nothing is a sure thing," Matt said dreamily, the warmth in the cab and the liquor in his blood lulling him into a kind of trance. He watched the lights, the steaming streets.

"This is bombproof, I swear. You told me yourself, you're in trouble."

Matt sighed. Ken, the talker, the wheeler dealer. Nothing had changed. "What is it you're into?" he asked sleepily.

"Viatical and life settlements," Ken answered eagerly. "Basically, we buy life insurance policies; we scoop them up for part of their value, then collect the full payout when they mature."

When Matt didn't reply right away, Ken leaned towards him, the leather of his jacket creaking against the vinyl. "What's the one sure thing?" he asked, suddenly intense.

Matt kept his forehead against the glass. He liked the coolness. "Yesterday, I might have said real estate but what do I know? The market's shit the bed."

"Real estate's a crap shoot compared to this."

"Gold, then."

The driver, who, until now, had been listening to a soccer match on the radio looked back; Matt could see the whites of his eyes in the rearview.

"Not gold."

"Securities. Mutual funds."

"No. You're thinking like the stock exchange. Think bigger. What's the one absolutely guaranteed thing in all of life?"

Matt sat up. He shook his head. "I don't know. Growing old?"

"Even more sure than that."

"What then?"

Now, the cab passed under a street lamp and the light fell over Ken's face so that it appeared queer and orange, the streaking drops of rain on the windows painting shadow tears overtop, like black tears streaming backwards over his queer orange cheeks. Matt recoiled momentarily, then Ken became shadowy blue again with only a gleam of light on his eyes. He leaned close, closer still, then whispered in Matt's ear: "*Everybody dies.*"

CHAPTER FIVE

The cottage sat alone at the end of a long, tree-lined lane. It was small and neat with cedar shingles scuffed a pale grey by the salt and wind. A lawn of rough, yellow grass sloped gently down to a gravel beach that arced in a wide crescent to a point of land about a mile distant. The surface of the water was calm, dark and glassy near the shore, then white and opaque further out where it merged with the colourless sky.

Annika got out of the car and stood trembling. Cool, bright air prickled on her skin. There was a whiteness all around her, a thin veil of fog that obscured the horizon and nearby islands; yet the light in it suggested a wideness to the landscape, the sky brightening as if it were just about to lift.

She stood still and listened: a soft, steady sound lapped at the edge of her awareness. There was a small swell, she realized, despite the water's unruffled surface. It gathered, then broke with a sigh, then pulled back, raking its glistening fingers across the small, grey pebbles on the beach, turning them over and dragging them back, then gathering again, sighing again, the rush of water, the clicking stones, in and out and in and out; it's slow steady rhythm was soothing, the sound just tickling the surface, drawing her attention to a far deeper silence underneath. She let out her breath and it seemed to spread out into the whiteness, the way a river fans out then comes to settle in the sea. She'd made it. After a hellish week of lawyers and doctors and signatures and contracts, she'd actually made it.

She took the key that the landlady had given her and walked slowly along a path of flagstones that were embedded deep in the earth. Rough grass curled up in clumps along their edges. Then she stepped up onto a small porch that ran along the front of the cottage and fumbled at the door. Her hands were cold and shaking and her fingers barely had the strength to turn the key. Just a little longer, she told herself. She mustered her concentration and clenched her gut, then the key turned and the lock slid back.

Inside, it was even colder than it was out. The landlady had told her the cottage hadn't been used since the summer. The frigid air was in the wood; it was in the walls.

The main floor consisted of one, long open room with yellow, plywood walls and broad pine floorboards. There was a staircase running up its center; the kitchen and bathroom were at one end, the woodstove at the other. A large window facing the sea ran along the lengthwise wall, while two smaller windows faced the woods on either side.

There was very little furniture: a small table with two chairs and a sagging loveseat near the stove were all the furnishings provided. The landlady had fussed about it being rustic but Annika was glad. In Seattle, amongst Hamish's friends, she'd felt pressure to care about houses, how they looked, how much they cost and she'd felt herself an imposter in that fluttering, cooing world with all those fussy women. This place would do nicely, she thought. There was a calming simplicity to it. A bareness that required nothing of her.

She climbed up the narrow, creaking stairs to the loft, a single room with sloped ceilings on either side. A black stove pipe ran up through the floor and into the peaked ceiling. There was a double bed pushed up against the wall. She sat down on the mattress and fingered the time worn quilt. A Star and twenty: it was a pattern her mother had liked. She could feel the cold in the heavy batten.

She went back down the stairs. The light was fading now and she crouched in front of the woodstove and set about making a fire. Whoever had been there before had left some old newspapers and kindling in a basket, and it wasn't long before the wood began to crackle and spit.

Annika left the grate open and remained crouching, holding her hands out in front of her, turning them over and over in the orange glow. It had been her job as a child to light the woodstove in the morning and now here she was with these much older hands, all sinews and veins and wrinkles, passing the warmth between them like a familiar orange ball. There was a sense of rightness to it, like she'd come full circle. The stove pipe creaked as the metal warmed and her thoughts began to drift: to Rose Prairie and her family, to those Summers firefighting, then to Seattle and the clouds and the mountains and the loneliness. And now here. This quiet, spare place.

The room darkened. She put another log on and then another. The flames leapt and roared and threw strange shadows on the ceiling: her hands like a child praying, her hair like a wild animal.

A deep tiredness came over her. It was so very quiet. Outside, the white blanket of fog had lifted and now the moon came up and the water shone silver, the black heaps of the nearby islands rising sharply from it. It was like no place she'd ever been before and yet she found it soothing, like she'd always known it in some deep part of her. She lay down on the hard boards in front of the fire, in the silver caress of the moonlight, and fell fast asleep.

The next morning, she was unloading the car when an old Ford pick-up pulled in the gravel drive. A tiny blonde girl in a sweatshirt and jeans hopped down from behind the wheel.

Annika stopped on the flagstone path with a box in her hands and watched as the girl got out and looked around, out to sea, then towards the point, then decisively and without hurry, began walking towards her. It couldn't be her, could it? Annika thought. The woman seemed so young. So small.

When the woman reached her, she immediately extended her hand. "Hello. Annika? I'm Sasha. It's nice to meet you."

So it *was* her. Sasha. The nurse. Annika stared at the strange spritely creature before her. The woman had wide moonish features and a jaunty ponytail. There were bone plugs through both her ears like someone from a tribal society.

Sasha stared back with unflinching green eyes.

Slowly, Annika put down the box. There was a heaviness, a portent to the nurse's arrival that thickened the air and made it difficult for Annika to breathe. This will be the last person on Earth that I see, she thought. She held out her hand. "Hello."

Sasha clasped Annika's hand in a warm firm grip and smiled. Up close, Annika could see there were deep, well-worn creases around the little woman's eyes. She was not that young, after all.

"It's great to finally meet you in person," Sasha said. "How are you feeling?" Her eyes never wavered from Annika's face. It was unnerving, how steady they were.

"Good. Fine. Tired maybe. Should we? Do you . . . Do you want to go inside?" Annika had no idea how it was supposed to work, or if she even wanted it to, now that she saw her. There were dolphins tattooed on the side of Sasha's neck near the hairline, nose to tail, in a ring.

"It looks like you're still settling in," Sasha said decisively. "I'll help you with your things."

"No, it's fine, really. We can go in. We can talk about the contract." Annika bent to pick up the box she'd set down but when she stood her vision tunneled and she staggered.

Sasha grabbed her arm. Her hands were surprisingly strong and muscular. "Let me help you."

"I'll just take this one in and we'll go and figure out about the payment and . . ."

Sasha didn't let go of her arm. She looked Annika full in the face. "I'm going to help you unload the car. Then, we're going to go inside, have some tea and talk about the details." Her voice was strong and firm and rather than grate against its sudden authority as she might have when she was younger, Annika felt overwhelmed by relief. It was the first time in months she'd felt sure of what to do. "Okay," she said weakly. "Let's do that."

Sasha had a precise way of moving, calculated but graceful, like a dancer in slow motion. She bent at the knees, placed her hands on either side of the boxes then lifted from the ground in a smooth, controlled motion. Annika could hear her breathing, slowly, deliberately in a way that pulled her own breath into its rhythm. It was calming, almost hypnotic and Annika felt her eyelids grow heavy, as if she might fall asleep just walking beside her.

They went back and forth from car to cottage and with each trip, Annika grew more and more tired. She allowed Sasha to go ahead, then, when she thought she was alone, she leaned against the car, rested her head against the cool metal and closed her eyes.

Then a hand was on her shoulder. Warm. Firm. Confident. "Let's go inside. I'll make tea." Annika followed wordlessly.

Inside, the little nurse moved about the tiny kitchen with those same precise movements, with that same measured breath. "This is such a peaceful place," she said. "Are you happy with it?" She ran the water. She put the kettle on the stove.

Annika stood and opened the cupboard to get the mugs then two hands were on her shoulders, pushing her gently back down. There was no hesitation in those hands, no question as to whether they should touch or not, they just went right ahead. "Sit down, now. Relax. You need to rest."

Annika slouched. Her thoughts were foggy and confused. The desire to sleep was almost overwhelming and yet she couldn't let herself. She thought about the divorce, how she'd not really understood it, how she'd just assumed that Hamish would be fair, and then this viaticals thing, how the broker had looked at her with his pale eyes and how the air had quickened just before she signed and how the quickening had made her feel bad, guilty, like she was doing something wrong. She didn't like contracts or lawyers or legal documents. She never had. "I just. I don't want to overstep boundaries here. I really think we need to . . ." Her eyelids fluttered.

Sasha leaned against the counter and watched her. "It's difficult to make an exact plan, Annika, because it's impossible to predict how things will progress. My rates are determined by the nurse's union, as we discussed. It's up to you, but what I'd like to do is start with two visits a day, then go to a live-in arrangement as needs change."

The dolphins on her neck were nose to tail. One time, when Annika had come home from school and reported that dolphins had the IQ of a seven-year-old child because that's what she'd learned in science class, she'd been made to kneel on the hard floor for telling lies. She shook herself. She tried to think. "The hours though. We should talk about the hours . . ."

Sasha poured the tea. Steam coiled up over her hands then slithered away. The fire cracked. Someone had lit it. Annika couldn't remember. Sasha handed her a mug. "Hey, I'm not here to screw anyone over. It's like we agreed on the phone. Trust me. Please. Let me help you." She had such an open, clear face.

Annika took the tea. The warmth bled into her fingers. She blinked twice, then closed her eyes.

Annika slept. She slept like she'd never slept before. Her body was greedy for sleep. The books she'd brought, ambitious titles she'd always thought to try, remained unpacked; the letter to her parents unfinished, a white piece of paper with Dear Mother and Father in her dark leaning cursive at the top and nothing more. All the awful things she'd imagined: the terrible indignities, the excruciating pain, being cheated by her hippie nurse, none of it happened. Instead, there was only this tiredness, a full body craving for rest as if she'd been awake for a thousand years.

Days and nights went by and she drifted in and out of sleep. Sometimes it was dark and sometimes it was light. Sometimes the heat travelled up the pipe tat tat tat like a small creature climbing.

She was still strong enough to make it to the washroom herself and to cook light meals and twice a day she made the descent, her head so heavy with sleep she feared it might topple her, forward or back, if she let go of the rail. Then, when she was back, safe in bed, she'd think, it's not happening yet. Not yet, for she was still able to do the stairs. As long as she was able to do the stairs, it wasn't happening. Then sleep would pull her back under.

Time went by. She dreamt about many things and the fact that they were end dreams, sick dreams didn't seem to matter. Sometimes her dreams were mundane. Sometimes foolish. Sometimes sexy. Sometimes weird. On the occasions when they seemed portentous or significant, she'd wake and think: remember, you must remember; yet remembering proved too arduous, reflection too tiring, and even regret, with its morbid tenacity, could not hold her mind.

Sasha came twice a day as they'd agreed. She went about preparing food and making tea, checking vitals with her firm, sure hands. Sometimes she sat cross-legged in the room where Annika slept, breathing in her slow, steady way. The first time Annika woke to find her there, she'd found it strange to find this grown woman sitting on the floor.

"What are you doing?"

"I'm meditating. I hope that's alright."

For a moment, Annika was irritated and thought about how the women in Rose Prairie used to whisper prayers with their thin pinched lips and eyes full of judgment and she didn't want it, she didn't want anything to do with it anymore but then the tiredness swept in again. "It's fine," she said and soon she came to look forward to it, this calm and silent presence in the room.

Weeks went by. Then a month. It was coming up to Christmas.

Then one morning, Annika woke to find that something was different. She lay perfectly still and listened, trying to figure out what it was. She could hear birds outside, thrushes sending their calls spiraling upwards into the trees. She could hear the waves. It took her a minute to realize it was not a sound that was different, but a feeling. A strange fluttering inside her.

She went down to the washroom and saw that Sasha had brought in a folding cot. It was leaning against the wall. There'd be a time when she couldn't do the stairs, she supposed. There were boxes of medical supplies on the floor. She walked over to them and touched the lids.

Sasha was at the stove, making soup, her back to the main room. She stopped what she was doing and stood very still.

Annika looked at the boxes. There were bed pans, gloves, iv bags. Dying supplies. She picked up a plastic, kidney shaped tray. It was for vomit, she knew. She knew its feeling in her hands, its exact dimensions, its curves and its weight and then all of a sudden it came back to her, a memory so clear and vivid it seemed impossible she could have forgotten it all this time.

"My aunt died at home," she said without looking up from the boxes. She turned the pan over and over in her hands. It was pale pink. "I don't know how I possibly could have forgotten that until now. I must be crazy. The cancer must be affecting my brain."

She heard Sasha exhale slowly. "Sometimes we repress things. It's not uncommon. Especially difficult things."

Annika frowned. She thought of the old house; she could see it square and bulking against the wispy, prairie sky; she thought of the footsteps on the floor and the curtains blowing in and felt this strange fluttering deep inside of her. "She wasn't that old," she continued in a daze.

She went over to the table and sat down. "She would only have been about 40, although she was considered a spinster in Rose Prairie. Like me, I suppose. Did you know that? That where I come from I'm already a spinster? That my life would be considered a tragedy, a failure?"

Sasha put the soup ladle down. She moved gracefully to the table and sat. Her movements were even more careful, more deliberate than usual.

"It's funny to think about that now because I remember my aunt as being so old, this gaunt, scary lady with brittle hair . . ." She shook her head. It felt incredible to put the connections together, incredible yet frightening all at once. What else did she not know? What else had she failed to understand?

"How did she die?" Sasha asked carefully.

How was it that she'd never made the connection to her own illness? It seemed impossible yet here it was. Annika frowned. "It was cancer. She died of cancer." She looked out the window at the stacks of cloud piling up offshore. Golden shafts of sunlight pierced through the spaces in between them and slanted down onto the grey surface of the water. She felt all turned up inside, like she didn't know anything anymore. The story kept coming. "It was a Saturday when she died so I was at home. I was ten at the time and in the kitchen, baking bread. Isn't that crazy? I was only ten years old and already doing all the baking and helping out on the farm. Why didn't I remember any of this before? Anyway, it was bright and sunny out and there was all this sweet, spring air moving through the house; it was blowing the curtains in, and I wanted to be out in it so badly, I remember that, that I felt guilty for the desire in me to run and skip and play while this great solemn thing was happening in the house."

"You were a child," Sasha said. She looked down at her hands, as if concentrating very hard on every word. Her breath came slow and steady.

"I was in the kitchen when I heard my mother yell, "Quick! Quick! Anni! It's time!" We'd gone through what I was to do and I ran so fast, my heart was pounding. I was so afraid, so afraid to screw up, that I wouldn't do it right and her soul would bounce back and be stuck for all eternity, like a bird hitting a window, you know? That's how I envisioned it: a bird hitting a window then fluttering about in a panic for the rest of all eternity. I ran upstairs and ripped the bedclothes off the beds and hung them over the mirrors. I even took the pillowcases and ran out into the drive and threw them over the rear views on the truck. When I came back in, my mother came out of the room and there were tears in her eyes and she said, "She's gone, she's left," and just as she said it, this sweetest of breezes came through the house and out the windows and we watched it move off; it shimmered in the aspen that lined the drive, then past and away, out into the fields where it bent the grass down so it was pale and silver and then it was gone. 'You did good, Anni, you did good,' my mother said. She was mostly a quiet person and didn't talk much. It was a secret, what we did. My father didn't believe in souls bouncing back; it wasn't something we learned at Church, but some of the women . . . they still believed in all that old stuff, stuff their mothers and grandmothers had passed on before they came there. Spirits. Omens. They didn't dare talk about it in front of the men. Their lives were so hard, those women, maybe too hard to even look at clearly, so they gave to ghosts and spirits all the things they couldn't say," Annika looked out at the sea. The clouds had pressed together now into a solid, purpling mass. Wind scurried across the grey water underneath. She felt the strange fluttering inside, quick and faint the way leaves shiver in an unfelt breeze.

"That's a beautiful story," Sasha said. Tears were running down her wide flat cheeks. They just slid, spilling naturally from her steady, green eyes.

Annika shook her head roughly. She didn't like the tears or how they quickened the flutter inside her. "It was medieval is what it was. I don't know how they expected us to live in the world, growing up the way we did. They were fundamentalists and refused, absolutely refused to change with the times. My brother is totally fucked up too . . ." She stood suddenly. The sound of the chair scraping against the floor was loud and jagged.

"Well, I'm glad you shared it any way."

Annika reached for the door. She wanted to get away from the strange flutter inside her, from Sasha's understanding moon eyes, from the dead air and the dying supplies. She thought of the wind as it had travelled through the house. She grabbed the doorknob, then stopped. "I want you to tell her that you did that." It was as if the flutter had a voice of its own, as if it were pushing words up and out before she had a chance to think them.

"Pardon?"

"I want you to tell her," she said, louder now. "I don't care if you actually do it or not, but I want you to tell my mother that you covered the mirrors. That I asked you to. It would make her happy."

Sasha spoke very quietly. "I would be honored."

Annika went outside. She hadn't been outside in weeks, she realized. She walked quickly on her shaky legs but couldn't get away from the strange, naked feeling inside her. She breathed deeply but couldn't dispel it. She stood on the gravel beach and looked out to where the clouds were threatening. The wind had kicked up and there were whitecaps cresting now and a rumble of thunder far off in the distance.

"It's okay, you're okay," she whispered and the wind came up and smoothed her hair back from her brow; it was cool and smooth, like a lover's hand pushing her hair from her forehead. She closed her eyes, trying to make sense of things, of the fact that she'd only remembered now. Her aunt had been almost the exact same age, they'd even looked like one another, she realized and somehow this fact brought everything else into question: the choices and the genes and the seeds . . . Maybe it would have happened anyway, she thought. Maybe it wouldn't have mattered what she'd done or what choices she'd made. She felt all mixed up. I know nothing about myself, she realized. I don't know anything anymore.

The thunder rumbled again and she found herself thinking of Hamish. It struck her as strange to find him there, in the cool, soothing touch of the offshore breeze, but there he was, fluttering up to the surface, not the icy, cruel post-divorce Hamish but the one before that, the one forgotten. There were so many forgotten things.

He'd had a deep voice, Hamish did. She used to put her head on his chest to hear it rumble deep inside him. His chest was broad and flat and her head had rested perfectly there, just below the shoulder. They used to lie in bed and he would tell her things, he would talk about his elaborate, detailed plans for the future, what he would do, the schools their kids would attend, the vacations they would take; he sketched for her the exact map of his future and she would lie and listen to the rumble beneath the words, like the Earth moving, like thunder and she'd liked how it made her feel, as if she were safe in the shelter of his warmth with a storm coming, but it occurred to her now that maybe he had, in fact, tried to tell her. He'd told her his dreams and she'd listened to the resonance only and maybe none of it had been so sudden after all.

She blinked tears away just as the first few drops of rain began to fall. They spattered on her forehead and on her face then Sasha was at the door of the cottage, in the yellow light yelling, "Quick! Anni! Quick! You'll catch a cold!" and Annika took one last look at the sea. It was loud and hissing now as the rain came across and as she drew in her breath she realized what was so strange, what was different in her. It was the hardness. It wasn't there anymore. She breathed deep and her breath went right down to the very center of her and then she ran towards the cottage and the warm yellow light and Sasha beckoning.

CHAPTER SIX

Big, fat, greasy raindrops splattered down on the roof of the car where Matt sat parked in front of an empty townhouse, drinking cold coffee from a paper cup and waiting for a client who he suspected was a no show. The neighbourhood, a new suburb about an hour from downtown, was close to schools and parks; on the website he'd called it family-oriented and community-minded, which might have been true after five o'clock when all the busy productive people got home from their busy productive lives; but at midday, in the cold and the rain, the streets were eerily deserted, like the soaked and silent countryside left behind by the frontlines of a war.

He watched the rain hit the pavement: a thousand tiny explosions on a sheet of running water. It was hypnotic, in a way, and part of him liked it, liked being here, though it was cold in the car. He could be truly alone during the days, his thoughts his own in a way they never were at home. He watched the rain and his mind drifted again to the name he hadn't expected to see; that spare, mean signature carved into the last page of the contract: ANNIKA TORREY.

Most women had an upright, loopy way of writing, a kind of apology in the lightness of their hand, but not this one. This one had a dark, leaning cursive, her signature an angry slash she'd practically carved into the page; he'd felt the tiny grooves with his fingertips when he'd signed his name next to it and it was this, more than anything, that his mind kept coming back to. Was she angry? Nervous? Why had she pressed so hard?

He took another sip of coffee, then checked his phone. The guy was already half an hour late. Five more minutes, he told himself. Five minutes, then he'd go. He settled back, wrapping his arms tight around his chest.

It was only 3:30, yet all around him Christmas lights were beginning to turn on, strands of hopeful glow-bugs making a doomed stand against the dreariness, against the cold wet night that was, even now, descending. On the lawn next door, someone had put up a creche: cheap, plastic statues of Mary, Joseph and Jesus surrounded by hay bales and what appeared to be a camel made of birch logs. The whole thing was an eyesore and he'd fretted about it at first, fearing potential clients would balk at the prospect of overtly religious, not to mention tacky, neighbours; but now, as the flood lights came on, casting long shadows of the Holy trio onto the soggy bales behind, he paused, filled with a strange ache, like longing, like loneliness.

He was not a religious man and never had been. Both his parents had moved away from their families at a young age and let go of any religious beliefs. They'd never taken him to Church and the Christmas story was one he understood only vaguely; yet something about the simplicity of the three figures on the lawn— man, woman and child—moved him almost to tears; the quiet of it, the hay, even the camel, made him want to lay his head down and rest, made all the striving and busyness of his life these days feel hopeless, cruel somehow.

He thought again of Annika Torrey. What was she doing with the last of her days? Did she have someone? Somewhere warm and dry and out of the rain? Had his money helped her? He hoped so.

He sighed heavily, then reached forward and started the car, glancing one last time at the Holy trio before pulling away. Was it a sacrilege, he wondered, to envy them?

The next day, he stood in his own driveway, watching Jen go back and forth as she loaded their things into the car. They were going to Anacortes to visit her parents for Christmas, the three of them travelling together in one vehicle the way he'd once imagined happy families to be; yet looking at Jen now, he was filled with anxiety. He couldn't help but see her as her parents would see her: their once confident, hopeful daughter so thin and downtrodden, so nervous she had to check and re-check every bag with her spidery hands. He closed his eyes. He wanted a drink, something strong and quick to sear his worried mind to stillness.

It was two days to Christmas and he *still* hadn't told Jen about his investment. He'd meant to do it; yet each time he came to it, he found he wasn't able and what had started as avoidance had morphed into something that felt like a lie. He watched as she hurried back into the house. The screen door slammed shut behind her.

He hadn't expected to feel this way. The way Ken had talked about it, the deal had made sense, even if it was a bit on the morbid side: this woman needed money right away; he needed money long term. She'd agreed to it; he'd agreed to it. It was a business transaction, nothing more. Yet, now, outside Ken's rationale and icy, pale charm, it felt different, shameful somehow, and he found himself wishing that Ken had just gone about it the normal way, grouping the policies together rather than cutting him a 'special deal' and going 'straight to the source.' Ken had stressed that this was a rare opportunity, that this was *pancreatic* cancer, as if it was a good thing and urged him to act quickly. Maybe too quickly. And there'd been the medical report with all these detail Matt hadn't expected to see and the shady lawyer he'd hired to look things over because he was too embarrassed to use his regular lawyer and then her name carved like that into the last page of the contract . . . There was no way he could explain this to Jen!

He watched helplessly as she came back out of the house carrying a basket of brightly wrapped presents. He felt sick, the enormity of what he'd done bearing down on him as he watched her. It was bad! He'd taken out a $50,000 line of credit against the house to pay for the fucking thing, and even though Jen took almost no interest in their finances, it was her money too. He looked at her pleadingly, hoping to catch her eye.

She stood, looked over at him, then frowned. "Can you watch him a little closer, please?" she scolded. "I told you to watch him, and you're not watching him at all." Then she bent back down to rearrange something in the trunk.

Matt looked to the end of the drive. Jacob. There he was in all his four-year-old glory, getting his feet soaked as he crouched next to a puddle, his wire-rimmed glasses streaked with dirt. Matt walked over. "Try not to get your feet wet, Bud," he said. "We want to look nice for Nanna and Poppa."

Jacob picked up a worm and dangled it in front of him.

"It's the eve of the eve, buddy, are you excited?" he asked, trying to muster up some of that old Christmas excitement he remembered as a child, but Jacob scrunched up his nose then went fishing in the puddle for more worms.

Jen closed the trunk. "There. I think that's it," she said. "Jakey, are you excited to see Nanna and Poppa?" she called over, sickly sweet.

Jacob looked up from where he was crouching. "I found four worms."

Matt clapped his hands. "Pitter patter let's get at'er," he said, aware of how much he sounded like his own Dad sometimes. His old man had been a great one for sayings: *Christmas, part deux* he used to say after the divorce, deux in a mocking exaggerated tone that made the holidays sound slightly squalid and naïve, although, to give him credit, the old man always had the best gifts: video games and pump-up sneakers and Tommy Hilfiger sweatshirts when they were first coming into style. It used to make his mother jealous, he remembered, because she couldn't afford the same, and he used to hide his Dad's presents from her, keeping them stashed in his backpack until he got to school.

He bent down and scooped Jacob up in his arms, holding him tight against his chest. "I love you, Bud," he whispered as he carried him over to the car. No matter how bad it was between him and Jen, he wouldn't put his own son through that, he vowed. Jacob would never, ever be torn in two: it was one of the promises he'd made to himself.

Soon, they were off, winding through the suburbs in their little Subaru wagon, then out onto the northbound Interstate where the road quickly became a total holiday shit show. People were rushing, braking for no reason, cutting each other off. Matt felt his stress levels rising. His head began to pound. Ahead of him, on the shoulder, a car did an impossible squeeze play and he had to jam on the brakes. "What the fuck?!" he exploded. Jen gave him a dirty look. "Did you see what that guy just did, though? People think just because its Christmas, they can do whatever the fuck they want!"

Jen glared at him a moment longer and didn't answer, then, she leaned forward and started screwing with the CD player. Soon, her and Jacob were singing along to a children's album while he leaned forward and tried to concentrate, his shoulders curving inwards as if guarding something dark and real against the inane little knives of the music. Then, just when he thought he couldn't take anymore, the city spat them out and they left the highway, driving North, then West along a quiet, winding road.

Traffic subsided. The forest closed in around them, huge groves of cedar and fir with glimpses of the water, grey and restless, between the pillars of their trunks.

The music ended. Jen sighed. "Ahhh. Finally. Seattle's not the sea. Not like out here."

He glanced over at her. The angry crease between her brows was gone. Her face looked soft and pretty, the way he remembered it. In the rearview, Jacob was sitting placidly, his pale, fair head against the glass, his long limbs dangling limply over the edges of the car seat.

"We'll walk down to the beach," Jen mused. "We'll take Jakey to the beach and then go to the Wildflower for a hot chocolate."

Tentatively, Matt put his hand on her leg and glanced again at her thin, young face with the forest rushing behind it. This was the Jen he knew, the one he'd fallen in love with.

"And we'll have a fire," she continued. "We'll have a fire down at WestPoint and roast marshmallows if there's a moon. Dad used to take us to do that when we were kids. It's so bright down there with the moon on the water, sometimes it's like daytime and you can see your shadow on the rocks. One Christmas it was like that."

The moon on the water: he liked it when she talked this way. It was easy to forget when she was rushing around Seattle looking like all the other busy moms, that Jen grew up in a place where wood smoke still hung on the air and people said hello to one another in the street and let their dogs roam free. It was easy to forget that she cared about things like the moon on the water, that she grew up building tree forts in the forest near her parents' house and that her growing up was not that long ago.

She turned towards him and smiled softly. She looked like a little girl when she smiled, and his heart swelled with the urge to protect her. How had everything gotten so screwed up? After Jacob was born, her doctor had told him she had postpartum depression, and he'd tried to help her, he'd rearranged his whole life to help her, but most of the time it just felt like she hated him and it hurt, especially since he'd tried so hard. Still, he wanted it to work. He would tell her, he resolved; he'd find a quiet time and tell her everything.

She sighed again then slid her hand over top of his and they drove in silence for a while, their fingers intertwined, both hands resting on top of her thigh, until Anacortes came into view.

His in-laws, Crystal and Ed, must have been watching for them out the window, because as soon as Matt turned the car onto the long gravel drive, they rushed out onto the porch, waving Matt in, their rambling, cedar-shake palace falling down behind them. It was an absolute monstrosity of a house, cobbled together over years of renovations, so sunken and grey, it seemed part of the forest floor.

"So it begins," Jen whispered in that dark and comic way she used to have. Matt slowed the car as Crystal came running out into the drive in baby steps, her arms held open in front of her, her great breasts bouncing up and down, a teal and silver poncho streaming out behind her.

"Jenny! My sweet Jenny!" Crystal cried, leaning in the open window and planting multiple kisses on Jen's face before the vehicle was even fully stopped. Crystal looked her daughter over with big, soul-searching eyes, then went around to the backseat where she flung open the door and began smooching Jacob. "Look at how big! Oh! My heavens! You're so big now!"

Matt got out and breathed the cool, fresh air. He looked around at the overgrown garden and the woodpile and the sheds. High above, the branches of the great fir trees sighed and shifted.

It was so completely different from where he'd grown up, he could never quite get used to it.

Now Ed came down into the drive, his hands thrust deep in his pockets, a small sheepish smile on his weathered face, as if Crystal's theatrics embarrassed him. Matt stepped forward and offered his hand. "Merry Christmas, Ed. Thanks for having us."

Ed was a carpenter and his hand was rough; it made Matt was conscious of how soft his own hand was. A blush rose to his cheeks. Ed had never been anything but kind; yet it would always be there, hanging in the air between them, what Matt had done to his daughter.

"Nana! Poppa!" Jacob was out of the car now, hopping up and down with excitement, then he was off chasing an orange cat into the bushes, through giant ferns and rotting logs and rough, papery salal. They all stood in the driveway, smiling after him, and then, suddenly Jeremy, Jen's brother, was there, appearing from the shadows, like a wraith. "Hey little sister," he said.

Jeremy was two years older than Jen but still lived in the basement of his parent's house where he wrote screenplays and tried to make connections as an artist, whatever that meant. His narrow face was permanently mocking yet he never missed a family event. He was always simply there, skulking in the background.

When it was Matt's turn, he hugged his brother in-law and felt Jeremy's thin chest draw inwards and away. Then Jeremy said in that sour mocking way he had, "How's life in the burbs?" and Matt felt his blush deepen.

That evening, once they'd settled in, they all came down and sat around the large country table where Crystal had laid out a feast: roasted potatoes, a huge roast beef, steamed carrots and pickles and onions and mustards, all in brightly coloured pottery dishes. The kitchen was bathed in a warm yellow light; in the darkened living room, a fire crackled in the woodstove.

Once everyone was seated, Ed stood at the head of the table and cut the meat while Matt poured the wine. The first time Matt had met his in-laws, he'd been so nervous he'd brought multiple bottles as a kind of peace offering, and since then it had evolved into a family tradition. He always came well supplied and they always drank up and maybe it was taking the easy way out but after a few drinks all the tension went away and the thing he'd done didn't seem to matter anymore: Ed would slap his back like they were brothers and Crystal would lean close and tell him things, heartfelt emotional things about life and family.

"So, tell me, Matt, how are your parents?" Crystal asked, as they passed the dishes around the table. She always asked about his parents, even though she'd only met them once, at the wedding.

"They're good. Really good. My Dad's got the RV down in New Mexico with Ginger . . ."

"Did I meet . . ?"

"No, that was Kathy."

Crystal nodded, her eyes wide and earnest.

"And my mother's doing really well," he jumped in quickly. "Fantastic really. She and Al went down to Florida to do Christmas on the beach. One of his kids has a condo there."

Jen leaned over and cut Jacob's meat. The knife scraped against the plate.

"Well good for her! I've always wanted to do that. Spend Christmas somewhere warm," Crystal smiled warmly and took a sip of her wine.

They ate. Matt watched the levels in the glasses. He asked Jeremy what he was working on and Jeremy told them about one of his plays, a weird plot about lesbians trapped in a flooded city after the apocalypse.

"Neat," Matt offered. Jeremy winced.

"And what about you, Jenny? What have you been up to?" Crystal asked brightly.

"Keeping busy," Jen said without looking. She held a piece of meat in front of Jacob, a tiny square suspended on the silver tines and suddenly they were all watching it. There was a kind of breathless waiting as the piece of meat hung in the air.

"Open up now, Jakey," Jen said. Jacob opened his mouth. "I started a yoga class," she said, then trailed off. "Okay, Jakey, chew, chew, chew."

"Sounds exhausting," Jeremy said dryly.

Jen blushed, ever so slightly. She held the fork in the air, her attention trained upon it.

"Jen's been doing a lot of work on the house," Matt jumped in. "She's doing all kinds of renos, figuring everything out all by herself. It's incredible. The job she's done. She just finished the floors in the basement and they look awesome." He was talking too fast and he knew it but couldn't seem to stop. "I'd say she's added $30,000 to the value of the house. At least. Probably more."

"You could work for me," Ed said, and put his gnarled hand gently on Jen's shoulder but she didn't respond. The fork hovered. They all looked at the fork.

"She totally could. She does really nice work. Super good," Matt said.

"Do you ever think about going back to school, Jenny? You could go and finish your degree, start writing again and . . . We could help you . . ." Crystal asked with her wide imploring eyes.

"Mom. Don't," Jen snapped.

There was silence. There was the fork hovering. There was the memory of their first meeting hanging over the table: Jen on the couch, crying, saying my life is over my life is over and him pouring glass after glass, promising to make it right. He got up suddenly, went to the counter then came back with another bottle. He stood like he used to stand at the bar with the label outwards, his hands swift and definite as he opened it. Everyone stopped watching the meat and watched his hands. It was like a magic trick. It was forgiveness in a bottle. He pulled the cork out with an air of ceremony.

Crystal flushed and said, "Oh, I really shouldn't," and held out her glass.

Ed smiled, his ruddy cheeks like polished apples and slid his glass silently towards Matt.

"I don't need it," Jeremy said. Matt stood over him and filled his glass.

"What about you, Jeremy?" Matt asked as he looked down at his brother in-law. "Are you all ready for Christmas?"

Jeremy sniffed, though his eyes sparked for he'd caught the irony. He was smart if nothing else. A smart, sour little rat. "I can't say I'm really that into the Christmas thing, Matt. I'll do turkey but other than that . . ."

Crystal scoffed and batted her hand at the air as if it were all nonsense. She leaned forward, her breasts swelling upwards as she pressed against the edge of the table. "Jeremy used to love Christmas. He'd be up at three, four, five in the morning on Christmas because he couldn't wait."

"I saw a documentary that said the average American spends $10,000 on Christmas. People go into debt each year. Does that not strike you as insane? People spending that much money to celebrate the birth of a dead Arab who may or may not have existed?"

"We used to call Jeremy the Christmas Kid," Crystal continued. She was feeling the booze now, Matt could tell. It didn't take much.

"It used to be a pagan festival before the Church co-opted it."

"He used to sing like an angel. A beautiful little blonde angel with this crystal-clear voice."

"It's not even his real birthday," Jeremy sniffed.

Jacob leaned forward with his eyes wide. He turned and stared at Uncle Jerry with open adulation. "An angel?"

"Oh yes!" Crystal turned to Jacob now, giving all her attention to her rapt little audience. She held the wine glass aloft at her side and rubies of light scattered across the table. "Uncle Jerry had a voice just like the sweetest of angels. People said he'd been sent from heaven."

Jacob was beside himself with excitement for he, Jacob, was also a great singer of carols.

Now Crystal turned to Ed. "Do you remember the night we moved to the new Church? With the children's choir?"

Ed was leaning back in his chair. He nodded slowly. "Hard to forget that," he said. "Hard to forget." He kept nodding.

"What happened?" Matt prodded. He was enjoying the pinched look on Jeremy's sour, rat face. "Tell me what happened."

"When we first moved to Anacortes, we used to go to Church. The old Lutheran Church was up the hill in this cute old-fashioned wooden building," Crystal began. "It was one of these old-style Churches, you know, but tiny. Anyway, more and more young families were moving to the area and soon the Church was too small for the population. At Christmas Mass there was standing room only. People packed in on top of one another and the heat!" She fanned herself as if the mere memory warmed the air.

"Each year there were casualties," Jen added, "You'd see them start to weave then bang! Down they'd go. The altar boys used to drop like flies."

Jen could be so funny when she relaxed, he thought. It was easy to forget. He smiled to encourage her but she didn't notice; she was absorbed in Crystal's story.

Crystal continued, "So they built the new Church down the hill closer to town. It was needed but a lot of the older parishioners didn't want it. They were sad, you see. They'd had their weddings, baptized their children in that old Church. Their parents, their grandparents were buried in the lot next door. It was important to them. Well, Reverend O'Donnell, he's retired now and this new guy, we don't even bother anymore, but Reverend O'Donnell was one of these people that just understood, you know? He just got people. Anyway, he organized a procession to carry the spirit of the old building and bring it into the new one. We walked at night on Christmas Eve. Each person carried a candle lit from the flames on the advent wreath in the old Church. The whole community came out." She was far away now, lost somewhere in this magic past. Matt looked around the table to find that Jen and Ed and Jeremy were there too. He was filled with a kind of ache, a loneliness.

"It was cold, cold and clear and there was snow on the trees and stars on the water and all the houses lit up for Christmas down the hill. We walked along the old road with the children's choir leading the way. Then Jeremy did this solo of O Holy Night. We didn't even know he was going to do it; it was a surprise . . ." Her eyes, which had been slowly filling with tears, brimmed over now.

Jeremy shook his head, "Jesus, Mom," he groaned while Ed continued his long slow nodding with his arms folded over his chest.

But Jacob was on the edge of his seat, vibrating with excitement. "Sing it, Nana!" he commanded.

"Jakey, you don't know that one. Uncle Jerry doesn't like to sing anymore," Jen said.

Crystal leaned over and looked Jacob in the eyes, "*Oh Holy Night, the stars are brightly shining, this is the night of the dear Savior's birth.*" Her voice was surprisingly good, rich and full of emotion. She placed her hand over her heart.

Jacob frowned.

"You don't know it, Jakey."

"*Long lay the world, in sin and error pining, until he appeared and the soul felt its worth,*" Crystal continued, tears falling freely now.

Jeremy stared down at the table. "Okay, we get it, mother."

It seemed for a moment that she was through. Her head drooped down and she rested her chin on her clavicle and just when Matt was sure it was over, she lifted her head and raised her eyebrows dramatically, "*A thrill of hope, the weary world rejoices!*" She was going all out now, hand gestures, trills.

"Okay."

"*For yonder breaks a new and glorious morn!*"

"Alright!"

"*Fall . . .*" she began but her voice broke on the high note and she settled back. "It was so beautiful when Jeremy sang it. I can't even describe it. His beautiful voice and the candles and the stars."

"People still talk about it," Ed nodded, "Hard to forget."

"Let's do Rudolph!" Jacob cried.

"No Jakey, we'll do Rudolph later. Not now."

"Rudolph!" he insisted and began, "Rudolph the red-nosed reindeer, had a very shiny nose . . ." He looked anxiously from one face to another and there was a desperation in it, a franticness, as if he sensed seams in their togetherness that no one else could see.

"And if you ever saw it, you would even say it glows!"

"Like a light bulb!" Matt joined in for he couldn't stand to see his son looking so anxious; yet his own voice, when he joined in, came out loud and honking and he felt singled out by it, stupid somehow: his loud honking voice in the wake of the stars and the candles and the cold, like a lightbulb in the wake of the weary souls rejoicing. And even though they all joined in and clapped their hands, even though Jeremy joined in in sourpuss monotone for "Like George Washington!" even though they knew all the words and continued on with Frosty the Snowman because Matt and Jacob didn't know any of the religious songs, Matt's own honking voice remained in his head.

Like a lightbulb.

Later, Matt was alone in the spare room with Jen. The house was quiet and he stood by the window watching the snow fall softly through the black shapes of the trees, a living curtain that made the world seem more still, more quiet by its motion.

"You never told me about any of that," he said. "I didn't even know that you used to go to Church."

"Well we did," she answered. She was already in bed, her nose in a book. "My parents were into the whole God thing for a while but not anymore. I guess the new minister is a real douchebag."

He watched the snow for a moment longer. It landed soft and disappeared into the still wet Earth. There was so much unsaid between them, so many secrets, so many lies. He turned to look at her in the lamplight. It unsettled him that she'd never said anything, that he hadn't known the story. They'd been together long enough. "Why didn't you ever tell me?"

"You never asked." She didn't look up. After a moment she added, "Anyway, it's not like we were ever Bible Thumpers."

Now the orange cat pushed its face through the crack in the door and its body slipped in after it. It sauntered over to the bed and hopped up beside her and her hand found it and stroked it, like she knew exactly how and where to pet it without looking. They circled round one another, the cat and the hand, while she continued to read the book, and he realized he'd never even asked whether she'd want a pet or not. He'd never even thought about it.

"I don't know, Jen . . . I mean I think it's important, that we try to be honest with each other . . . That we tell each other . . ."

She looked up. "What do you want to know?"

"I mean, your parents . . . Do they . . ." He paused, searching for the words. He didn't know how to ask; his parents had never talked about God or spirit or anything like that at all. "Do they believe in God and all that?"

Now her face became dark and mocking in the way he remembered. "Crystal just likes to believe in things: God, angels, the perils of too much gluten, tarot cards, reiki, aliens. If there's emotion to wrought from an experience, it's good enough for her. Crystal's a Believer and Ed just does whatever's easiest." Her hand continued stroking the cat, like they knew each other, yet it was a new cat, one he'd never seen before.

He remembered the first time he'd ever seen her. Some of the kitchen guys were having their free beer after shift and were talking at the bar about earthquakes. They were talking about the Big One and what they'd do if it ever happened and she'd been standing at the waitress station waiting for the drinks, this new, very young, very beautiful girl, a summer hire in her first year of University. One of the guys asked, "What do you think, new girl, are you scared of the Big One?" And she'd looked right at him until he stopped smirking, then she'd narrowed her eyes and said, "I think Gaia's going to shake her tectonic plates and cast us all into the sea and that we'll probably deserve it," then she'd flounced away in her little tartan skirt and they'd all stared after her as she smiled sweetly at the customers as if nothing had even happened. He'd been smitten. He'd wanted to know her then, to find out all about her. He looked at her now in the lamplight. So much had happened since. He tried again. "I just, you know, I know it hasn't been easy but sometimes I feel like I hardly know you . . ."

"Well. It's not like we spent much time getting to know one another," she snapped and there was such dry and sudden anger in her voice that he recoiled as if he'd been slapped. Immediately, she began to lavish attention on the cat, picking it up and kissing its face while he stood alone at the window, watching.

"Good Kitty. What a nice kitty, you are," she cooed.

He turned away and looked back at the black and silent forest and he was filled with a sudden anger. A rage of frustration, like pounding on a locked door.

"Ssssss sssss, ssssss" she whispered into the cat's ear.

And he found himself thinking about his own secrets, piling them up in his mind against her refusal with a kind of bitter pleasure. He stood alone at the window and the name he'd wanted to forget slashed suddenly through his mind: Annika. Annika. Annika.

CHAPTER SEVEN

Annika woke and lay perfectly still. Feeling. Assessing. She half-expected to find the pain and tiredness had returned but instead she felt a bit stronger than the day before, a bit more alive. I am dying, I am dying, I am dying, she reminded herself; yet there was an excited tingle deep inside her, a bubbling up of possibility that came on each new breath.

She went downstairs, lit the fire, then made herself a coffee and took it out onto the porch where she sat wrapped in a blanket in an old Adirondack chair, staring out at the humped blue shapes of the islands on the horizon. Dying, dying, dying, this is it, the end, it's over, she told herself and still the grey jays came swooping down through the branches of the nearby trees where they flitted about, soft and silent and curious, and the squirrels chattered and chased one another, and the sea mist prickled on her skin.

A month passed, then another. Her strength returned day by day.

Sasha's visits were reduced to once every three days now, in the afternoons, when they'd go walking with Sasha's dogs. The walks were short at first, just to the end of the drive, then they ventured further out along the road, passed houses and cottages that were nestled into the hills and dips of the island's shoreline. On each of these walks Annika felt a small thrill of discovery: a creek chuckling through the waxy clumps of sword ferns, an elaborate gate at the end of a long drive, a great arbutus spanning the road. She felt as if she'd woken up from a terrible dream to find herself transported to a strange and magical landscape. Then she'd remind herself: I am dying.

Unlike most of the people Annika knew, Sasha was not afraid to talk about death. For several years before starting her nursing practice in Saltery Bay, Sasha had travelled the world, volunteering at hospices in different countries, learning how different cultures dealt with death. "There's this beautiful realignment of priorities that happens before the end," she explained one day after Annika had, once again, brought the conversation back to death. They were walking along the gravel road towards town, a low grey blanket of cloud hanging above them. "Things that used to matter don't matter anymore. Old hurts. Old angers. I know you don't believe me now, but I've seen a lot of deaths and it's often quite peaceful."

Annika considered this. She watched the dogs as they bounded back and forth between the road and the woods, rustling in the salal. There was a black lab and a goofy white mutt about the same size. Max and Kia. Now they stopped and pricked their ears forward, their noses quivering as they searched the air, and she found herself listening and quivering also, noticing things she wouldn't normally see. She drank the cool, spring air in great, eager gulps, then, remembering, looked down at her feet on the gravel. "What about accidents though?" she asked. "What about people who die suddenly?"

"The body is merciful, Annika," Sasha replied. "I truly believe it. I've heard too many stories of near-death experiences to believe they're a coincidence. People all report a very similar experience: a white light and a tremendous feeling of peace."

Annika didn't know what to think. Sasha came from a completely different world from the one she'd known: Sasha's parents were hippies and had carted their daughter around to Buddhist temples and communal farms before settling on a small homestead to raise goats and children. Many of Sasha's beliefs struck Annika as strange, a wild pastiche of ideas and cultures; still, it made her feel lighter somehow, to think that there was more than one way to look at things.

They continued walking. They were further now, further than they'd ever walked before. "Are you getting tired? Do you want to turn back?" Sasha kept asking but Annika felt good; she felt a quickening of excitement as the townsite, a cluster of grey buildings at the harbor's edge, came into view. During her illness, she'd barely given the town a second thought but suddenly she was filled with a desire to go there, to be out amongst other people for a while.

They kept walking. The gravel turned to pavement. Sasha called the dogs and clipped them onto their leashes. When they reached the main street, Annika felt a warm rush of satisfaction. "We finally made it!" she said. She hadn't realized it had been a goal until this moment. "Let me take you for a coffee to celebrate."

Sasha was looking at her with a strange expression, as if slightly puzzled and unbelieving. She did not respond right away, then nodded slowly. "Yes. I know a place." Annika frowned, unsure if she'd done something to make Sasha upset.

They passed several shops with crafty wooden signs out front. There was an art gallery, a bookstore, a wine store and a small grocery. All the buildings were a weathered grey colour with neat white trim, an understated tidiness that suggested affluence, the kind of money that's lost the need to yell. The streets were quiet, almost empty; but the people they did pass were friendly and had a pleasant, comfortable look. They all said hello to Sasha and smiled warmly at Annika, as if they already knew her.

The coffee shop, the Java Jive, was in the corner of a one-story building that also housed the hardware store. A For Sale sign was hanging in the front window. Sasha tied the dogs to a post, looked at Annika with that same puzzled expression, then opened the door and went inside. Annika followed.

Inside, the space was simple but cozy with two large windows overlooking the harbor, dark wooden floors and a collection of brightly coloured chairs and tables scattered around the room. After so many months confined to the cottage, Annika couldn't stop looking around. She ordered a coffee, then sat next to the window drinking in the scenery. From where she sat, she could the main street ramping down onto the ferry dock and public wharf. Beyond this, at the end of the harbor, was a small marina with several rows of white sailboats bobbing in their slips, their masts tickling up against the flat light of the sky. She sighed happily, cupping her cold hands around the warm porcelain of her mug. She wanted to savor every detail, to enjoy each moment. When she looked back up, Sasha was watching her closely.

"You know, Annika," Sasha began slowly, choosing her words with care. "When we started our walks, I never thought that we'd get this far. I assumed that your feeling better was a small reprieve, a bump before the illness really took hold. I've seen that happen before. Now, I'm not sure what I believe." Sasha's green eyes were sincere and searching. Annika looked away. "I've looked after a number of people with the exact same diagnosis as you, the same prognosis, and I've never heard of anyone bouncing back like this. I mean, your skin is glowing, your hair is shiny . . . It's amazing, but strange."

Annika's hands tightened around the mug. She both wanted Sasha to say it and not to say it, lest the words make it real, lest the words turn what was now only a feeling into something more definite, something that could be reversed, that could be refuted or denied.

"I mean, I'm happy to keep being your nurse for as long as you want me," Sasha continued, "But I feel like I'm beyond the scope of my understanding. I don't think I can offer you any real useful advice at this point . . . I think you should go back to see your doctor, to find out what's happening."

Annika looked down into her coffee again. She felt excited and frightened and lonely all at once. She didn't know how to feel.

Sasha gripped her hand overtop the mug. "Annika, don't be afraid. This is a good thing! An amazing thing . . ." Her voice was suddenly thick with emotion. "Every day that you're healthy is a gift. Think of it as an absolute gift!"

Annika nodded. She was terrified.

Two weeks later, she was back in Dr. Zagar's office, sitting in the same small examining room with the high window and the table and the eye chart and the stool, only now the sun through the window was warm and gold. Almost six months had passed since her initial diagnosis.

Dr. Zagar came in and sat down. Her grey trousers climbed up her shins. She looked down at her chart, then at Annika, then at her chart again.

I am dying, I am dying, I am dying, Annika thought loudly, in the front of her mind, trying to beat back the excitement that was bubbling up from the pit of her stomach.

The doctor took off her glasses. She set them on the counter. "In all my years, I've never heard of anything like this happening, not with a cancer so advanced. Certainly never with pancreatic cancer."

Annika pressed her hands together. They were shaking. "What? What's happened?" she asked.

The doctor looked into her eyes. "The tumor is gone. It's literally not there anymore, except for a tiny speck no bigger than a . . . than a grain of sand. If it weren't for the scarring, I'd be tempted to believe it had never existed at all."

Annika closed her eyes. "Will it come back?"

"I don't know, to be honest. It might. It might not. We'll keep checking on it, of course, and we'll get you started on a course of chemo right away to zap any of it that's left, but I can't really tell you anything conclusive at this point, because . . . because this is a one in a million case. I'd call it a miracle if I believed in those things."

The sun was warm on Annika's face. When she opened her eyes, she could see dust motes lifting lazily on the air. The doctor's face appeared soft and honeyed and feminine. I'm alive, she thought. I'm alive. She could barely keep herself from laughing.

When it was time to leave, she paused in the doorway. "Dr. Zagar?" she asked.

The doctor looked up from her clipboard.

"Whatever happened to that picture, the one that used to hang out in the waiting room, the one called 'The Doctor'?"

The doctor frowned. "Oh, that one. I keep it at home now; too many people complained that it was macabre. Why do you ask?"

"I liked it," Annika said simply.

The doctor tilted her head slightly, regarding Annika curiously, then she smiled and nodded. "So did I."

It was a Friday evening, and, aware that she'd be hard-pressed to make the last ferry, Annika decided to stay in Seattle for the night. She splurged on a hotel room, something she'd never done before. She felt determined, on some level, to do things differently this time.

It was a clear, cold evening and, after settling into her room, she went for a walk along the seawall. The water was still and black and she could see the city lights reflected there, shimmering just under the surface so that all the world was doubled: the glittering skyline and the Ferris wheel and the strings of coloured lights in the masts of the boats; the lamp posts that followed the seawall shimmering and waving like a string of faery torches, leading the way to a magical gathering forever out of view.

There were decisions that had to be made, she knew: work and money and where to live; yet her mind rushed away every time she tried to focus on these details. She wanted to drink in the lights, the cold, to just feel alive for a night.

Well-dressed, attractive people walked by her on their way to the restaurants and bars, hands plunged deep in their pockets, their faces bright and pale as underwater moons and she felt herself being drawn along, as if enchanted by the lights, following the crowds towards the market and the pier where all the night life was. How was it that on a cold, clear night this rainy, dreary city could transform itself into something so exquisitely beautiful? How was it she'd never noticed before? She kept walking and soon she was standing in front of the Old Triangle, an upscale bar where her co-workers from Lifeline Insurance used to come on the last Friday of every month. During the entire time she'd worked a Lifeline, she'd never once joined them, even though they'd always invited her. They would be here tonight, she realized, if nothing had changed.

She stood for a time watching the diners in the windows, their faces gentle in the candlelight. She put her hand on the door; she could feel her own heartbeat in her fingertips as they gripped the ornate, metal handle. Then, without thinking much of anything, she took a deep breath and pulled it open. It felt like a wild, daring thing to do. It felt like a new way to be.

Immediately, warm air rushed over her, tinkling with the sounds of conversation and clattering silverware. The room was specked with twinkling lights, tiny candles on each table that were reflected in the glassware; the bottles behind the bar glittering under dim overhead lights; the rude plaster and rough finish of the pub's interior providing a charming contrast; the lights like faraway cities surrounded by darkened hills. She could have stood there all night, just listening and looking, but then Beverly was there beside her in the entrance.

"Oh my God!" Beverly exclaimed. She wore a sleek black dress and her hair was pinned up to show off her toned shoulders. "Annika? Annika! I can't believe it's really you!"

"You look great, Beverly."

They hugged, then Beverly put her hands on Annika's shoulders and looked deep into her eyes. "How are you doing? I can't believe it. I couldn't believe it when I found out."

"I'm good. It's . . . it's much better for now." She'd thought she'd been prepared to talk about it but Beverly's intensity was overwhelming. She looked down.

Beverly lowered her head and came up from underneath with her eyes, rooting for eye contact the way an attention-seeking dog will push its muzzle under your hand until you pet it. "Annika . . . We've all been so worried."

Annika had to smile. Her father's dog used to do just that. "Well, you can stop now! I have good news: I just came back from the doctor: it's in remission." She linked her arm in Beverly's and Beverly grinned as if something rare and wonderful were happening.

She squeezed Annika's arm. "Come on. Everyone is going to be super excited you're here. They're going to be shocked. I should warn you, though: they're all wasted. It's a bit of a gong show, really." They walked arm in arm through the tinkling, flickering air to a large table surrounded by familiar faces.

"Hi everyone."

Conversation stopped. They all turned to stare, then finally, Ray hollered, "Annika Bo-Bannika! The lost sheep of Lifeline! The prodigal daughter of new applications!" His sandy hair was standing on end and his narrow face was bright red and wild-eyed; he looked like one of those Japanese monkeys that sit in the hot pools and Annika burst out laughing.

"Hello, Ray. I can see some things haven't changed," she said. Ray was one of these composed, sand-coloured men who was instantly transformed into a raging maniac at the mere mention of a drink.

Now everyone was greeting her and welcoming her back. They were all there: Tiffany and Rehab and John and Tyler and two people she didn't know. If there was any strangeness, no one let on. Annika found a chair and pulled it up between Tiffany and Rehab.

Tiffany touched her arm. "How are you doing? Are you? I mean, you look . . ." she fumbled. Tiffany had been her manager, a constantly frazzled woman with dry, poofy hair.

Annika realized she had better just come out and say it. "I wanted to let everyone know I'm doing much better now. The cancer is in remission. I really appreciated all your well wishes. It meant a lot." It came out with far more confidence than she'd expected and they all raised their glasses and toasted her health. She wondered why she'd never come before.

"Well, let me fill you in on what you missed," said John. He pressed his thin lips together and stared silently into his drink, some kind of syrupy amber liquid in a snifter, before looking back up at Annika. "That's it. That's all you missed."

Tyler, the department's nod out to youthful hipness with his tight pants and ironic delivery, countered, "Oh come on now, John. There was that memo seven days ago and some *very* entertaining email threads. Oh, and there was Ray, totally killing it at the Christmas party." Tyler's sleeves were rolled up to display his tattoos, flowers and faeries in greens and blues, a kind of magical garden that seemed a strange contrast to his clipped manner of talking. They were beautiful, Annika thought. She wondered why she'd never asked him about them.

A waitress came and Annika ordered a glass of wine. She felt a kind of reflexive guilt for spending the money, the ghost of her parents' frugality even now; yet another part of her rebelled against it, that newly woken part that was determined not to travel the same lonely path. When the wine came, she took a sip and held it in her mouth, holding it carefully, then she swallowed and she could feel it spreading out inside her, pale and cold and delicate, like snow melting into the Earth.

She sipped her wine and listened to the banter and watched her former co-workers twinkling faces. She'd spent so much time annoyed at who they were not, at the compromises she'd slid into when she'd moved to the city with Hamish, that she hadn't ever really seen them. Now they drank and ate and were charming and gracious and she marveled at how beautiful they were.

Everyone kept switching seats and eventually she found herself next to Ray, who was already lit up like Christmas. "Beverly told me that you're going to Spain," Annika said. "That's exciting."

"Finally get to tick it off the ol' bucket list," he said, then froze.

"The bucket list," she mused.

"I mean, I'm excited to go," he corrected himself. "I've wanted to go for a long time."

"What else is on your bucket list?"

"Ummm . . ." His eyes darted about anxiously. "Well . . ."

"It's okay," she laughed. "I'm not about to drop dead. I really am just curious." She took another sip of wine and held it in her mouth. They used to send her forwards in her email, links to blogs about fads or silly videos and she'd always just deleted them, for they'd struck her as a waste of time, but now she really was curious. What did other people dream about? What did they want to do before they died? She wanted to know.

"Ummm . . . Greece. Definitely the Greek Islands. Santorini on a sailboat, you know?" Ray said cautiously.

"That would be beautiful," she encouraged.

"And the pyramids. I mean, c'mon. Everybody's got to see the pyramids," he said, bolder now.

She thought of the dusty gold world of ancient Egypt and Moses and Pharaoh and all the plagues and nodded seriously.

Beverly, who'd been listening in, put down her vodka soda. "I want to try paragliding," she said. "That's my new life goal."

Beverly was very definite about it and Annika could suddenly picture it: there it was in bold and vivid detail: a verdant hillside near the ocean, a spandex-clad Beverly launching out into the sharp, sparkling air in tandem with a Mexican hunk, the two of them flying out over the glittering water with Al on the cliffside watching, wringing his hands and worrying over her ovaries, breathing deeply and trying to channel the calm and surrender they'd told him about at the fertility clinic, while above him this ungainly bird swooped and dove, its shadow passing over the rocks, its shadow passing over the bald dome of his worried head, an awkward miracle, a two-headed Icarus reaching towards the sun and screaming 'waaahoooo! waahooo! this is the coolest thing ever!'

Now Rehab leaned close as if she were imparting a great secret: "I want to ride a horse. In the ocean." She covered her mouth with her hand and giggled. Hee. Hee. Hee.

"You're wild, Rehab," teased Tyler. "Totally out of control."

But it *was* wild, Annika thought. It was wild and amazing and incredible. She could see it: an absurd white steed pounding through the surf, Rehab hanging onto the mane, her headscarf trailing out like a pennant behind her, riding and laughing in her jolly, infectious way: hee hee heeeee!

"There's the Great Wall of China," Ray continued.

"I'd like to see Cirque du Soleil in Las Vegas," Tyler said, at which point John rolled his eyes.

"There's the Taj Mahal."

"Guy Laliberte's an artistic genius. I don't see any reason to be a snob about it."

"There's Machu Pichu."

"There's partying with Guy Laliberte. *On the fucking moon!*"

"There's Angkor Wat."

"Swimming with the dolphins." Hee. Hee. Hee.

Now everyone was jumping in, adding their two cents and Annika sat spellbound, enchanted by the dreams that were being paraded before her, desires that would have struck her as frivolous before, in litany became a kind of poem, a caravan of desire.

"The complete works of William Shakespeare."

"Pay down my mortgage."

"There's this town in Germany where you can go and watch the entirety of Wagner's Ring Cycle all in one shot. They seat you in uncomfortable chairs, so you stay awake."

"Learn to play the guitar, then serenade my husband on his birthday."

They went tinkling past, these pretty horses all done up with longing, so close she felt she could almost touch them, and suddenly, without warning, she found herself lonely, achingly lonely for the cottage in Saltery Bay.

Ray interrupted her thoughts. He threw his arm around her shoulder. "What about you, Bo-Bannika? You're being awfully pensive, young Missy!"

They all turned to look, their faces still soft with their own dreams. Annika didn't know what to say. Her mind raced, yet she couldn't think and as her silence went on, she saw them keen to her panic; she could feel their awareness sharpen to the question's significance. What do you want to do before you die? Even the sounds of the restaurant seemed to be waiting. Conversation around her went into a lull. "I don't know, really I . . ." she stammered. "I want to live somewhere quiet. I want a quiet, peaceful place." As she spoke, she remembered a dream she'd forgotten, something she used to talk about before she'd met Hamish, at the end of her firefighting days. "I've always thought about opening a café or a Bed and Breakfast, something like that. A place where I could be my own boss and people could come and relax. Where they could just come and be themselves."

She looked around. Everyone was silent. Blood crept up into her face.

"But Annika," Tyler said after a long silence. "Why would you want a rewarding life in peaceful place when you could go to Germany with John and sit in an uncomfortable chair for twelve hours?"

Rehab punched Tyler on the arm. "You. You are such a kidder."

Then the sounds of the restaurant rushed back in and the crisis passed. Annika sat back and sipped the wine, her thoughts returning again and again to Saltery Bay and the café she'd visited with Sasha. Maybe it was possible to start again, she thought. Maybe it was possible to leave the past behind.

A week later, however, she was back at the cancer clinic and all her old fears had returned. She felt a tightness in her chest, like she couldn't breathe.

The clinic faced the interior of the hospital so there were no windows to the outside; the air was dead and smelled strongly of antiseptic. There was a hint of sweetness underneath that made Annika feel sick, a kind of undertone, like a drunk that tries to hide the booze on their breath with a breath mint but fails. It was like that here: all the pastel lights and soft tones and lemony freshness couldn't quite mask the smell of death, couldn't quite hide the suffering that was happening in the rooms all around.

A young nurse in pink scrubs walked past and Annika tried to smile but it felt more like a grimace. The staff here were friendly and professional to a fault, yet they unnerved her; there was a tidiness, a neatness to the way they talked that reminded her of that other clinic, the fertility one, a way of speaking that turned sex and death into something clean and polished. A thing. A fact. An object. It was meant to make things easier, she knew, but somehow it didn't. It felt like a lie to her, this neatness, this over-simplification that caused the depths of her, the complicated parts, to cry out with loneliness for everything that went unacknowledged.

She tried to breathe deeply to calm herself, but the tightness in her chest remained.

Dr. Zagar wanted to start her with chemotherapy right away. To zap it, she'd said, just to make sure. In principle, it sounded like a good idea, yet the actual logistics of arranging it, felt impossibly complicated. For starters, Annika had given up her apartment and didn't have a place to stay in Seattle, which meant either travelling back and forth to Saltery Bay or finding a place to rent. For the past three days, she'd driven around, looking for apartments, and every minute she'd spent on the roads reminded her of why she'd hated it here in the first place. Everything she looked at was either too expensive or too depressing. She was staying in a cheap hostel for the time being, surrounded by kids who were one step away from the street.

She waited; the tightness in her chest ratcheting up with every minute she spent in that dead, enclosed space. The feeling was depressingly familiar: she'd had it towards the end when it was clear things weren't working out between her and Hamish. At that time, Dr. Zagar had dismissed it as anxiety, and maybe it was, yet she couldn't help feel that it was this very tightening that had made her sick in the first place, that her heart had simply closed into a knot and never let go.

Suddenly she stood. She didn't want to be here. Couldn't be here. Walking quickly, she left the hospital. She didn't think much of anything, only that she wanted, needed to leave. She missed the cottage. She missed Sasha. She thought of the sea, of a big wide sky above her and decided she would take her chances.

PART TWO

CHAPTER EIGHT

It happened on a Monday at the beginning of October. It was not quite noon yet when Matt ducked into a pub, an upscale Irish place with a grand old bar in the center, the tiers of bottles lit up like a temple and taps on all four sides. He took a seat and ordered a scotch. Several men in suits were tucked away in a dark-paneled booth and there was a woman at the bar across from him doing a crossword, a plump redhead with catty glasses, the kind that were popular in the fifties, a half-empty pint glass on the bar in front of her. She was closer to his age than Jen and wasn't overtly sexy, not in the way he ordinarily defined it; yet he felt attracted to her right away. He liked the fact that she was here before noon on a Monday, drinking by herself. Who were any of them kidding, anyway? He flashed her a smile and she smiled back, rouging slightly.

The bartender slid his drink in front of him. Matt closed his eyes and held the liquor in his mouth, trying to place his mind into the whiteness of the burn, to sear his worries away. The bank had called and left a message on his phone and he hadn't yet mustered the courage to call them back. He knew what it was about: his line of credit was maxed out and the automatic payment for the mortgage must have bounced. He sipped his drink, his mind scrabbling over the various combinations of loans and credit cards that might keep them afloat a while longer. Six months to a year, Ken had told him, and now that year was almost up. He'd be getting a much-needed injection of cash any day.

He ordered another scotch and watched the waitress as she went about the room, wiping the surface of each table with a rag.

There was something strange about her. She had a pretty, slim face and long, dark hair; a lean stretch of thigh was visible between her black bobby socks and short skirt; yet there was a stockiness to her upper body that was incongruent with her limbs, a thickness in the middle. It wasn't until she bent over a nearby table that he realized she was pregnant.

He looked away and swirled his drink. The ice cubes clicked softly against the sides of his glass.

Jen had kept working right up until the last month, out of stubbornness or pride he wasn't sure. She'd been huge at the end, awkward to look at, and they'd stuck her on lunches, the dead times, the B team. She didn't fit the image anymore. Still, she'd refused to quit and would come back to his apartment after each of her shifts crying. He'd told her to take the time off but she wouldn't do it. He took another sip and held it in his mouth. The night that Jacob was born he'd been working, he remembered. The bar had been hopping, a real party vibe and he'd been in the flow, his hands flying, the jokes cracking when he got the call that she was in labor. Before he'd left for the hospital, he'd ordered a staff shooter, the A team pressing up around him in their sexy little outfits. "Matty Matt's going to be a Daddy!" they'd cooed and then they'd all knocked one back, then another, and then he'd taken a taxi out to the hospital with that fire still in him, with the music still throbbing in his ears. It wasn't until he saw Jen's face, her frightened, naked face, that he'd actually understood the enormity of the changes that were about to happen, and then it was too late, then he was there, stumbling around the delivery room, trying to hide the tequila on his breath.

Matty Matt's going to be a Daddy!

He closed his eyes and tried to hold the burn, to prolong it as it went down.

Then the crossword cat said, "Hey. Turn that up for a second."

He opened his eyes and watched as the bartender put down his rag and reached for the remote.

The television above the bar showed a reporter standing in front of the New York stock exchange and crowds of people milling about. "Investors are panicking here as the afternoon wears on," the reporter said. "It's absolute mayhem here on Wall Street. With only a few hours left to close, this stands to be the worst crisis in over 50 years." Now the screen showed a series of graphs with steeply dropping slopes.

The two businessmen came over and leaned against the bar. The pregnant waitress stood still in the middle of the room, holding a tray of empty glassware. They all watched the television. The crossword cat whispered, "I can't believe this is actually happening."

The screen switched to the inside of the stock exchange where men in their shirt sleeves were holding their heads and walking around with stunned expressions. A handsome young man stood in the middle of the floor watching the numbers on a screen above him, then he crumpled to his knees and there was something about the slow-motion way that he went down, in stages like a ruined horse buckling, that was immediately recognizable. It was the way you imagine giving up in dreams, crumpling slow to the pavement as the world rushes on ahead of you.

"I can't believe it," one of the businessmen echoed.

"I can't fucking believe it," said the other and Matt joined the chorus of incredulity even though none of them were truly surprised. There'd been talk already. There'd been warning signs. The news was just a confirmation, really, of what everybody already knew, a creeping dread made physical by this man crumpling to his knees. Matt felt his scalp crawl as if from sudden cold.

Outside, the sun kept shining. Cars and people went by the front windows, just as they had before. The waitress resumed her rounds, wiping tables and collecting glasses; yet it all felt suddenly precarious, as if the brightness of the day might shatter, sending the windows showering inwards in a million deadly shards. The moment seemed to stretch on, taut and discordant and strangely empty, then a single, panicked thought flooded Matt's brain: Jen and Jacob. He had to get back to them. It was irrational, he knew, yet the feeling was so overwhelming he couldn't deny it.

He set his glass down on the bar, then hurried out to his car.

He was probably over the limit, he thought as he peeled away from the curb. He'd driven in far worse states, however, and he'd always managed fine. It was a matter of focus. He weaved in and out of the slow-moving lanes until he came to the Interchange where traffic slowed to a crawl. He sat there looking at the great, shimmering line of vehicles that stretched away towards the horizon. He was drunker than he'd originally thought; this worried him. Suddenly, a siren began to wail, rising up from the lines of cars like a long, thin line of smoke. He glanced in the rearview but couldn't see the cherry.

C'mon, c'mon. He tapped his hand on the steering wheel, then fished in his wallet for a penny and placed it on the dash in front of him. Chew a penny and it fucks the breathalyzer. Where had he heard that? An urban legend, a Ken thing most likely, but at least it was something. At least it felt like he was taking action.

He glanced in the rearview. The sirens were moving off now, towards downtown and it occurred to him that people might be looting, fleeing the city. He turned up the radio but there was no news of the crisis, only traffic reports and the inane flirtations of Kelly and Mike on 92.7 ROCKS. I'm going crazy, he thought. I'm losing my fucking mind, still he couldn't shake the prickling sense of disaster that tingled across his scalp.

By the time he arrived home it was mid-afternoon. The front of the house was bathed in a soft, golden light and Jen's car was in the driveway. They were home.

He opened the front door, near desperate for the sound of their voices, for their cheerful chatter to reassure him, but the house was quiet. It smelled of paint. "Hello? Hello?" He called out and his own voice echoed back to him. "Jen? Jacob?"

He went upstairs. The door to Jacob's room was partially opened and he peered inside, unsure of what he expected to see.

They were in there, snuggled together on Jacob's bed. Jen had her head propped up on the headboard and was reading a story while Jacob snuggled against her. The afternoon light fell across the room and lay rich and golden in Jen's shiny hair; it glowed in Jacob's eyelids, that perfect translucence where the delicate fringe of his eyelash met the lid of his downcast eye.

"Hello?"

They looked up. "Jacob had his frenulum out today," Jen said. Her thin hand smoothed Jacob's pale hair back from his forehead. "He was a very brave boy."

Matt stared in wonderment. Frenulums. Bravery.

"My mouth feels like a balloon, Daddy."

"Like a balloon?"

"It feels puffy like a balloon underneath."

Matt took a tentative step into the quiet space. The slanting gold light threw animal shadows on the walls: cats and bears and elephants, Jacob's gentle guardians in a wicker basket on the floor. Jacob's frenulum! That little piece of skin that connects your lip to your gums; his was too long; it was going to make a gap in between his teeth, he remembered now. Had she told him the appointment was today? He didn't remember her telling him.

He tiptoed towards the bed, aware of his own towering bulk, his fumbling awkwardness. "Did it hurt, buddy?"

"It hurt like a pinching but I didn't cry at all and then Mummy and me had milkshakes."

"Mmmmm. That sounds yummy. What flavor did you have?" He stood next to the bed holding his crumpled jacket in his hand.

"I had chocolate. Mummy had strawberry."

"I called you. I didn't know if you were coming or not," Jen said. Her voice was even, strangely neutral. He couldn't tell if she was angry or just stating a fact.

He stood, twisting the coat.

Jacob slid ever closer to Jen and tapped the empty space on the bed beside him. "Daddy."

Matt sat and Jacob beamed, snuggling deep between both parents for maximum contact. It was a miracle, Matt thought, this sidelong warmth against him.

"We're reading Wally Walrus goes to school," Jen supplied in that same, strange neutral tone. "Wally Walrus was bigger than the other seals. Much bigger. 'Can you do this?' the slippery seals asked then they slid down the icy slide into the blue, blue water."

"Look Daddy! The Walrus is stuck!"

Matt reached his arm around Jen's shoulder. He bent down and kissed Jacob's fine pale hair, breathing in the clean, baby-powder scent of Jacob's shampoo and then his own breath bounced back at him, smoky and sour with booze.

Jen turned the page and he saw that her jaw was set. There was a hardness round her mouth and a crinkle between her brows that he'd missed. Maybe he'd wanted to miss it. He tried breathing only through his nose but the smell was still there.

Afterwards, in the hallway, she hissed, "Where were you?"

"Hey, Jen. Sorry I missed it. Look, traffic was backed up and . . . Have you watched the news?"

"Were you out drinking? I told you his appointment was today."

"No, Jen. It's not like . . ."

"So what? Did you have some pretty little client to entertain?"

"No. Jen. Honestly, I don't remember you telling me it was today and I just went to have a drink because . . . Jesus, I rushed all the way back here to make sure you were alright. Have you heard what's going on?"

She raised her eyebrows and waited and the way she did it, with that mocking, overly dramatic arch and her hand on her hip, it made the world economic crisis seem pathetic.

"The economy is tanking," he said, aware that it sounded like an excuse. "The stock market crashed and . . ." The men, he wanted to tell her, the men on Wall Street were falling to their knees.

She rolled her eyes as if she didn't believe him. "Well. You could have at least called to say you weren't coming. He was expecting you to be there." She turned on her heel and stomped downstairs.

He retreated to the spare room where they kept the computer. The room was mostly bare, one of the few she hadn't gotten around to with her renovations. There was a desk and a chair and a few unpacked boxes along the wall, filled with books mostly, novels and old textbooks from the time before she'd met him. He felt badly about missing Jacob's appointment although the kid seemed to have fared okay without him. Lately, he kept forgetting things. Whole chunks of time went missing. It worried him.

He logged onto the computer and went straight to the news for updates. The same urgency, the panic he'd felt at the bar screamed at him from the headlines and he felt calmed by it, somehow. It was real. It was happening. His reaction wasn't crazy after all.

He could hear Jen downstairs cleaning up in the kitchen. He looked over his shoulder at the bare room, now filling with shadow, then at the closed door, then, satisfied he was truly alone, he typed in a familiar web address. Instantly, a picture of an attractive young couple filled the screen. They were smiling at one another, standing in a bright, airy room with hardwood floors and whitewalls and cardboard boxes piled up behind them; then the picture morphed into that of a child lying in a sunny field and blowing on a dandelion gone to seed, the magic paratroopers drifting upwards into the blue, blue sky. Make your money make sense, the caption read.

He took a deep breath, then logged into their account. The numbers made his stomach turn. We're going to have to sell the house, he realized, although he'd be fucked if he could flip it now. He was so busy mentally tallying the what ifs and various combinations of debt that would make it somehow more palatable, that he didn't hear Jen come back upstairs. When the door opened, he started. He reached for the mouse and clicked the browser closed. "Hey!" he said, wheeling.

"What were you doing?" she asked in a slow measured way that was laced with accusation. She was a sharp, angular shadow against the yellow light in the hall.

"Nothing! Just checking my email."

"So why did you close it then? Why did you panic like that?"

He could smell his own breath like a rank beast hunkering in the dark. "You startled me, that's all." He should have turned on the light, he thought. It would have made things better, less suspicious somehow, if he'd only done that.

Her thin shadow didn't move. There was a long silence then she said icily, "I was going to tell you that I warmed up some left-overs, but I guess you're busy with other things." Then she turned and stalked off and he felt something snap inside him.

He thrashed about wildly in the computer chair and gave the middle finger to the floor where he could hear her downstairs slamming the dishes around and mouthed FUCK YOU then he gave the finger to the computer screen and to the window and to the ceiling. A shred, a tiny shred of self-control prevented him from screaming, from actually going ahead and smashing his fist through the screen with its stupid screensaver of a mountain lake that he'd never even fucking been to, and the fact that this small shred still existed, the fact that he couldn't, that he didn't just go ahead and punch it, made him even angrier. He balled his hands into fists and punched at the air. He couldn't do anything! He couldn't fucking do anything! Everything he did, every least thing, was some kind of strike against him. Come home early, come home late, what did it matter, he was already accused. Jesus, he was mad. I'm sooooo fucking sorry I ruined your life, he wanted to scream. You had sex with me too! You fucked me too!

He sat there for a while, then he got up and went downstairs where he crashed about the liquor cabinet. Why should he have rules for himself when everyone else seemed to do whatever the fuck they wanted? He poured a HUGE glass of scotch but she stayed in the kitchen and didn't get to appreciate it so he stomped back upstairs and returned to the computer.

He sat there in the dark with this reckless anger battering around inside him, then he thought of something he could do. Over the past year he'd thought about doing it many times, but something had always stopped him. Ken had been so grave, so serious, warning him several times: 'Always through me, you understand? If you have any questions, any problems, you come through me,' his pale eyes boring into Matt in such a way that Matt had felt like he'd already done something wrong. Fuck him, Matt thought now. It was his money and if Ken hadn't wanted him to know her name he could have just gone and done things the regular way instead of cutting through the red tape, instead of 'hooking him up direct.' There wasn't any harm in it, anyway. It was just a search, that was all.

He typed 'Annika Torrey, WA' into Google.

There were multiple results. At the top of the list was a link to a tourism website for Saltery Bay, a small town in the San Juan Islands. It showed a directory of local businesses. Halfway down the list was a place called Twisted Anni's with a little star beside it saying NEW! Coffee, muffins, cinnamon buns, open year-round. Contact Annika Torrey, then a phone number and a mailing address. It can't be her, he thought. There must be another Annika Torrey; yet his heart had begun to pound wildly in his chest.

The next link was to a photo in a weekly newspaper, *The Saltery Bay Tribune*. The picture showed a busy outdoor market. There was a table covered in produce, another in what looked like sweaters. In the aisle between the booths were three lines of dancers, women mostly, but with a few bearded and pony-tailed men thrown in. All the dancers had their hands in the air and were in slightly different phases of a lunge to the left. The caption read: Flashmob! Members of the Healing Journeys Meet-up treated shoppers to an impromptu dance performance at last week's farmer's market. From left to right the dancers are . . . followed by a list of names. Matt leaned forward. He held his breath.

Annika Torrey was in the back row, on the end. She was slim, wearing jeans and a plain white T-shirt, and had a mass of thick, dark hair that was twisted into a braid that hung down over one shoulder. She was beautiful, in a way, with sharp, haughty cheekbones and big, dark eyes. Unlike the other dancers she was not smiling and appeared deep in concentration. Intense. It couldn't be her, he told himself again, yet he remembered the medical report. He remembered that he'd imagined her to be attractive: 5'8 and 135 lbs. He thought about the dark, angry slash of her signature pressed into the page. Healing from what? The article didn't say.

The next link was from Island Life magazine, again about Twisted Anni's Bakery Café. "Torrey, 39, came to Saltery Bay a year ago." He caught his breath. He remembered that too. That she was the same age as him. She was quoted: "I came here looking for a quiet place away from the city and I liked it so much I decided to stay and try to make a life here. I've always toyed around with the idea of owning my own business. You come to a point in your life when you realize that we're only here for a short time and you might as well make the most of it."

He stared at the screen for some time. It was her. It had to be her. He took a long drink of Scotch but it didn't make him feel any better. The booze just seemed to seep under his skin and make him feel hot. He went back to the web page with her photograph and stared at it. She didn't look sick. He'd always imagined people with cancer having no hair, but he supposed that was only if they were getting radiation.

He sat there in the dark, drinking and looking at the photo. He looked up viatical settlements, hoping, perhaps, for reassurance but the more he dug, the more he came across stories of fraud and bad behavior. Faked medical records. Brokers selling fake policies. A total gong show in the eighties with the AIDS crisis.

His face began to burn. Why would a dying person start a café? Even if you lived longer than predicted, you wouldn't start a new business. The more he thought about it, the more it didn't make sense. She could have forged the medical records, lied about her illness then started a new life with his money. Or maybe Ken had lied. Ken! That opportunistic little shit, he thought. He should have known.

He polished off the Scotch and decided he had to do something. No one else was going to help him. He'd called Ken the week previous to check in and Ken had brushed him off with non-comital bullshit. He'd told Matt to be patient, that if he'd wanted medical reports he should have specified that in the contract. Fuck him, Matt thought. He'd ask her himself. He wrote the address of the café down on a small scrap of paper, then opened a new document and began to type, his fingers pounding down on the keys: "Dear Ms. Torrey . . ."

Chapter Nine

Annika arrived at the healing circle early and sat alone at the table, watching tendrils of smoke unfurl from the glowing ember at the end of a stick of incense. The smoke rose and twisted, then spread out into wraithlike fingers that seemed to beckon ominously as they curled upwards into the peak of the high timber-framed ceiling.

Only a week ago, she'd felt safe here. The beautiful house, the delicate china tea cups and herbal teas and quiet music had made her feel cared for and she'd dared to hope, to believe that healing—from cancer, from heartbreak, from life—might actually be possible. Then she'd received the letter. Receiving it *did* something to her, let the air out somehow, made everything around her flat and dull and ugly. She was aware of her own creeping cynicism, of a ragged whisper inside her brain, mocking her efforts to build a better life, to be healthy and whole.

The doorbell rang, jarring her from her trance-like fixation on the smoke. She heard Marion, an aspiring energy healer who hosted the weekly therapy group, go out to answer it. Soon, familiar voices drifted in from the hall.

Annika sighed and turned to the large bay window, hoping the bright day outside might lend her some of its optimism. It was a beautiful afternoon: the sun was sparkling on the water and the shapes of the nearby islands were cut in crisp, fine lines into the pale strip of blue where the sky touched down. On the lawn directly in front of the window, Marion's husband Helmut was working, arranging what appeared to be rusted sections of pipe onto an orange tarp that was spread out over the yellow grass. He stooped, then stood upright, clasping his hands behind his back as he assessed his loot, a tall athletic man with a silver crew-cut. Helmut was often around the house, working on the property, but never joined in his wife's healing sessions. He was always alone, quiet and contained. Annika watched him closely.

Amongst the Saltery Bay healing community, it was rumored that Helmut was a sociopath, a man so ruined by violence he'd lost the ability to feel, a claim greased along by Marion, who, after several glasses of wine liked to corner anyone who would listen with her marital woes. "You have no idea what he's like," she'd say, then her eyes would go misty and she'd shake her head, as if to rid herself of some terrible memory. Helmut's past didn't help him either: his parents were Austrian immigrants who'd moved to the States shortly after World War II and then Helmut himself had spent the majority of his adult life in the military, serving in an unknown capacity at a number of overseas postings, a position which, if the beautiful house was any indication, had earned him a great deal of money. Yet, despite all these rumors, Annika couldn't help but feel drawn to him. She watched as he walked over to his pickup and lifted something heavy from the back: in the bright crisp air, with the sun on his face, he seemed to her to be healthy and strong.

Now, the other participants began to filter in from the hall and she turned around to greet them. Barry and Kat and Susan arrived close together, then stood around the tea station, fixing their drinks and exchanging news of their week. Shortly after, Doug and Velma arrived and their group was complete. Once everyone was settled, Marion came in and sounded the chime.

"Welcome all," she said in a deep, mysterious voice, running her palms over the flawless white linen tablecloth. Standing at the head of the table in her flowing white dress, her smooth, golden skin aglow in the sunlight, Marion appeared otherworldly, like a prophet or a movie star. She pushed her sleek, black bob behind her ears with two fingers. "I hope everyone had a relaxed and healing week and were able to think about the things we discussed. Today, I'd like to begin our session with a guided meditation." In a slow, graceful motion, she reached over to the small table beside her and turned on the CD player. She asked everyone to close their eyes.

The music began, a mix of Celtic drums and pipes that crept along like fingers of mist creeping down over the hills. "You're sitting by a pool, looking into the water," Marion said in the low, steady voice she used for the meditations. "You feel good there, as you sit by the water's edge; you feel safe and relaxed. There is nothing to think about or worry about as you sit looking down into the clear, clean water, breathing deeply, steadily, your mind as still as the clear, clear water."

Annika listened as the breath of the others fell into a rhythm, rising and falling in unison like waves on the shore; it was peaceful, hypnotic even, yet she was unable to settle into it. She felt restless, the way she used to in Church, sitting in the hard pew with the sweet spring air coming through the open door. Since receiving the letter, she hadn't been able to focus. She hadn't been able to sit still at all.

She opened her eyes and looked at the faces around the table, each one deep in concentration, unaware of her watching, then she looked around the room, as if searching for her lost peace, but she could not find it. Today, the great living room with its high ceilings and wide windows appeared to her cavernous and bare; the friendly glow from the rose quartz lamps lost to the brightness in the window; the vivid colours of the Native American artwork washed out and over-exposed. Marion and Helmut had built the house several years earlier as a new beginning after the death of their daughter and they'd spared no expense; it was all perfect, all new; yet there was something false about it, a dream built by people who'd lost their ability to dream, who dreamed of what dreams should be.

Annika turned back to the window. She watched Helmut as he hauled a hose out of the shed with brisk, athletic competence. When her gaze returned to the table, she started: Marion had caught her.

Marion regarded her sternly, then silently passed her hand over her own eyes in that calm, lissome way she had, motioning for Annika to rejoin the meditation.

Annika closed her eyes again and tried to focus but the sun from the window made the backs of her eyelids glow and squirm, a liquid fire of reds and yellows. Suddenly she felt angry. What did Marion, with her pampered grief, really know about anything? Her only qualification was her own untouchable loss, a grief she held as whiter, purer somehow than the rest of their squalid compromises and mistakes . . . Annika shook her head. Stop, she chastened herself. It was cruel to think of Marion that way.

"Now look deep into the water. What do you see? What new awareness comes?"

They were supposed to envision a clear, cold pool, Annika knew, in which some vision or insight would appear, but today she saw only the backs of her own eyelids like squirming petrie dishes of her own blood.

"Now I want you to take this new awareness, this thing you've discovered and take it to your secret place, that place which is all your own, where it can be considered and cherished, where it can be turned over and over thoughtfully like a cool and precious stone. Breathe deeply and go now to your secret places, bringing this new awareness with you."

The secret places! The secret places that weren't secret at all! The secret places that were, in fact, so painfully obvious they seemed almost a pornography, a pornography of loneliness and need. She could go around the table and name them: there was Marion who dreamed of a crystal palace and pretty dresses and her daughter still alive; Kat, an obese diabetic with multiple health problems, who travelled to a gypsy carnival and danced with abandon round a fire; Barry, an ex-lawyer and ex-husband recently diagnosed with Parkinson's, who dreamed no further than a backyard barbecue with cold beer and easy laughter and a wife's forgiveness; Susan, the thin silver-haired celiac recently divorced after a life of doing exactly what she was supposed to, who rode wild horses on the Mongol steppes with a fur-clad warrior prince; and Paul and Velma, a symbiotic old hippie couple suffering form 30 years of political disappointments, who travelled back in time to a barefoot and hopeful love in a mud-slick field. There was nothing secret about any of it!

Irritated, Annika opened her eyes again and regarded them harshly; yet there was something so child-like and trusting about them sitting there with their eyes closed that her irritation quickly softened and turned into an exasperated affection, the desire to shake them and hold them all at once, to shield them and show them at the same time: don't you see? Don't you see that your dreams cannot protect you? That the world is brutal, that its consequence shall come to bear regardless of what you do?

She sighed and closed her eyes, remembering what Sasha, who'd recommended she come here in the first place, had told her: "There's no right way, Annika, only that you choose to heal. Everything that comes after, whether its yoga or religion or chemotherapy, everything is secondary to that intention." And Annika *did* want to heal. She *did* want to try. Breathing deeply, she willed her mind to her own wide horizon, to a summer field shifting in the breeze.

The music ended and there was a gentle opening of eyes.

The next part of the session was a group discussion where they each took turns sharing the troubles and triumphs of their lives. When no one volunteered to begin, Marion looked at Annika. "Annika, you seem distracted today. Is there anything you'd like to share?"

Maybe it was her irritation flashing again at Marion's prissy innocence, or maybe it was just there, like a splinter ready to come out, because she found that she wanted to tell them. She wanted to tell them about the letter and Matt Campbell and the whole squalid affair so they would see, so they would understand.

She took a deep breath, then began: "When I was first diagnosed with cancer, I sold my life insurance policy for cash. I had a policy through my work and no dependents so that's how I got the money to come here." She looked around the table: the faces were blank and uncomprehending. She tried again: "It's called a viatical settlement: I got paid part of the money up front with the understanding that my investor will get the full death benefit when I die. I know it probably sounds a bit morbid, but I didn't have any savings and I couldn't imagine dying in a hospital all cooped up with no living air, you know . . ." The faces were still empty and confused but she soldiered on: "Anyway, I ended up getting better, so I used the rest of the money to start the café and since then I feel like things have been going well. I've been try-ing to move on, slowly figuring stuff out, but then last week I got a letter in the mail from my investor. He beat around the bush, but the gist of it was: when did I plan on dying."

For a moment, no one spoke or moved at all. It wasn't a long moment, but long enough for all her loneliness to come rushing back, forcing its way into the shocked gap of their understanding, pushing it wider. How could these people begin to understand? she thought bitterly. They all had money. They all had second homes and cottages and families who they complained about, adult children who didn't visit or call enough but who were part of their lives nonetheless. They had no idea what it meant to be alone.

Now they all began to murmur and shift and look at her with wide, caring eyes. Susan, who normally kept her silver head bowed against her bony collarbone when someone else was shar-ing, looked up. "That's not right, Annika," she offered. "They shouldn't be contacting you. Maybe you should call the police."

Annika shrugged. "Apparently, they can. They did." A hard-ness had crept into her voice. "No one forced me to sign the contract. I took the money. I made that choice."

The sound of a compressor started up, hammering into the silence. Annika looked out the window; Helmut was spraying his loot with a pressure washer.

Marion frowned but said nothing.

"Well don't let them make you feel bad for a second," said Velma. Her small voice was nearly lost to the roar of the machine but her eyes were blazing fury. "They're nothing but a bunch of vultures, a bunch of capitalist vultures."

"People wonder why the system is crashing," Doug added, chin firm with indignation. "I say it deserves to crash when I hear a story like that."

They were warming up now, mustering their outraged sup-port, all but Marion who continued to frown.

"Don't let them get to you, Annika. You stay healthy and strong and stick it to those bastards," Velma rallied.

"Live forever just for spite," Barry twinkled. "Make their goddamn grandchildren inherit the premiums."

Marion motioned for calm, holding her hands to each side and pressing down like she was pressing on a bellows. Her big watery eyes couldn't hide her irritation. "Let's focus on Annika, not on what's wrong with the world." That was one of her rules: to keep discussion in the personal. "How did you feel, Annika, when you read the letter?"

How did she feel? Blood rushed to Annika's face. Sometimes she wanted to smack Marion, to wake her up from her dreamy earnestness. What did she want to hear, exactly? That after receiving the letter, Annika had sat on the floor for two hours, staring into space in the place the cot had been? That it had felt cold, her blood had felt cold, that death could leak back into a room, into a life, just like that? "It made me really fucking angry," Annika spat.

Fucking. Annika didn't usually swear but the word broke from her lips with all the pent-up fury of a rodeo bronc and for a moment she felt pleased by the shock it created: by Marion's frozen face like a stunned fish in her watery little world, by Susan who literally cringed.

Across the table, Barry started to shake. His white-blond head was bowed and his hands were folded in front of him, so Annika couldn't tell if he was laughing or if it was his Parkinson's acting up. Cups rattled on their saucers. It would be just like him to find it funny, she thought with a measure of affection, and she might have even laughed herself to relieve the tension except that the rest of them were all so wide-eyed and serious. They sat in silence, breathing deeply and letting it be until her outburst seemed an absurd and awkward thing between them. She found herself missing the firefighters, her friends from so many years ago, when they were all young and full of life, free in their joy and their speech and their anger; she thought about those vivid young men punching holes in hotel room walls on drunken nights off; she remembered their bruised hands in the mornings. How real, how raw it had all been!

Now, around her, these much older, much more comfortable people continued to sit in silence until she felt she had to say something. "Okay, I'm sorry. I'm just frustrated, that's all. I feel like I've been doing well and this . . . it's like a cold hand dragging me back, I don't know how to describe it."

"Okay. It's okay to have setbacks, right?" Marion said, her voice overly bright and hopeful. "Remember what we learned the last time? That growth is like a spiral? That we come back to the same place again and again but each time with a bit more insight and awareness than before. So here we are again. Anger."

Outside, the compressor stopped. The silence rang.

"What makes you angry?" Marion pressed.

"I don't know. The tone of it . . . It was so sloppy and aggressive, like he was accusing me of something but wouldn't just come out and say it . . ."

Marion leaned forward, her dark eyes welling up with tears. "You know, when Emma died, I was so angry I thought I would literally explode," she whispered. Here it was: the trump card, the mother of all grief. "I went after the driver in the courts. I spent all my time on lawsuits but it was wasted energy. I was putting up a wall around my own hurt, looking at the world when what I needed to do was look inside."

Annika looked down at the table. It was too much. It was not the same problem at all.

"Don't put up a wall, Annika. It's okay to feel hurt. We're here to take down walls, to erase boundaries."

"Maybe walls keep the bad guys out," said a dry male voice. Helmut. He was standing in the doorway, leaning against the jamb. It was unclear how long he'd been there.

Marion's face went white. "I'm so sorry," she said. She reached across the table and placed her hand on top of Annika's. "I'm so sorry for this interruption. Please excuse me."

Annika nodded, though in truth she was glad Helmut had intervened. She wished now that she hadn't spoken at all.

Marion got up and went out into the hall. "Jesus, Helmut! You cannot come in here without knocking! People are sharing very personal stories." Her words grew increasingly muffled as they moved away. Barry looked across at Annika and mouthed 'uh-oh.' The muffled hissing went on and on.

"Poor Marion," Kat sighed, her chins trembling as she brought her tea cup to her lips. She was a strange person, grey and remote, existing in a bubble of solitude outside the busy drama of the world.

"I don't know how she does it," the tight-lipped Susan shook her head. "I don't know how she stands him."

Eventually, Marion came back, her beautiful face all twisted up like a little girl trying not to cry. Helmut followed behind her, seemingly unfazed. He fixed them all with his steady grey eyes. "I would like to apologize for the interruption. My intention was not to disturb, but to tell you that I have found several useful items on my latest salvage mission to the dump: a water pump with brass fittings, a bidet and several sections of very usable copper pipe. Please, you are welcome to take a look on your way out." Then he was gone.

Marion hung her head. Her lower lip began to tremble, then tears began to fall.

"Oh dear," Velma said and reached her arm around Marion's shoulders. "Oh my, it's hard. Life is so very hard."

"I'm so sorry everyone. Here I am, supposed to be mediating and I can't even . . . He can't even . . ."

"It's fine, Marion. No one is upset. We understand you're both going through a lot. No one is here to judge."

"He doesn't respect . . . He just . . . spending all his time at that goddamn dump . . ." Her voice was completely different than it had been during the meditations; now it was high and strained. "I've told him that he doesn't have to join, that he doesn't have to talk about it but just to let me have this one hour every week, just to let me have this one thing and he can't even . . . he has to come in here and make a mockery of it . . ."

Kat reached out from her envelope of greyness and touched Marion's arm, her pillowy white hand barely touching Marion's lean, golden skin before retreating back. "He's hurt in his own way, just like the rest of us," she said. "He just shows it different is all."

Annika looked out the window to where Helmut was walking away towards the water, tall, erect and muscular and she couldn't help but wonder if, perhaps, he knew a thing or two about healing that the rest of them did not.

On her way home, Annika stopped at the café to make sure the new girl she'd hired for the weekends was making out okay, so she didn't get back to the cottage until early evening. When she opened the door, her cat, Zebedee, swirled about her legs, curling his body and tail around her shins. She bent and picked him up and he pushed his whiskers against her cheek. She'd been unsure about adopting a pet and had hemmed and hawed over it until Barry and Susan had shown up one day with a little tabby kitten and a promise they'd look after it, should her health fail again.

She held the warm, purring cat tight against her. The sun was already down, though the sky through the window was still pale where it met the water. There was a fog bank sitting just beyond the islands, an ominous grey blanket that moved out over the larger waters of the Juan de Fuca Strait during the daytime, then crept back in at night, as the air cooled. Even as she watched, she could see it creeping closer.

She turned on the lamp, then crouched to light the fire, remaining by the grate as the kindling caught, the silence heavy all around her. She'd tried to make the cottage more comfortable, more home-like since her illness; yet tonight its essential bareness leapt out at her, like a round of bone sticking up from the earth in a summer field, a stark white reminder of coyotes and wolves and the lean of winter. The empty space where Sasha had kept the cot yawned against the wall. Quickly, she shoved another log on the fire, then stood. The fog was almost at the point now, running its shadow fingers up the blonde flank of the hillside. Watching it, her skin crawled with sudden dread and she found herself wishing, almost desperately, for company, for someone, anyone, for another human voice to distract her.

"Okay, Zebedee," she said out loud, her words over-bright and jarring. "What next?"

She headed to the kitchen where she began to cut vegetables for dinner. She tried to focus on the small tasks, the papery skin of the onion, the knife biting down through the layers of flesh, one after another. This was how she tried to live now, always in the present, focusing on the small details of her existence, on the running of the café. What free time she had, she filled with the healing group and healthy activities; yet tonight doubts she'd brushed aside found her: had she made a mistake selling her policy? Would she be able to make a go of it here? Maybe she should have listened to Dr. Zagar and opted for the chemo. She worried that she'd chosen wrong.

Outside, darkness came down and the fog rolled up onto the beach. Soon, the little cottage was surrounded. When she looked up again, the view to the ocean had disappeared and she was met by her own startled reflection.

Chapter Ten

The letter, the letter, the letter . . . Matt lay awake, thinking about the letter. Beside him, Jen's steady breath counted out his lost hours of sleep while his mind rushed and scrabbled over shameful scenarios and possibilities: this Annika person could call the cops; she could call Ken and then what would he say? That he'd been snooping? Stalking her on the internet? She could find out where he worked and trash him in one of those online forums for home buyers; he'd been so fucking sauced when he'd wrote the thing, he'd even put his home address on it and now it was out there, physically out there in the world and there was nothing he could do to get it back.

Finally, he couldn't stand it. He got up and crept down the darkened stairs to the kitchen where he poured himself a drink, hoping and praying please please please that the burn would sear his squirming mind to stillness but the burn did nothing. It was as if someone had punched a hole in his stomach so that the booze simply leaked out and collected under his skin, a greasy, subcutaneous layer of booze that made him feel flabby and inflamed. "Fuck," he said aloud, knocked back the rest then crept back up to his room, his guilty feet feeling carefully for each stair, his breath short and shallow as he tiptoed past his son's room like a thief in his own house.

The next day he drove around drinking gas station coffee and trying to decide his next move. He felt half-crazed, full of delirious energy the way Jacob was when he needed a nap, that kind of half-crying, half-laughing mania with an emptiness at the core.

He decided to go out to the Regional Office. They had a message board there where they posted training and job opportunities. Leo, his supervisor, was always good for a bit of advice. Leo would help him get back on track, he thought as he drove. He needed a sale and needed one fast. Leo would know what to do.

He parked the car in an alley behind the building then walked around to the tidy storefront with the listings pasted up in the large window. The coffee shops and restaurants that lined the usually bustling street seemed eerily quiet and he found himself wondering if it was a holiday; with so much waiting and worrying he'd lost track of what day it was.

Inside, the waiting room was deserted. The pamphlets they put out each morning were still in a perfect fan on the coffee table. A small placard on top of the secretary's empty desk read 'Be back in 20 minutes.' He went down the hall to look at the bulletin board but there was nothing useful: a volunteer opportunity with Habitat for Humanity, a fundraiser for the United Way, that was all. He continued on to Leo's office. The door was slightly ajar. He pushed it open, unsure of what he would find.

Leo was crouched on the floor, emptying his book shelf into a large cardboard box. The small office was crammed with boxes and the walls, once a gallery of framed photos showing smiling new homeowners, were bare. Matt stood in the doorway, dumbfounded: Leo was leaving.

"Hey, where do you think you're going?" he said finally, trying hard to sound like his old, jovial work self. "It's only a bit of froth."

Leo looked up, then stood in a swift, athletic motion. "Pop goes the fucking weasel," he said. He was wearing jeans and a grey sweatshirt with the sleeves pushed up over his hairy, muscular forearms. With his gold ring and gold watch glinting in the grey light, he looked tough in a trashy way, like a mobster on a Saturday morning. Leo, of the elegant suits, the big white smile.

Matt stared, unsure of what to say next. Ordinarily, Leo would have filled the silence with a joke or small talk, but today he simply stood there wiping his hands on his jeans.

"So where are you headed?" Matt stammered. "Setting up shop somewhere else?"

"Nah. I'm done with this racket. Deb and I are pulling the plug and heading out to North Dakota. I've got some work lined up out there . . ." Leo paused, frowned at the floor, then leaned his hip against the edge of the desk and peered at Matt with tired grey eyes. "How about you? How are you weathering the storm?"

"I'm . . ." He almost said 'keeping busy' or 'staying positive' but in the quiet office with Leo looking like Tony Soprano, it seemed pointless to keep pretending. He shrugged. "I haven't had so much as a phone call in a month. I've just been . . . I don't even know what I've been doing, to be honest. Hoping for a turnaround, I guess."

Leo pursed his lips and nodded slowly as if Matt were simply confirming something he already knew, as if the hours, the aimless driving, the coffee shops and unanswered calls were just facts of life. It felt good to say it too; it felt like a drink after a long day, that hissssss-psssssst-aaahh of release, so Matt continued, "The bank is after me for that monstrosity of a house and I haven't had sex in six months. So there you go."

Leo continued nodding in that slow, steady way. "Well. That just about sums it up, I guess. I thought Deb and I were through about a month ago. The stress. You know."

Matt wandered in and picked up a picture from a stack of photos that was sitting on top of the desk. It showed Leo standing next to a sold sign, a young couple, his brilliant teeth. "So what's in North Dakota? How's the market out there?"

Leo let out a small puff of air as if Matt was being ironic, then he crouched back down beside the box. "I got a gig welding for an oil company out there. There's a ton of work right now if you're willing to travel. This whole fracking thing is taking off."

Matt flipped through more pictures, trying to get his head around it. It seemed too weird, too different from his image of them: Leo with his slick rhetoric, his charming smile, standing at the front of the room in one of his gorgeous suits and lecturing them on how to build a network, and Deb with her new boobs busting out the top of her dress at the Christmas party, sending back her chicken because it was too dry; now here Leo was looking like a guy you didn't want to fuck with. How did that work? "So, did you just apply for a job or what? I mean, do you need training or . . ."

"Nah," Leo said, as he piled stacks of computer paper into the box. "I've already got my ticket. My Dad owned a body shop when I was growing up and I went to trade school right out of high school. I worked at the shipyard a bunch of years before I got involved in this mess." He ripped a strip of packing tape with his teeth, his brilliant teeth. "Deb's got a job lined up too. She's going to hotshot."

"Hotshot?"

"It's kind of like a remote location courier, you know, if they need parts or something. The pay is decent." He stood with the box in his hands, forearms bulging. He paused a moment, then added, "Deb likes to drive," before pushing past Matt and out into the hall.

Deb likes to drive. As if it all made sense.

The rest of the day, Matt drove around. He went to check on a couple of his listings and felt a jolt of surprise to find that his signs were still there and the houses were still standing as if everything was still absolutely fine and normal and the world wasn't going to shit. At three, he broke down and went to Starbucks where he bought some sweet over-priced drink that gave him the shakes then he drove around some more, out to the suburbs where he stared at empty houses in empty neighbourhoods.

He kept thinking about Leo and Deb and their new life in North Dakota. He imagined going out there himself. He imagined the three of them, Jen and Jacob and himself, driving out there under a wide blue sky, packed into the car with all their things piled up in back, the three of them roaring away to another life, to a fresh start. He was still fit enough to do the work, he reasoned. He could get on as a roughneck; it might even be nice to work for a regular pay cheque for a while, to stop all this worrying and scrabbling and speculating and just put his head down and work . . . A kind of calm came over him. Yes, he thought, he'd like to just work; he'd never been any good at the real estate thing anyway.

He went to the Elephant Castle, ordered a beer, then took it to a booth near the back where he sat with his phone, working up the courage to call Leo and ask about a job. He was just about to do it, when his phone rang, the vibration causing it to glide ominously along the varnished surface of the table, sliding towards him as if being nudged by an invisible hand. He was filled with sudden dread. He looked down at the display: it was Ken. "Hello?" he answered, slouching down in the booth.

Ken said he wanted to meet for a drink. He said there was something important that he needed to talk to Matt about but wouldn't say what it was. Matt didn't press him too hard. He closed his eyes and hung his head and said he'd be there. Tonight, yes, at 8:30, yes, he'd be there, he said.

When he hung up, he sat for a long time, staring into space in the dim light of the bar. Ken hadn't sounded angry; he'd sounded like his usual self, yet Matt knew him well enough not to trust him; he'd seen Ken's playfulness flash to anger enough times and what else could it be? It had to be the letter. There was nothing else. By the time he left the bar, Matt's thoughts of a new life had vanished and returned to this one thing: the letter, the letter, the letter.

Later that night, Matt walked into a pretentious downtown nightclub that throbbed and pulsed with blue light and young bodies as if the crash had never happened. He found Ken lounging on a leather sofa, quaffing back a martini and was surprised that Ken had invited another friend to their little rendezvous, a young man named Justin who kept pulling his lips back in an exaggerated smile so that his teeth glowed ghostly blue under the black lights. Matt didn't know what to make of it. He stood in front of the sofa staring at the two of them, trying to assess Ken's mood, then Ken laughed and said, "Quit being so uptight, Matty. Sit your ass down here and have a drink with us."

So, Matt drank. They ordered one round, then another. Ken and Justin began to smile wider and talk louder. Their eyes wandered loosely to the bar with its blue glow and world-weary female bartender, then to the groups of girls with their bare legs scissoring underneath the high glass tables as they leaned forward and whispered to one another over cosmic coloured drinks, their dark-lined eyes darting about to see who was watching.

Matt kept an eye on Ken. He kept drinking and watching and little by little the booze seemed to seep under his skin and he felt his consciousness peel like a blister off the real-time version of himself so that he became both at once: he was good ol' goofy Matty, smiling at Ken's stories, laughing at all the right times but he was also hanging just above the action, watching himself smile and laugh, a presence that was cold and calculating and removed. The feeling was strange and powerful.

"So, I had to go to the doctor the other day," Ken announced with steady, pale sincerity. "I had these little porcelain splinters in my ass. It was a fucking embarrassment. Half an hour, pants down on the table."

Justin guffawed, lips curling back from his flashing teeth, then he glanced around to make sure the girls with their scissoring legs noticed what a fantastic time he was having.

"Time for a new toilet seat or what?" Matt quipped, his irritation with Ken's endless stories simmering just below the words.

"No man, it wasn't that. Isabella threw a plate at my head and it smashed all over the floor. The woman is crazy. She's totally insane when she's angry." He said this with a great display of wide-eyed amazement, awe even, as if female craziness was an erotic blessing, a great sexual windfall he'd stumbled into. Matt wanted to smack him.

"So how'd the splinters wind up in your ass then?" Justin prodded. Matt groaned inwardly. They were so predictable, like a bad movie.

Ken raised his eyebrows and regarded them as if he were a great sage of female ways. "Anger is a type of passion," he replied. For the first time in his life, Matt felt wholly outside the power of Ken's charm. He felt unreachable somehow, like he'd grown beyond it.

"So we're fighting and throwing plates and screaming, then all of a sudden we're kissing and going at it. Our clothes are coming off and she's pushing me down to the floor. Best sex of my life."

Now Justin jumped in with a story about a Brazilian ballet dancer he'd hooked up with. "I don't know if it's a cultural thing or what but I didn't even know some of this stuff was possible. I was like a project for her, a quaint Canadian boy that had to be re-educated." Matt's eyes wandered around the room.

"And what about the foxy, young Mrs. Campbell?" Ken asked, calling his attention back.

"Jen? Yeah, she's good. She's doing lots of work on the house, redoing all the floors in the basement . . ." He could see their eyes glaze over; he could see Justin's eyes flicker to the girls with their dangerous black-rimmed eyes over the bowls of their drinks and their long smooth legs crossing and uncrossing underneath and suddenly he felt mean and cruel. Suddenly he wanted to hammer them with the drudgery of life. He wanted to rub their noses in it. You think you know but you don't know, he wanted to say, how different those scissoring girls will turn out to be outside the violet lights. "She's got Jacob in pre-school twice a week," he went on. "She's been taking a yoga class."

"Yoga's cool," Ken offered.

"I met this yoga instructor online once," Justin began and Matt sat smiling and nodding and watching himself smile and nod as Justin explained how natural and flexible this woman had been. "You know, an anus was just a thing to her. Same as a foot or a hand. It was wild."

They traded stories a while longer, then talked about the crash but briefly, in a superficial poor-suckers kind of way, then Justin wandered over to the bar to cast his teeth and eyes about and Matt and Ken were alone.

Ken was nodding to the thump of the music, looking out across the sea of pulsing bodies on the dance floor, his eyes glazed and far away and, for a moment, Matt had the sense that their old roles had been reversed, that he was clear and sharp while Ken was clumsy with liquor, then Ken turned towards him and was instantly sober, his blue eyes sharp as ever. It was as if someone had flipped a switch. "So Matty, you going to tell me what's up?"

Matt's sense of being outside himself came crashing down. His face began to burn. "What do you mean, what's up? Nothing's up. I'm having a drink, that's what's up."

Ken looked at him hard in that psychologizing way he used to use to drag the truth out back when they were still in high school, that look that said, 'I already know so don't bother hiding; I know you better than you know yourself."

"You asked me to come here," Matt stammered. "Here I am, drinking."

Ken continued to regard him silently and Matt felt wretched and transparent under his gaze. The moment stretched on, Ken staring him down, regarding him like a wounded animal until the tension was so unbearable Matt thought he might break and admit what he'd done just to put an end to it; he could feel the desire to confess rising up inside him, to end it, to end all the gut-twisting not-knowing tension and just get it over with, but then Ken shook his head and looked away. "Alright, Matty. Don't get your knickers in a knot. You just seem a bit off, that's all. Distant."

"I'm not distant. I'm right here aren't I?"

"You forget Matty, that I know you and it's pretty fucking obvious that something's bugging you. You were never any good at keeping secrets."

What did it mean? Was he fishing? Bluffing? What? Matt thought he might pass out with the stress of it. "There's nothing," he managed. "Woman stress. Money stress. I don't know. The usual shit."

"If you need money, Matty, I can . . ."

"I don't need any more help with money, thanks," he snapped and immediately he regretted it. He was strung out, he realized, still half crazed by his sleepless night.

Ken didn't respond. He looked out at the dance floor and sipped his drink. When he finally turned back to Matt he looked tired, sad even. "Look, Matty, if you want to talk about that contract, we can talk about it tomorrow. Not tonight, though. Tonight is special. Tonight, I wanted to ask you something personal."

Matt's mouth was dry. He could barely speak. "What? What is it?"

Ken leaned forward so his face was very close. Matt could smell his aftershave. "Well, as you know, my girlfriend Isabella and I are getting married and we're starting to plan the wedding.

I wanted to ask you, since you're my oldest friend and all, if you'd stand for me at the wedding?"

Matt hung his head. He looked down at the dark tiles between his feet. He wanted to feel warmth inside him; he wanted to feel happiness for his friend, to be overwhelmed by memory, by nostalgia, by something, yet all he felt was relief that it had not been this other thing.

"Matty?"

Matt looked up. Ken's blue eyes searched his face. "Of course," he said. "I'd be honored."

They embraced and Ken thumped his back so that the impact reverberated through Matt's chest, echoing through him as if he were hollow inside. Quickly, Matt called for drinks to celebrate; he called for shooters; he called for dancing; yet he was unable to shake the sense that the keen and watchful part of him that stood apart was still there, watching, judging, even as he congratulated his friend, even as they walked arm in arm to the bar.

Several hours later, Matt hurried along the wet sidewalk, hunched under his umbrella. It was late and the streets were quiet except for the hiss of the rain. The reflections of the streetlights were smeared on the glistening pavement and somehow this made him lonely, like looking at the lights on the highway outside of River City used to make him lonely. He walked on, passed city hall then passed the library where he saw a young man and woman huddled under the awning, their lower bodies wrapped in a pile of blankets and sleeping bags. They were talking quietly to one another, the steam of their breath back lit as it passed between them, the girl's cheeks pink and round despite her poverty, the weedy young man leaning close to her, speaking excitedly, about what? about the world's problems maybe or politics maybe, or dreams; the young man's eyes were so bright and hopeful that Matt felt embarrassed as he passed; he felt embarrassed for the hollow knocking of his good shoes in the steaming, whispering street.

When he got to where he'd parked his car, he got in, put a penny on the dash like a kind of talisman, then headed home on the wet, black streets. It was late and there was very little traffic; yet each time the headlights of another vehicle approached in the opposite lane, he was filled with a horrible panic. He used to get it sometimes in high places, whenever he stood at the edge of a balcony or a cliff. It wasn't vertigo the way others described it, but a sense that he couldn't quite trust himself not to jump, that his body might just do it, that it might just launch him out into nothing against his own will, not a suicide wish but a lack of trust, that he might jump, that he might steer into the opposite lane, that the self could slide out from under conscious control and act on its own dark and poorly understood intention.

Another week went by and still Matt couldn't sleep. He checked the post box every day but there was nothing, only bills and threatening letters from the bank. At night, he kept returning to the computer to look at the picture online. Annika Torrey. He kept staring at it, trying to make some sense of it, but the more he looked, the more confused he felt. Twisted Anni's. Saltery Bay. Ken's pale and steady eyes. There was a lie here somewhere yet he couldn't pinpoint what it was.

Eventually, he called Ken again to ask if there'd been any news about his contract but Ken just sounded annoyed and told him to be patient. He said there were no exact time frames, no way to predict these things. He didn't offer anything more. He asked Matt about Jacob. He talked about the wedding plans.

But Matt couldn't stop thinking about it. Saltery Bay. Twisted Anni's. Was this woman sick? Had she stolen his money? He started doing research, looking into cases of fraud; it was like a wormhole. Back in the eighties during the AIDS crisis it had been the wild west. They'd regulated things since but could he really trust Ken? It would still be possible for someone to fake a medical record, wouldn't it? He kept going over and over it in his mind.

Finally, he decided he needed to do something, to take some kind of action. If Ken wanted to behave like an obfuscating fuck and this woman wouldn't even bother answer his letter, then he'd go down there and find out what was happening for himself. Was she sick or not? At least if he knew, he could make a plan. At least then he'd know.

The next day, he packed a duffel bag full of clothes and told Jen that he was going on a little road trip to look into an investment opportunity on the San Juan Islands. He said that business was slow in Seattle and he wanted to look at other options. The funny thing was, he thought as he pulled away, it didn't even feel like a lie.

CHAPTER ELEVEN

Annika had Barry over to dinner sometimes. It was only dinner and it made sense that she would, that they would get together in this way because they both lived alone and it was quiet in the off season. She busied herself about the kitchen, thinking it would be nice to put the candles out, but as she rummaged in the bottom drawer she paused, then closed it, worried that candles would send the wrong message. She didn't want things to get confused.

Outside, darkness came down and the fog crept up the shoreline. She tended the fire, then went out to the woodpile with the basket she used to carry the wood. The night was so thick and heavy she had to navigate by feel, her hair standing on end as she piled up the logs in her basket then she hurried back, slamming the door behind her, relieved to be inside again with the warm, comforting smell of the roast cooking in the oven. She checked it, then sat down, then got up again. She rubbed the steam from the corners of the windows and looked out but there was only darkness.

At five past six Barry arrived. He was wearing a dark button-down shirt tucked neatly into his jeans and he stood in her doorway holding two bottles of wine, one in each hand. He grinned at her in his lopsided way and she was glad; she felt a kind of full body relief to have someone there. She took the bottles and thought to kiss him lightly on the cheeks the way the French do, the way she used to do when Hamish had friends over. How she'd hated those dinner parties with all their affectation and chatter and people she had nothing in common with, that pretentious kiss kiss kiss in the doorway; yet how she missed them now sometimes. There had been a lightness to them, a frivolity that didn't ask too much; sometimes it was nice. She leaned in close and saw Barry's eyes twinkle, then she pulled back, took the wine and said, "Hey Barry, make yourself at home."

"Smells delicious, Anni." He stepped in and immediately stooped to scoop up Zebedee who'd made the mistake of coming near. Zebedee was tolerant though not affectionate towards Barry and sat in his arms with his silver limbs sticking out stiffly as Barry whispered "sssss sssss sssss, what a good pussy. Aren't you a good pussy?"

Annika set the wine on the counter and watched him out of the corner of her eye. He was barely able to support the cat and yet he still twinkled with his juvenile humor. Pussy. Honestly!

And yet a smile tugged at her lips. Sometimes Barry reminded her of the guys on the fire crew, after they'd accepted her. That easy rapport. The foolish banter. Those young, strong men . . . It was strange, she thought, to have reached an age where people were not just who they were now but who they used to be also. She looked at Barry: here was the class clown with his pussy jokes, here the handsome lawyer, here the shaking cripple. Sadness filled her.

The handsome man he must have been was so close, so close to the surface sometimes, it was right there, almost touchable and somehow its presence made his decline all the more poignant. Being with him she oscillated between irritated amusement and the desire to take his face in her hands and say, I know. I understand.

Now he put the cat down and came over to the counter. He was shaking badly. He opened the cupboard and reached for the wine glasses and she paused, unsure of whether to help him or not. She decided not. She wouldn't want people pandering to her should she face the same. She thought back to her relationship with the stairs during her illness. Sometimes she thought the stairs had kept her alive. He took the glasses down and they chittered against one another but he got them safely to the steady surface of the counter.

"Red or white?"

"Red. I cooked a roast." She handed him a corkscrew and turned away.

"Red meat and wine. Will you look at us? We're just a couple of Healing Journey rebels." He handed Annika her glass.

"Back of the bus!" she quipped as she clinked his glass. "I'm even serving regular plain old gluten-filled white dinner rolls."

"Sweet blasphemy. Susan would have an absolute shit." He smiled, and there it was again, the ghost of a dashing man.

Annika turned quickly then set down her glass. She crouched to check the roast. Heat from the stove blasted her in the face.

Barry made his way over to the couch and lowered himself down. He picked up the book she'd been reading, then set it down. "I enjoyed your little F bomb at Marion's the other day."

Annika sliced into the roast and blood came out onto the plate. "I don't know what got into me. It just came out. I knew you were laughing!"

"Well, what can I say? Your little 'fucking' was the most action any of that crew has seen in a long time."

Annika started to laugh then was quiet. It was a dangerous thing to do, to let sex out in the open, she thought, even as a joke. She set the meat on the table and turned back to get the potatoes.

"So you never actually said what you plan to do." His voice was serious now. "Are you going to write them back or what?"

Annika pursed her lips as she set the steaming pots on the cork board. "I don't know. At first, I thought I would write him and ask him not to contact me but, I just . . . I don't even know if it's worth responding to."

"What do you mean him?"

"Him. The investor."

"I thought you had to go through a broker in Seattle. I admit I was curious. I looked into it."

"I did. I did it all through a licensed broker I found online. But it wasn't the broker. It was him. It was the guy who bought my policy. Matthew Campbell. That's who contacted me."

Barry came to the table and sat down. He was uncharacteristically silent as she scooped food onto his plate. After a time, he said, "I'm a bit concerned here, Anni. I've been thinking about it and I don't think that's the usual way of going about things. May I see that letter?"

"To be honest, Barry, I really don't want to talk about it anymore."

"You know Annika, I was a lawyer for many years and if this person is contacting you now... I'm actually very worried here. If you want me to do anything, I could take a look . . ." The mischief in him was gone now and he was fatherly, lawyerly.

She shook her head. "No. The last thing I need right now is some kind of legal battle. I've had enough of courts with the divorce. No one ever wins by it."

"I could just . . ."

"No, Barry. Please. I did it. I signed the contract. I took the money. I'll deal with it." She drank her wine. Her face had begun to burn.

He was not letting up. "It is a big deal though. You said yourself, at Marion's, that you were upset and you have quite a legitimate reason to be. I don't think you're appreciating the seriousness of this."

"Well I shouldn't have brought it up then."

They ate in silence for a moment. Their knives scraped on the plates.

Finally, he said, "You know Velma was right. These people are vultures and I hope for your sake, Anni, that you don't take any of this personally."

She put down her fork and looked at him. A cold chill ran through her. "It is though. It is personal."

"It's some asshole trying to make a quick buck that's what it is." He was angry now. He shook his head. There was wine on his lips.

"It can't be more personal. It's my policy. My life. I went into that office on my own volition and signed a contract, knowing full well what it meant. That's how it is, Barry. I took that money. Me. Annika." She made a fist and held it against her chest where the cancer had been.

"No, no, no. Okay. No," His voice was almost pleading, begging. "You can't look at it like that. I don't want you to look at it that way. Think about it. It's not even a thing. It's an event that may or may not happen for a very long time, its possibilities, speculation. It's part of a very complicated, corrupt system."

Annika poured another glass of wine. Her hands were shaking worse than his and she was overcome with an almost violent urge to show him, to make him understand. "My mother used to have envelopes and she'd divide the money into it. The coins and the bills. The money was real. It was allocated for specific things. For flour. For milk. For eggs. And we got that money from the market. We got it for beef. For alfalfa. For hay." She ground the words in, blunt and short as if to bludgeon him with their realness. "And I don't care what you say, it's not really complicated at all. Everything is connected to something real."

He winced as if each word caused him physical pain, then they sat there with the empty plates and the wine bottle dead between them. The cottage smelled like red. "Not everyone is out to get you, you know," he said after what seemed a long time. She looked away. "Not everyone has some twisted ulterior motive."

She stood up. Her chair scraped on the floor. She went and put another log on the fire and crouched before it, watching cities burn and crumble in the grate. His voice from behind her continued on. "I worry about you, you know. Here you are, this beautiful intelligent woman and you hold everyone away at arm's length."

She closed her eyes. Not this, she thought. Barry, don't do this. She stood and came back to the table and began clearing the plates. She tried to keep a lightness in her voice. "What are you talking about, arm's length? I go to Healing Journeys and spill my guts don't I? I'm involved in the community here; I have people over for dinner; I host the jam night. I don't know what you're talking about, arm's length. I'm right in the thick of it." She began to run the water.

"Ha! You're baking cinnamon buns and going to therapy like it's a fucking penance. Living like a monk out here on the point . . ."

They'd drunk too much she thought, that was all it was, he was drunk and getting wound up.

"What I'm talking about is connection. Friendship. *Trust*," he said.

"Well, we're friends aren't we Barry?" she asked, though her words came out strangled. Don't, she thought, please don't. She put on the coffee. They would sober up. It would be fine.

"Friends let friends help one another," he said darkly and she ignored it.

"And Healing Journeys," she added brightly, "Healing Journeys is all about connection."

"Healing Journeys is bullshit. You know it. I know it."

She sat back down as the coffee started to drip. She felt rattled. His accusations seemed to be coming out of nowhere.

"I mean, do you ever do anything just for fun, Anni?" he implored.

"What is this? An intervention?"

"What do you even like to do? I've known you for six months now and I still don't know what you do for fun."

"Barry stop."

"And what about men? Dating? You're still a young woman. Don't you ever miss having that in your life?"

She stood up again to hide the burning in her face. She was angry now, that he should come here, acting like a friend . . . She got out the mugs. "How would it be fair though? To go out and date someone when I've got what amounts to a time bomb inside me. It could come back now. It could come back any day."

"Jesus Christ Annika, no one's trading in futures anymore. I'm talking about having a good time. About just being with another person. About love."

She set down the mugs and scraped the plates into the garbage. "Everyone wants something, Barry," she said evenly but her anger showed through.

"Jesus, I'm not talking about that! I'm not talking about me! Did you think? You did! No, no, I'm talking about enjoying yourself every once in a while. A nice evening? A smile?" He tried to catch her eye but she wouldn't look at him. "Okay, now we're going to have a lesson in male-female relations," he said. He rubbed his palms together then got up and went over to the small stack of CD's and the portable player she'd bought at the thrift store as she stood at the counter wrapping the roast beef in tinfoil.

"Ah ha!" she heard him say but ignored it. She opened the fridge and the whiteness glared at her. Butter. Milk. Eggs. The barest necessities. What do you do for fun, Anni? Do you do anything for fun? She shut it quickly.

Music filled the room and then Leonard Cohen's low and rasping voice: "Dance me to your beauty with a burning violin . . ." She turned and there he was with his arms spread theatrically, inviting her to dance.

"No."

"Oh but yes."

"Lift me like an olive branch and be my homeward dove," he sang along. "Dance me to the end of love."

"I'm not."

"But you are. You are." He was off balance and if she didn't grab him he was going to fall, he was going to tip right over and fall on his stupid hopeful face and even though she was angry she wouldn't let that happen. She would never let that happen to him. She took his hand and was drawn into his embrace and they began to lurch about the cottage. She held herself upright so as not to press too tight against him.

"Let me see your beauty when the witnesses are gone," he whispered in her ear.

"Barry," she scolded.

He leaned his head close until they were almost cheek to cheek. She could feel the heat of his skin, smell his aftershave. A man's smell. No. no. no, she thought as memories came unbidden. There was such a thing as too much loneliness, she knew, and she was close now, dangerously close to that threshold where thoughts no longer matter, where want becomes a tidal wave, a torrent. There was that weakness in her legs, that thickening of the air that happens just before. She'd let it build up; she'd let there be too much and now here it came all at once, rushing, flocking to his touch the way it flocks to a simple kindness, all the loneliness of a lifetime rushing to a touch, rushing all at once to be relieved. She was afraid that she would not be able control it, that she would do now whatever he asked of her and that he would ask and he seemed to grow stronger for her weakness and she remembered how she'd felt this way before, in the off season, one winter when she'd been lonelier than usual and a man named Hamish had smiled her way and how the decision that hadn't been a decision at all but a falling down, a helpless tumbling in a tidal wave of loneliness, had swept her to a cold, grey city away from the things she'd loved most.

"You know, Anni," Barry said casually, "You act like I'm some snot-nosed kid asking you to the prom and that's sweet but it's not like that. I'm not looking for anything from you. Cinderella's over for me and do you want to know something?"

Her knees, almost buckling. The warmth of hands on her back. The torrents of loneliness rushing. "What?"

"It's a goddamn relief." He laughed in her ear. "Now will you just relax. It's just a dance. I'm not going to grab your ass . . . Unless, of course, you want me to . . ."

She groaned.

"What's that? Did you want me to?"

"No!" It came out as a kind of squeal, a flirtatious squeal that was strange to her own ears. They danced and she felt herself lean closer, melting towards him. Her head grew heavy and it dipped forward and she snapped it back and he whispered, "Just let it, let it," and she rested her head on his shoulder, and a voice inside screamed don't don't don't and there was the loneliness, rushing to be relieved. Then the music ended and he let her go and said, "Taa daa!"

"Taa daa?"

"That's it, that's all. You can relax now. That's all I was after, a dance with a pretty lady. Now was that so bad?"

She felt shaken, confused, torn up inside by the awful secret that she might have said yes if he'd asked her to go upstairs. She didn't know that she would have said. "I'm sorry, Barry. I didn't mean to imply . . ."

"Stop. Just stop being sorry. You're lovely. I'm your friend. People can be friends, you know."

She served the coffee with shaking hands and they talked for a while then he stood to leave. "I'll see you later tonight, then?" he asked.

She felt a panic at the thought of him leaving, at being alone again even for a short while. "Yes. You'll see me."

"See you soon. Thanks for the grub. Delicious as usual."

"Goodbye, Barry."

"Goodbye, Annika."

She watched him go, dancing from flagstone to flagstone, his shaking all but gone now. Then the fog consumed him.

She sat alone in the cottage staring at her bare, yellow walls. She touched her cheek where it had brushed against his and then she sat for some time.

She went upstairs and took out her tin of old things. She took off the cover and took out the silver earrings Hamish had given her when they were first married and held them up to her ears. The cool silver against her warm, golden skin gave her face a dramatic symmetry; Hamish's mother once said she looked like a queen, though it wasn't quite a compliment. Now, she fingered the matching bracelet, clasped it round her wrist and put the earrings in. She had to push a bit to break through the skin that had grown over the holes in her ears. She dabbed the blood with her forefinger, then brushed the tangles from her hair and stared at herself in the mirror.

She was smaller than before, having lost the muscle she'd built up in her traps and shoulders to the illness. The smallness made her hair look bigger, her eyes larger, her cheekbones sharper. There was something spare and essential about her face and she thought she'd never looked so much like herself before, never so . . . she shook her head and took the earrings out. It was stupid. It was jam night. It was Saltery Bay. And yet . . . other women did it, didn't they? They wore jewelry? Fussed over their appearance? It didn't have to mean anything. She put the earrings back in. The torn skin burned. Why not? Why shouldn't she? She put on her best sweater and was on her way.

She walked out onto the gravel road, feeling her way in the dark. The town down the hill was an orange smear in the fog and the air was wet and cold on her skin. She walked now whenever she could. It made her feel alive.

She'd got the idea for a Jam night in a marketing book about small business. Most of the book had been simple common-sense advice but there'd been a few good ideas. One was to host social events as a way of advertising, a way to get your name out there, and she'd thought that an open-mike night would go over well with so many healing types keen to bare their souls. She'd been right. People absolutely loved it. It was as if the town had been waiting for it, bursting with creativity and hidden talent that only needed an opportunity to express itself.

When she got to town, the streets were quiet. After September the tourists left and now it was only the locals: hippies and the fishermen and retirees. She turned down a side road, then stopped to admire her own storefront.

Twisted Anni's.

A piece of bleached driftwood with white Christmas lights wrapped around it hung above the door. The hand painted letters had come out more angular than she'd meant them to, but it was all a work in progress. She'd meant for 'twisted' to refer to her cinnamon rolls but the fishermen in town had all taken to calling her Twisted Anni. Here comes Twisted Anni, they'd say and she liked it. Twisted Anni! they'd yell when they saw her across the street, as if she were some kind of rock star and it was so ridiculous, so absurd, it made her giggle. Twisted Anni. What would they say in Rose Prairie if they ever knew?

The door was unlocked and she let herself in. Meg, one of the local girls she'd hired was already there, helping to set up. Thin and pretty with a medusa of blonde dreadlocks twisted on top her head, Meg was one of these confident young people who spoke in a low, world-weary voice as if she knew the dark truth of the world and was only humoring you with small talk. She looked up from the fridge which she was filling with beer and exclaimed, "Look at you, Annika! You look beautiful. What's the occasion?"

"No occasion. I'm just . . . I thought I'd try to look civilized for once."

Meg raised her eyebrows knowingly but said nothing.

Annika went around the room with a bucket of tea lights, placing a few on each table, then lighting them. The café, a plain rectangular room with hardwood floors, looked magical with all the twinkling lights and she felt a warm flush of pride as she looked around. It was a fairly basic operation but she'd taken great pains to make it nice. On Sasha's advice, she'd kept her menu simple: coffee, tea, a few baked goods, but people liked her bread and rolls and she was able to stay afloat. It was all she'd really hoped for, to make enough money to be able to stay. She went behind the counter, then dragged the mic and amp from the storage closet while Meg went back and forth with cases of beer. Annika put out little plastic glasses for wine, then, after surveying the room, she opened the till and turned the card in the door to open.

Slowly, people began to show up and she smiled and greeted each of them at the door, taking the names for the open mic. Barry arrived with Marion and Susan who were both done up in their pewter jewelry and long, flowing cotton capes. They gushed and flitted about when they saw her and Barry pointed to her ears and said, "You're gorgeous!" There was nothing awkward about him after their dance and she felt a pang of loneliness as she watched him escort Marion and Susan, one on each arm, showering them with his trembling attention, then she checked herself. It was stupid. She was glad he was happy. She didn't want him that way.

Then Sasha and her partner Cosmo arrived, two short, luminescent elves with wide, earnest faces and bright white teeth. Cosmo trained therapy animals and the two of them had a dream of running their own hospice one day. They gave Annika long meaningful hugs and Sasha kissed her on the forehead and said she looked well.

The small room was rapidly filling up: there was a group of Meg's friends and Greg, another hire, and his friends and a skulking teen named Liam who came by himself although his mother was there also with Kat and Velma; there were the Goldsteins and the monkey lady and several people she'd seen but didn't know, and then Helmut arrived with two lean, wolfish men who were visiting. Helmut and his friends sat at a different table from Marion who kept glancing over at them and whispering urgently in Susan's ear.

At nine, Annika helped Liam, who was first on the list, set up. He grunted a few words into the mic then blasted them all with epic riffs on his guitar, his thin sallow face a mask of utter seriousness, sweat beading on his feathery upper lip, his greasy hair pulled back in a red bandana. She stood behind the till and smiled to herself as she watched the audience do their best not to cringe, his mother and her friends being wide-eyed and open-faced and impossible to shock. After it was over, they showered him with attention and he took their praise like dirty money: his mouth twisting into a smile; his skin aflame with the shame of it.

Next up was Kat who wrote poetry. It took her some time to get her bulk up to the front. She leaned on her cane and looked grey and mottled and unhealthy until she began to speak and the light came on in her face. She had a beautiful face, really, like a sad, youthful woman looking out the round porthole of a sinking ship.

Kat spoke about love. She spoke about loneliness and being trapped, about being in a world where you couldn't touch others, where you see them and know them but are separated somehow. Annika looked around: at Barry beaming with his two dates, at Cosmo and Sasha; even Helmut, it seemed, had found a kindred.

She sighed.

Then the door swung open and a man she'd never seen before stood in the entrance. He was tall and handsome and she liked him immediately for, despite the expensive coat, he had a look on his face that was exactly as lost and lonely as she felt inside.

CHAPTER TWELVE

Matt got up from the hotel room bed and looked out the window to find the view obscured by fog. Even the parking lot directly below was barely visible, the fluorescent sign at the entrance a blur of colour, the streetlamps down the hill faint smudges of light suspended in the darkness. Saltery Bay, he reminded himself again. I'm at the Captain's Inn in Saltery Bay and yet a queer doubt remained, a strange dream-like feeling, like he'd been cut adrift and was floating, a floating man in a floating hotel at the edge of the world.

He lay back down on the double bed. There were football highlights on the TV. The talking heads talked. He drank a beer, then another. On the ferry ride over, he'd imagined that this would be a kind of personal vacation, a night off from Daddy duty with a few beers and sports on TV and no one to tell him otherwise; but now he felt trapped and listless. The hotel lobby, with its nautical theme and rope trim, had been quaint and tidy, but the room itself was shabby and cheap. Everything in it was beige or tan, the only decoration a nondescript still life of brown flowers in a brown vase. The whole place smelled faintly of smoke.

Restless, he put on his coat, went outside and started walking in the direction of the town. It was down the hill by the water, he knew, yet he couldn't see it for the fog. Christ, it was black out! He walked along, then came to a stretch of road with no streetlights where he had to feel for the pavement with every step, unsure of what angle it rose or fell. It made him dizzy, made the whole world seem off-kilter and strange, as if the very ground were playing tricks on him. He'd had this feeling before, one time when he'd gone down to Mexico, back when he was single. He'd gone on a boat tour and been fine onboard, unfazed by the choppy seas, but then, back on land, he'd been barely able to stand, the whole world pitching and rolling beneath him.

He inched along until he came to an intersection where the streetlamps started again, then he followed them down the hill. Soon, he came to a cluster of buildings that he assumed was the downtown. He passed a health food store, a massage clinic, a small grocery and a barber shop but they were all closed. There was no one else in the streets.

Then he heard music, a single guitar screeching out a bad cover of Guns and Roses. Thank God, he thought. He wanted to sit down somewhere and have a drink, no matter how awful the band, to get out of the cold, deserted street and be around other people for a while. He began walking towards the sound but then the music stopped and didn't start up again. He wandered for a while looking for the bar but couldn't find it. He was just about to give up and go back to the hotel when he looked up and realized he was standing in front of the café. Twisted Anni's. It was right in front of him, a small unpretentious shop next to the hardware store. He stood and stared.

It was getting late but there were still lights on inside. This struck him as odd for a coffee shop. He took a step closer. The windows were foggy with condensation, yet he sensed that the place was full of people. He stood in the street, unsure of what to do.

It wasn't at all like he'd expected. In his most bitter fantasies, he'd imagined it would be a brand new, over-priced joint with five dollar coffees and organic nut bars but this place looked more like a beach bar, kind of run down and shabby with a strange, driftwood sign hanging above the entrance; the letters that had been carved into the bone-white wood were irregular and got smaller at the end, the last 's' barely making it on, as if the carver had run out of room.

He took another step towards the door. His plan had been to find it the following day, to enjoy his night off, then go and have a coffee in the morning and ask around for Annika. That was all he'd intended to do. Now, here it was, right in front of him. Open. He stood there, undecided. He could feel the fog, like a physical presence, pressing in at his back. A chill ran through him. He put a hand on the doorknob, his heartbeat in his fingertips.

He took a deep breath, opened the door and stepped inside.

Warmth flooded over him, but his relief was short-lived. He'd bumbled into some kind of meeting, he realized. The hushed and solemn crowd turned their faces towards the door as he entered, then they turned back to the front where an enormous woman was leaning on a cane and reading from a notepad. The woman was grossly overweight, a great tube of fat hanging down over her lower abdomen, her vast thighs stretching the wide expanse of her polyester pants.

"Can't you see?" the woman said in a thick, rich voice that seemed to well up from deep inside her. "A lifetime of accretion, of landscapes and lovers and dreams, these layers of a self and still love, like a buried treasure, waiting to be found . . ."

Panic seized him. She was talking about her vagina.

A chair! A chair! His left nut for a chair! He could feel the crowd's awareness on him as he stood awkwardly in the doorway. People kept turning and looking back at him, twisting around in their seats and looking back until he felt huge and conspicuous, his black wool coat and neatly cut hair already marking him a stranger, someone who didn't belong; he could tell right away what kind of scene this was and knew how he must appear to them: Mr. Seattle, Mr. Frat Boy Matty Matt, the kind of guy who barged into rooms and told pussy jokes and made fun of fat chicks and was purposely ruining this woman's moment in the spotlight; oh yes, he knew how it all must seem but where? Where could he sit? It was packed.

Now, a trembling, lopsided man with a white-blonde ponytail caught his eye, shifted over and patted an empty seat beside him. Matt nearly wept for gratitude. He picked his way through the crowd as inconspicuously as possible then settled in beside the man and mouthed "thank-you." The man's eyes twinkled merrily. The two women at the table beside him smiled benevolently then turned their rapt attention back to the front. They were both extremely thin and were dressed in long, flowing capes like medieval fairies.

The poetess continued her search for the buried love as Matt looked around the room. There were quite a few Crystal look-a-likes: braless middle-aged women listening intently; a group of younger hippie girls; some hawkish older men with silver crew cuts and furrowed brows; and a group of young men pinching the wicks on the tea lights and dipping their fingers in the wax.

Then he saw her.

She was standing behind the counter with her arms folded, perfectly still, her long dark hair cascading around her shoulders.

Annika.

He'd expected she would be here but hadn't been prepared, hadn't thought he would . . . He shook his head. She was beautiful. He'd seen her in the photo and could tell she was attractive but here, in the candlelight, with her standing there . . .

She wasn't sexy in the way he would ordinarily define it. She was too skinny, for one thing, her shoulders too square, her bones too raw; and she was older too, he could tell by her face. Younger women had a prettiness that flushed up from within, something florid and changeable that could be made to blush or scowl or smile and that was all part of it, part of the attraction; but this woman's face had a set, a stateliness, as if nothing a man could do would change it. He couldn't pull his eyes away.

"This love, this love is buried deep," the fat woman concluded then she closed her eyes and there was an incredible silence that drew itself out for so long Matt was afraid that no one would clap. Then, as if on cue, the entire room broke into thunderous applause. The young men at the front made loud whistling sounds and one of them yelled, "Boo-yah!" then one of the fairies at Matt's table leaned in so he could see the deep scoop of her collarbone and said, "That was so brave. Don't you think that was brave of her?"

"It takes a lot of guts," Matt agreed then blushed; he didn't want her to think he was poking fun, making reference to actual guts as in belly fat, so he rambled on, "I mean, I couldn't do it, you know? I wouldn't have the courage to open myself up that way." Both fairies beamed at him like he was the very paragon of open-mindedness, then suddenly the poetess lumbered down among them and everyone leaned towards her and said, well done, well done, beautiful, beautiful and he wanted them to know that he wasn't a judgmental prick; he wanted them to see he could appreciate this kind of thing so he put his hand on the woman's round shoulder and said, "I'm sorry for barging in. I thought your poem was awesome," and she smiled at him so openly, so honestly, that he momentarily forgot why he was there. He felt good, appreciated, like he was part of something even though he'd only been there just ten minutes. It was hard to explain. He leaned back in his chair then remembered his mission. He looked again towards the counter but Annika was gone.

Jesus, he needed a drink. It was all so strange and his head was already fuzzy from the beers in the hotel. He would drink one beer then leave and come back in the morning, he resolved. That had been his plan in the first place: a simple reconnaissance mission to find out what the hell was going on. He tried to muster his outrage at Annika, at the possibility that this woman had screwed him out of fifty grand, but the atmosphere was so odd and she was so beautiful, he was unable to stay angry for long. He felt like he'd wandered onto another planet.

There was a lull in the entertainment and he stood up to get a beer. He'd get one for the Trembler too, he decided, as a thank-you for saving him. He stood at the counter waiting for the dreadlocked chick to come back, then Annika was standing in front of him looking him full in the face.

"Welcome to our jam night," she said. "You looked a bit surprised when you came in. I hope you're enjoying it." There was a disquieting steadiness about her. No extra motions, no nervous fluttering of hands. She just stood there.

"I kind of barged in at an inopportune moment, I guess, but everyone is super-friendly," he stammered and almost winced at super. Her eyes were grey and steady. "I heard the music so I was expecting a band but I like poetry. I can do poetry. I'm a sensitive guy, you know?" Jesus Christ where did *that* come from? he wondered, appalled at himself. Bullshit was pouring out of him, unimpeded, apparently, by the jackhammering in his chest.

There was a spark of humor in her eye, a slight twist to her mouth. "Well, that's good to hear, because we're very into self-expression here in Saltery Bay. This night's only getting started."

"I love poetry. I wrote a sonnet in high school."

"I can put you on the list if you'd like."

"Maybe not. Motorbikes and suicide. I'd be embarrassed. I've evolved." Jesus. Where was it coming from?

She smiled. "What can I get for you?"

"I'll have two beer. What do you have?"

"We've only got the one kind. Rock Island IPA."

"Perfect."

She fished two bottles from a cooler behind the till and brought them up to the counter. Her hands were surprisingly mannish. They were broad and muscular like farmers hands and he watched them closely as they fumbled awkwardly with the bottle opener. They looked like they belonged to someone else, not this pretty, frail woman with the beautiful earrings and shiny hair. The contradiction bothered him and now he did feel angry. There was a lie here somewhere, he just couldn't say what it was.

He paid her and took the bottles. "Thanks, maybe I'll talk to you later," he said, somewhat coldly.

"I'd like that."

It struck him as odd that she would say that and again he felt confused. It was such an odd, odd place. He turned back towards the crowd and saw that the Trembler was watching him with twinkling, knowing eyes. He saw that they were all watching him. Jesus. One beer, he reminded himself, one beer and he was gone.

An older woman with long, faded blonde hair was setting up a harp at the front. The instrument was gold and impossibly ornate, like something from one of the castles he'd visited in Europe. The woman herself wore a gauzy blue dress and looked like an aging minstrel, a fairy queen from another era. Beside her, a short, impish man with a neatly trimmed goatee took a violin out of a satin lined case and settled it under his chin. The wood was dark and lustrous against his dusty leather vest, the kind with a logo emblazoned across the back that bikers wear.

The Trembler leaned close. "These two are a real treat. Ed and Linda Goldstein. They both used to play at the Met, then toured on their own for a number of years."

"What are they doing here? It's a funny change of scene." Matt asked. His eyes followed Annika behind the counter. She looked impossibly healthy. Her skin glowed. He didn't know what to think.

"That's Saltery Bay for you," the Trembler continued. "A lot of these islands are like that. They're crawling with artists and talented people from all over the world. See that man over there? He was a reporter for CNN and that lady? She's a sculptor; she shows her work all over the world, and that other lady beside her?" He pointed to a diminutive old woman with a long silver braid, "She used to be the head of zoology at Cambridge. She's big into primates."

"Monkeys," Matt encouraged vaguely. Annika had disappeared again. She was somewhere in the back.

"Now she's got this beautiful property where she runs an animal rehab. Each month she brings a couple of her monkeys to the hospice to cheer the patients."

Matt snapped to attention. "Hospice?"

"Oh yeah, there's actually a hospice here now and quite a few private health practitioners. You wouldn't know it based on the size of this place but you probably have more alternative health care options here than on the mainland. There's all kinds of clinics and wellness retreats and spas. You can't get a drink after nine but if you want your chakras balanced. Woohoo. Place to be."

"So the hospice, is that for cancer, or what?"

"It's not a treatment center. It offers end of life care. People come for all kinds of reasons, though I'm sure it sees its fair share of cancer patients. We all come to the sea to die," he mused philosophically, then he looked around the room and appeared to reconsider, "Or to be reborn," he added and winked.

What the fuck did *that* mean? Matt sipped his beer. His head was reeling. Maybe she *was* sick. But the hair, the skin . . . She'd opened a café for fuck sake! Nothing made sense.

The musicians started to play and Matt settled back into his chair. He watched the woman's hands on the harp, her long elegant fingers, plucking and flowing as the music filled the room. They were good, virtuoso even; he could tell right away. It was not the kind of music he usually listened to but he liked it. There was a haunting purity to it, a sadness, and he felt his mind travelling with it until he felt like he was far, far away. He would get their CD, he decided. Jen would be surprised that he knew about the Goldsteins at all; she'd be surprised that he was into that kind of thing, that he had such eclectic taste in music. He'd tell her he'd seen them in this quaint little local place and then he snapped to and remembered why he was there.

He looked again for Annika but couldn't find her.

After three songs, the Goldsteins came down and a man stood up and told a joke about fishing and women at which point all the fairies in the room booed and groaned, then there was another lull in the entertainment and people turned towards one another and started talking. The two fairies dove into an intense tete a tete, the subject of which, Matt gathered, was some nefarious he.

The Trembler leaned close again. "So, what brings you to town?"

He'd prepared a story, a cover, but the blood still came to his face with the lie. "I'm looking to buy a property here, you know, to get away from the city . . ."

The man nodded. There was a keenness in his eye despite the slowness of his speech. "I hear you. I used to practice law before the Parkinson's." He held up his hand so Matt could watch it shake. "I'm not quite as smooth in the courtroom as I used to be. I came looking for a change of pace." Now he held the hand out. "I'm Barry."

"I'm Ma . . ." Matt began, then halted, thinking suddenly of the letter, of the need for caution. "I'm Michael." The man had this maddening twinkle like he already knew your thoughts and found them hilarious.

Then Annika came and sat down across the table.

Matt stared.

"This is Annika. She owns the joint," Barry supplied. "Annika, this is Ma . . . Michael."

Annika extended her mannish hand. Her grip was firm and strong.

"Awesome place you got here Annika. Super fun show."

Super.

She smiled. "It's pretty basic right now, but it's a start."

"Michael is a . . ." Barry began, then he whispered in Matt's ear, "What are you?"

"I'm a real estate agent . . ." Matt stammered then wondered if he should have said it; it was not part of his cover story. "Or, I was . . ." he corrected. Annika watched his face with her steady, agate eyes.

"Michael here wants to be reborn as a part-time gardener like the rest of us." The old man seemed to be relishing this role, twinkling all the while. "Annika here is a firefighter turned desk jockey turned café owner extraordinaire." Then he leaned in close again and said in a mock whisper, "And she's also single."

"Jesus Barry!" Annika exclaimed and cuffed the old man on the shoulder. She looked at Matt. "I'm so sorry. These old people don't get out enough. Please ignore him."

Barry cackled. The two fairies looked up from their emoting and smiled knowingly and then it dawned on him what all the twinkling was about: they were aiming to set him up. He almost laughed out loud for relief.

The Trembler put an arm around his shoulder as if they were the best of friends. "That's how it is here in Saltery Bay. Everyone knows everything about everybody else. If you buy a place here, you'll figure it out pretty quick. And since we're shar- ing . . . How about you Mr. Ma . . . Michael? It's not that often we get tall, dark strangers wandering in."

The Fairies leaned forward and looked at him eagerly. Conversation around him petered out and it seemed the whole room was waiting, holding its breath. His fingers sought his wed- ding band, yet he found it wasn't there. The nakedness surprised him, then he remembered taking it off. He'd taken it off in the car. He'd twisted it off and put it in the glove compartment when he was barely out of the driveway with Jen's latest grievance still ringing in his ears. It was one of the stories he'd told himself, part of his cover. He remembered, yet the nakedness surprised him.

They were watching him. Waiting.

"I guess I'm not officially a divorcee yet but . . ." He could feel their want, their desire for intrigue pulling him towards his expected role. The tall, dark stranger. "But I'm in the process. Is that what it's called? A process?" He wondered if maybe it were true.

Barry twinkled. "That about describes it."

The Fairies beamed. The dark-haired one placed a hand on his arm. "Saltery Bay is such a supportive community. It's a great place to heal." Her eyes were wide and dark and earnest.

The other one, the near skeletal one with the silver hair, nodded seriously, "Love is so much more honest after marriage. You get all the bullshit out of the way."

Annika took it all in with her steady eyes and haughty face and he felt foolish under her gaze. He wondered if she'd noticed his hand searching for the ring. He was pretty sure she had.

She excused herself and went back behind the counter. He got up to get another beer, hoping to talk to her again, but it was the other girl that served him. The intermission ended and a bluesy, barefoot girl played the guitar and there was another poet and then a fiddler and then a young man who did a jig and played the spoons to the uproarious laughter of his wick pinching buddies.

Eventually people began to filter out. Annika came back to the table and Barry and the Fairies got up immediately, as if they'd planned it. They joined the group of men with silver crew cuts. Matt was alone at a table with Annika.

He twisted the beer bottle in his hand, aware that the opportunity to find out about her was basically being handed to him on a platter, yet he fumbled for words. She was truly a beautiful woman. "So firefighting. Wow. You don't look like a firefighter." ·

She smiled. "It was a long time ago. There was a forest fire training center near where my family had a farm, and I tried out, just out of high school. One of the foremen helped me get a job. I was young and strong. I doubt if I could do it anymore."

"But it must have been hard, no? I've heard it's super hard-core." She didn't look like she could lift anything but those hands . . . the set of her face. There were so many contradictions about her that he didn't understand. She didn't act like a liar and yet there was a lie somewhere. He could feel it.

"It is and it isn't," she said. "Physically it's the most demanding thing I've ever done. It's dirty, hard work and when there's a fire you work long, long hours. During my later years, I was on a Heli-access crew and the training was intense, but the stress was mostly physical." Her face became reflexive now as she remembered. "The goal, the danger was always obvious and I liked that. Fire. Smoke. You can smell it. Feel it. There's a simplicity to knowing exactly what you should do that I liked. My other job, working at an insurance agency, I always felt unsure. Did I say the right thing? Did I piss someone off? There were all kinds of politics to navigate. I found the firefighting easier, in a weird way."

Matt was caught between his sense of understanding and his awareness of the opportunity to find out more. "So why did you stop then, if you liked it so much?"

"Well, I'm telling you all this in retrospect," she laughed. "I did it for almost ten years, ten seasons anyway, and towards the end I was physically tired. Each year when the season finished, everyone else went back to their other lives, their real lives they called them, to their families and houses, but I didn't have any of that. My family didn't like how I was living, they're strict Christians who still believe in traditional roles for men and women so they considered what I was doing a sin. We stopped speaking after I left home, so I didn't have any family to go back to. Firefighting *was* my real life. In the winters, when the work ended, I never knew what to do. I tried working other jobs, waitressing, that kind of thing. I rented an apartment, even. Then the guys on my crew slowly began to drop off, getting married, having kids and moving on to other things . . . all my friends were leaving. Anyway, long story short, I met a man in the off season who had a good job in Seattle and I thought I was in love. Loneliness will do that, I suppose. I moved to Seattle, took an office management course and that was the end of my firefighting career. I still miss it, though," she said, then shook her head abruptly. "I'm so sorry. I don't know what's gotten into me. I don't usually ramble on about myself like this."

"Don't apologize. Please! I get it. I totally get it," Matt said, then all of a sudden he was telling her about Kato's and how he'd loved tending bar there and how he'd been good at it, how he'd felt like he'd discovered a truth about the world and how that truth had lived in his hands and in his body but then everything had gotten confused and complicated. Being Michael was easier than being Matt, in a way, and she kept nodding her head like she knew what he was talking about and each time he tried to get the conversation back around to her health, he found himself telling her something else. It felt good to be understood.

"I was trying to be responsible," he said pleadingly, as if she might absolve him.

She watched him with her steady eyes. "Don't be too hard on yourself. Trying to be something you're not can actually kill you, you know," she said. She made a fist and held it in the V of her ribs and it struck him as a weird thing to do and weirder still was that he understood.

Now people started coming over and saying, "Thank-you, Anni." "Goodnight, Anni." "This is so good for the community, Anni," and even though he'd just met her he felt strangely proud, like they were thanking him too, like he was part of it somehow.

The Trembler and the Fairies came over, trailed by the man with the silver crew cut. The Fairies made a great fuss over Annika and hugged Matt to their bony breasts as if he were a long-lost son, then the Trembler hugged him, then hugged Annika and Matt heard him whisper in her ear, "Enjoy your life."

When it was the man with the silver crew cut's turn, he was far less friendly. He glared at Matt during the goodbyes then stepped up to the table with his hands clasped behind his back. "Are you fine, Annika? I can drive you home, if you wish." He looked at Matt meaningfully.

Annika stood and kissed him on each cheek in the European way. "Thank-you Helmut, but I'm fine."

"There is one more space in the truck."

"I'm fine. Really. Goodnight."

The man gave Matt one more deadly look then walked out. When the door closed behind him, they were alone. "Do you have some angry ex-boyfriend I should know about?" Matt joked.

She laughed. "No, that's just Helmut. He's a friend. Mostly he just drives around in an old truck and refurbishes things he finds at the dump but if you ever need anyone killed, that would be your guy."

She smiled easily but somehow, in the now empty room, their friendly connection was broken. He felt a chill inside him. He shouldn't be here, he realized. He shouldn't be here at all.

And perhaps she felt it too, for her smile dropped away and she stood quickly and shook her head. "I really should clean up now."

This was the moment to leave; he was aware that he should leave, yet he didn't.

Then he was helping her, moving with brusque efficiency, wiping tables and gathering bottles, his hands moving, moving as if he'd worked there all his life. He liked how it felt; it made him feel how he used to feel after a good night at the bar.

He was taking a box of bottles to the storeroom when he brushed past her behind the counter. There wasn't much room there and as his body brushed against hers the air grew heavy with awareness. A man and woman. Alone.

He put the box away. His heart began to thud harder in his chest.

"Well. Thank-you," she said as they stood facing one another. "I really enjoyed our conversation but I have to get going now." Yet she didn't go. Not right away. Instead, she seemed to hesitate, to pause, to fumble with something in her hands. He took a step closer. He could feel his heart, da dum, da dum, asking what next? What next? The awful daring of it drawing him on even though he knew, he knew he should end it.

She stood in front of him, looking down. The air was so thick he could barely breathe.

And he found himself saying, "Why don't we go someplace else and have a drink? I'm really enjoying talking to you and wouldn't mind a nightcap. It's not so late."

He was almost certain she was going to say no for she didn't seem like the hooking up type, and he wanted her to say it; he wanted her to cut him off, to end the da dum, da dum of the awful tension that was building, but then her expression seemed to change, as if she were remembering something. "Well," she said slowly. "Okay. You could come back to my place for a bit. If you want to, that is."

They were standing very close now and he could feel his heart in his veins; he could feel it in his groin, the blood pounding what next? what next? the tension mounting until it was near unbearable and then, at the very height of it, at the excruciating peak of it, time seemed to stand still and there was this sharp little intake of breath, a kind of heart hitch at the top of the fall, that critical point where life could go either way, and then he was falling, he was letting himself go and his hand slid oh it just slid into the small of her back as if it were someone else's hand pulling her against him and she melted so easily; she made it so easy. What the fuck am I doing? he thought as his mouth found hers. And yet it didn't feel like a choice anymore but more of a sliding, like one foot in front of the next and the next on a road already decided.

When they got outside, the world was still cloaked in fog and the air was icy cold, a slick, penetrating cold that froze the desire in him almost instantly. He looked down at the strange woman beside him. The warmth of familiarity, the kind words of her friends that had collected around her, that had glowed like a sort of halo in the candlelight, vanished in the darkness. She was suddenly strange to him, silent and unknowable.

They walked side by side through the icy, prickling air and he had to fight to keep from shivering. She was wearing a flimsy jacket and seemed unbothered by the cold. What kind of person was this, he wondered. He would have one drink and leave, he promised himself. He'd ask her point blank about her health. He'd say that Barry had told him she'd been sick. One drink and he'd go.

They kept walking and she pointed out a few landmarks, properties for sale which he couldn't see. He commented on the quiet. He said that it was peaceful.

They walked uphill towards where the fog lay thicker and blacker and soon the town behind them was an orange smear, like a fire burning behind a cloud. The air smelled of woodsmoke and he could hear waves sighing somewhere on his right. The pavement became a gravel road.

She said, "If you do end up moving here, you could open a bar. People need an alternative to the Sports Bar. You saw how busy open-mic night was. A cute little Tiki bar or something like that would do really well here."

It was almost uncanny that she would suggest it. There'd been a few years when he'd thought seriously about this very thing. He'd even gone down to Mexico with a few guys from work and they'd toured the beaches looking for ideas. He'd talked to people, taken notes on prices, menus, that sort of thing. It smarted, in a way, to hear her talk about his abandoned dreams in this cold, dark place.

"Rent is surprisingly reasonable considering where we are and the municipality is trying to recruit small business. They helped me out a lot," she continued.

"I doubt I could afford it," he said bitterly.

She grew quiet and he wondered if she'd caught the edge in his voice; or maybe she was mulling over the inconsistency, for hadn't he said he was going to buy property? Quickly, he threw his arm around her shoulder and pulled her close. "What I mean is, I don't really know what's going to happen, with my finances. With the divorce and everything. Right now I'm just considering my options. You know, getting the lay of the land."

She allowed herself to be pressed sidelong against him but her body felt stiff and thin; there was no warmth in it.

"This way," she said and they turned onto a road of packed Earth with grass coming up through and there was a sense of the darkness narrowing around them. "I've been through many changes recently," she said thoughtfully. "People always talk about change like it's a conscious choice; they talk about changing their lives as if it's this big, sudden decision that they have to make, but I think it's rarely ever like that. By the time you get to a point where you're confronted with a major decision, by the time the crisis arrives, you've likely already decided. You've been deciding all along and the crisis is really just the consequence making itself known, forcing you to admit to the choices you've already made."

Her voice sounded strange and prophetic in the dark. He could barely see her. He wanted to leave, to run away, yet he walked on.

Now there was a sense of widening in the way that sound travelled. There was a low, steady sigh of waves breaking nearby and they walked along a path with dry coarse grass coming up between worn flagstones and then they were next to a building. Matt ran his hand along the rough, wood shingles, then stepped up onto the porch.

"This is it," she said. "My home."

He watched her back. Her hair was huge from the mist, her body small and hunched as she fumbled with the lock, like an old woman, like a witch. What kind of person would live out here all alone? He ached suddenly for Jen and Jacob, for their bright clean house and cheery, mindless chatter. I'm so sorry, he thought, but he didn't turn around.

It was cold inside, so cold he could see his breath. It struck him as shocking, insane even, that someone in this day and age would let it get that cold. A cat came swirling about his feet.

"That's Zebedee," she said.

Zebedee.

The light came on and revealed bare, yellow walls. There was no television, no dishwasher, no appliances other than the fridge and an ancient CD player on the floor. He felt a creeping sense of dread. He'd been to other women's houses over the years; he'd been to rooms and dorms and apartments and even in the dingiest student dives there'd always been some small feminine touch; women always left some clue to themselves:

jewelry on the nightstand, a photo taped to the fridge, something that told you who they were, but here there was nothing. The bareness shocked him. He didn't know what it meant, only that he didn't want to see it. He wished that he could unsee.

"I'm sorry about the cold," she said. "It warms up quickly with the fire."

He watched as she crouched down in front of the woodstove. He watched her blunt, muscular fingers on the matches, her knees at severe angles with no apparent discomfort, as if she were used to crouching that way. He'd seen poor people crouch that way in Mexico, cooking skewers of chicken over small coal fires at a bus stop.

"Please make yourself at home," she said. "There's wine in the fridge if you want and there's a blanket on the couch if you're cold. It should only take a few minutes to get warm."

He went to the fridge. Inside it was practically bare. Butter. Onions. Something wrapped in foil. He felt like voyeur, looking into that fridge with its poverty food, with its bareness. It shamed him. He shouldn't have come here, he knew; he shouldn't have allowed it to get this far; yet even as he stood, he felt another part of him, that flinty, hardened part of him breaking off and standing outside it all, searching the desolate little cottage for signs, for clues to the lie, whatever and wherever it was.

"I have some leftover roast beef if you're hungry. I could make us some sandwiches."

"No. No thanks." He found two glasses, opened the wine, poured and went back to the fire.

She was still crouched there with the orange light leaping up onto her face and his heart sank even lower. He saw in the firelight that he'd been wrong in his first assessment of her: her face wasn't strong or set at all but rather poised on the very brink, on the very edge of its own ruin, like a beautiful statue about to crumble.

She stood. "I hope this is alright. It's a little rustic, I guess. Sometimes I don't think . . ."

He smiled with the corners of his mouth. "It's fine. Super cozy. Here, have some wine." But it wasn't fine. The long walk, the discomfort, the damp in his clothes: he wished that none of it mattered to him but it did. He felt angry at her for letting her house be so cold, for naming her cat Zebedee. One drink and he'd leave, he told himself. He'd say fuck the whole thing and talk to a lawyer instead. He should have done that in the first place, he admonished himself.

She sat next to him on the couch and stared into the fire. She didn't say anything; she just sat there staring at the flames as they flickered and danced in the grate. The silence grew huge and heavy, full of accusation somehow. He was aware of himself in it, aware of his wife at home and his debts piling up and all the mistakes he'd made. Beside him, this strange, lonely woman sat, saying nothing, doing nothing, his guilty thoughts piling up as the silence stretched on, and finally he could no longer stand it. 'Come here,' he said and grabbed Annika by the shoulders. His words came out choked, as if he were being strangled.

He kissed her on the mouth, his lips pressing hard against hers, now harder, as if to crush himself out, to grind that mean and watchful part of himself out. I'm sorry. I'm so sorry, he said when she pulled away and looked at him with hurt in her eyes, and he was sorry and wished he hadn't done it; he wished he hadn't done many things and the questioning in her eyes made all his regrets tumble into one. Now he kissed her gently trying to take it back, all of it, every least thing in the hope that she would see, that she would understand who he really was and that he didn't mean it. He kissed her and kissed her and when she softened into him it felt like a kind of forgiveness and he was overwhelmed with gratitude that she didn't hate him, that she didn't hold it against him and then his desire swelled again; his initial attraction swelled again and he felt, in that moment, that his desire for her was real. Soon, she led him upstairs to a small room and a hard bed and he kissed her over and over and he wanted to crawl inside her to hide from that cruel and watchful thing in himself and he made love like an apology but still it was there.

CHAPTER THIRTEEN

Annika lay completely still, listening to the wind while the man slept peacefully beside her. Sometime during the night, the fog had lifted and the wind had come rushing in, whining and moaning at the top of the stovepipe like a hungry dog. A square of moonlight appeared on the floor next to the bed, then faded to darkness, then came again, then faded again and finally it stayed, filling the room with a cool, soft light that outlined the man's face in silver. He looked beautiful to her in the moonlight, ageless, aglow with a cold fire, like a marble statue. She watched his chest rise up and down. His weight made the small bed sag in the middle and she kept her body rigid, up and out of the trough he created. She didn't want to wake him and didn't know, at this point, if it was okay to curl up against him.

Eventually, the cold got her out of bed. The fire was out. He wasn't used to the cold, she reminded herself. She'd seen him shivering on the walk home, even with that big coat, and there was a softness to him that made her think he liked his creature comforts. It wasn't manly or tough, she supposed, yet it intrigued her, for she'd never allowed herself to want those things, never allowed herself to miss the everyday comforts most people lived by now. She imagined he was a regular guy, that he went to ball games and drank beer and watched television. Imagine that, she mused. Going to a ball game? She'd never been to a ball game. With Hamish it had been all about status and dinner parties with his over-mortgaged friends, and the healing crowd here was so intense. Wouldn't it be great to just go to a movie? she thought. To go to a stupid, Hollywood blockbuster movie and eat popcorn? Maybe he would take her on a date, a real date. Maybe he would want to . . . stop. Stop. What am I doing?

She tiptoed down the stairs. There were streaks of silver running on the water, a quick streaking brilliance incongruent with the stale wine taste in her mouth.

She crouched by the grate and crumpled up pieces of newspaper: Nation teeters on fiscal cliff, the headline read before the paper's ragged edge crumpled inwards then burst into flame. She arranged the kindling on top, put a log on and shut the grate.

The wine glasses were still half full, abandoned on the small table and, looking at them, a memory of his urgent kisses bubbled up and broke in her mind, hot shame flowering across her face: the way she'd melted into him and the fact that she'd cried afterwards, tears streaming from her eyes in a kind of full body release and him a total stranger . . . She shook her head abruptly. I'll make coffee, she thought quickly, he looks like he likes coffee, then she busied herself in the kitchen, her thoughts chasing one another like the squalls of wind across the bay.

The coffee had just started to boil when she heard him upstairs. The boards above her creaked, then she heard him on the stairs, then he was right there, in her living room with his shirt untucked and his hair in disarray, his face still soft with sleep.

"Good morning," she said, "I hope you slept well." She realized she hadn't turned any lights on and flicked on the lamp.

He blinked. "I did. Thank-you." He looked around and rubbed his head. "Wow. Now that you can see, the view here is spectacular. Stunning."

He was huge in the tiny room. He went and stood before the fire.

"Please keep sleeping if you like. Unfortunately, I have to go and open at the café, otherwise I'd . . ." she trailed off.

He kept looking around and rubbing his head. His hair stood on end like a little boy.

"Do you like coffee? I made coffee."

He stood there a moment longer then came up behind her at the counter, wrapping his arms around her waist and pulling her close. His chin rested on her shoulder as if he were used to such intimacies. "I had a good time last night," he said. "You were sweet."

The sandpaper on his cheek sent shocks through her entire body, yet she felt there was something strange, almost mechanical about his words. You were sweet. What did it mean? She shivered.

He took the coffee and went over to the couch where he flopped down and leaned back and closed his eyes. "My head is killing me," he moaned.

She went and got him some aspirin and a glass of water, then stood by the fire, unsure of what to do next. He stayed on the couch with his eyes closed.

"I'm sorry I have to run out on you. You're welcome to stay here and relax, if you want. If you want to, you can stop by the café later or . . ." She bit her lip and stopped herself. She put another log on then gently wrapped the blanket round his shoulders. "Good-bye, Michael."

"Good-bye, Annika."

The light was beginning to pale when she reached the café. She went about her routines, putting the coffee on, getting the cinnamon buns in the oven, feeling distracted and flighty. Conversations replayed themselves in her mind. Looks, gestures. When she'd first brought him back to the cottage, she'd wondered if she'd made a mistake, but then he'd kissed her, he'd kissed her all over with such urgency. She shivered then turned to find the coffee was overflowing.

At 7:30 she unlocked the till and flipped the sign in the door to open. She bent over and was arranging the muffins in the display case when the bell above the door jingled. She started up quickly but it was only Renee, another middle-aged divorcee who liked to read the paper with a poppy-seed muffin.

He won't come, she told herself. He's not coming, then the bell jingled again and her heart skipped again but it was only Roddy.

"Twisted Anni! You're looking lovely as usual," he said.

Roddy was a tall, grizzled man somewhere in his fifties who owned one of the fishing boats. Annika suspected he had a bit of a crush on her. One time he'd shown up drunk at jam night and explained to her in great length why one half of his face was more weathered than the other, something about always facing west in the afternoons, and he'd been quite earnest about it as if he were apologizing for not being more handsome. She hadn't had the heart to tell him that she'd never noticed the difference.

She handed him his bun in a brown paper sack. "You're not going out there today are you?"

"No, dear, no. Work to do on the boat. There's always something. Boats, you know." He leaned in and gave her a wink. He was a winker.

"Behave yourself now," she scolded and he liked that and tipped his ball cap and was off. She sighed, then sighed again. She looked out at the sunshine and the whitecaps on the water. Here she was, almost forty and only now beginning to understand the wide-eyed excitement of those high school girls she'd once envied. The bell jingled again and she whirled around hopefully.

Barry. He shuffled in, his eyes trained upon her like laser beams. "So?" he asked as he approached the counter.

"Hello, sir," she said formally. "What may I do for you this morning?" She didn't know if she wanted to tell him. Not yet, anyway.

"So how was the rest of your night?" he pressed.

"This is a café, you know. People eat here. They order things."

"Well, if you're going to be that way, I'll have two coffees and two buns to go. Helmut's outside. We're on our way to the dump for a little salvage mission, but I refuse to leave until you've spilled the beans."

She shrugged and pursed her lips. "There's nothing to spill. What you saw was all there was. We chatted a while longer then he went back to his hotel and I went home."

Barry narrowed his eyes and studied her face. She handed him the coffees. "Okay, be coy if you must. At the very least, I hope you got his number. He seemed like a nice guy."

She shrugged again. "He knows where I am."

"Aaaniiikaa!" he said in a long drawn out way, as if he already knew her secret. She handed him the buns but didn't meet his eyes. "Don't you worry, girl. He'll call you."

"How do you know?"

"Because the guy would be absolutely crazy not to." He smiled his lopsided smile. "And I don't care what the end result was, you looked like you were having fun."

"I drank too much," she sniffed.

He cackled merrily and turned to go. She came around to help him with the door.

Helmut was parked across the street. He gave her a nod but didn't smile and suddenly another bubble of memory came rising up, this one caustic: 'You were sweet' he'd whispered in her ear, his body so warm, his voice so stilted.

All day she waited and every hour he didn't show was a disappointment and these piled up until at last she felt angry, although mostly at herself. She was being ridiculous, acting like a child. She did the dishes in the back room, barely able to fight back tears. It was foolish to hope, she told herself, foolish to attach expectations to a drunken hook-up, and that was all it was really: a drunken hook-up. She thought the words bluntly, roughly, over and over as if to grind out any delusion. Sex is just sex, isn't that what they said? Like crushing out a cigarette. Like ripping a band-aid. Enjoy, Barry had whispered in her ear, as if love were a glass of wine.

Suddenly, the bell jingled again, and she felt annoyed at the way her heart quickened. "It's not him, she told herself, stop being such a stupid . . ."

But it was him. He was standing in the doorway with his hands thrust deep into his pockets, half turned away, unable to meet her eyes. He looked terrible; his face was so haggard and pained, he looked like a man with a war going on inside him. She walked over to where he stood. Without speaking, she put her arms around him.

CHAPTER FOURTEEN

Matt stayed. He didn't know why.

At first, he felt more like a convalescent than a lover. He lay on her sofa in front of the fire with a blanket wrapped around him, unable to think, unable to speak, his mind a curious blank. He felt *hollow*, weak, so worn out by months of anxiety he couldn't even move, but Annika was gentle. She padded softly around the cottage, preparing dinner, stoking the fire and making sure he was comfortable. She didn't ask questions and her quiet acceptance of him, lying alcoholic worm that he was, felt so unexpected, so undeserved, he thought he might weep. How long had it been since he'd felt a caring hand across his brow? How long since someone touched him with genuine warmth, free of obligation or resentment? He couldn't remember how long.

Later, when they made love, it was quiet, soft. He lay very still and let her explore his body. Her movements were careful; her kisses light; her fingers just grazing his skin, tracing the lines of his body with a feathery wonder, as if there was something amazing about him; as if his chest, his legs, his thighs were a miracle, not just muscle, not a meal ticket, not a mistake, and he felt something in him surrender to her lightness, submit to it, like a horse that comes to bridle with its head bent low.

Time seemed to pass in a fog. He was aware of it passing, aware of obligations and responsibilities, of debts and resentments that were circling, circling somewhere just beyond the periphery of the tiny cottage, beyond the warm safety of her bed. Yes, his own life was out there, yet each time he started to think about it, his mind rushed away. He held Annika tighter, kissed her longer.

On the morning of the second day, they went walking on the beach. It was still foggy and the sun, as it rose, turned the haze a dazzling white. The only thing visible was a small stretch of beach and the woman by his side and it was possible to imagine they were the only two people on Earth.

When they came to the end of the beach, Annika sat down on a log while Matt skipped stones. The action reminded him of being a kid: the focused movement, the coolness of the stones in his hand, the ripples spreading outwards on the glassy surface of the water, circles within circles expanding. He crouched down and scanned the gravel in front of him, looking for the perfect stone, then he found it: smooth, flat, almost square. Finding it gave him a silly amount of pleasure, and it skipped wonderfully, too. Ten, eleven, twelve times before passing out of view. He turned and grinned at Annika. "Did you see it? That's how it's done," he boasted. He could feel the lines of his deep, childish grin even after his face relaxed, as if they'd been creased there, his flesh unused to bending that way.

He turned and sat down next to Annika, putting his arm around her and pulling her close. She smiled at him, then rested her head on his shoulder in a way that was so natural, so simple and trusting, it reminded him of Jacob. Jacob. Just like that, the magnitude of the lie, of who he was and why he was here, hit him with full force. If he had been standing, it would have staggered him; the weight of it would have driven him to his knees. For a moment, the brightness in the air seemed to dim, as if something large and ominous were passing overhead, searching, circling above the fog, while he sat on the log holding his breath, hoping for it to pass.

Now, Annika looked up at him. Her searching, grey eyes and clear, fresh skin caused him almost physical pain. What was he even doing here? What did he hope to achieve? She didn't seem to him like the kind of person who would commit a fraud. In another life, he might have . . .

"I'm glad you're here, Michael," she said with genuine warmth.

He closed his eyes. "So am I," he answered, then tensed, holding his breath; but the shadow did not return.

That afternoon, he helped her split fire wood. They worked silently; there seemed no need to talk. He chopped while she collected the pieces, then stacked them in the woodshed. Each time he hefted the maul, he thought about how good it felt: the thwack of the axe ringing out in the quiet afternoon, the whiteness of the new wood as it fell away on either side, the strength in his own hands, like something newly woken.

And it seemed like this strength, this usefulness, remained awake in his hands when he made love to her afterwards, so he didn't have to think, his hands just knew what to do, moving over her body with a confidence that allowed her to trust him as they came together on a blanket in front of the fire, their skin alive and prickling, their cheeks still rosy from the cold.

Later, they cooked supper and listened to the radio. He opened a bottle of wine and they chopped vegetables and talked about politics along with the radio show. It was nice to talk with a woman his own age, he thought. With Jen there was always this gap, despite her natural intelligence; not of knowledge but of something else, some kind of aesthetic understanding, something that had to do with the eerie green glow of the first Gulf War, of being an adult already when the towers fell, of having email cut your life in half. It was hard to explain, but he felt it when he was with Annika, this basic understanding, like he didn't need to explain himself all the time or weigh each word for how it might oppress her.

On the radio, the pundits switched from the fiscal crisis to health care. He stood up, then poured them each another glass. The fire in the woodstove cracked. The cat lay purring on the sofa. He sipped his wine, enjoying the warmth, the simplicity, only half listening as the program droned on about nationalized health insurance.

At the counter, Annika paused from chopping an onion. "I don't know about that," she said, wrinkling her nose. "It seems to me that the health care system fails a lot of people in the middle too, not just the desperately poor. There's a lot of people that fall through the cracks." She took a sip of wine, held it in her mouth, then looked at the window. She seemed to be thinking deeply. "It forces people to extremes; it makes them do extreme things."

He frowned. Something in her demeanor had changed; there was a tension, a seriousness that wasn't there before. His heart began to pound. "Is throwing money at a bunch of middle men really going to change things, though?" he argued brashly, taking a position he didn't really believe. "It's not going to stop costs from spiraling."

She looked at him with a sad, tired expression that he didn't understand, then she looked away again, at the window. Why did she keep looking there? What did she see? Him? Her? The dark? He sensed that the lie was somewhere close.

"Hamish used to say the same thing, and I don't disagree, entirely. It just feels so . . . so unnecessarily brutal. I mean, do the consequences of being sick need to be so . . . so harsh?" Now, she began doing things quickly, sliding the onions into the pan, filling a pot with water. Was it too quick? Did the quickness mean something?

"Hamish?!" Matt exclaimed, joking to conceal the edge of his own excitement, his own quickening pulse. "Hamish? What kind of name is Hamish anyway? He sounds like an Amish farm-boy." It was the first time he'd heard her call her ex-husband by name.

Annika turned to look at him now, tilting her head in a curious way. There was so much he didn't understand about her, so many hidden things. "You're not entirely wrong. Hamish did come from a traditional, rural family, although they weren't Amish," she explained, as if there was some way he might have known this. "On the surface, he was an urban, modern guy but in lots of ways he was still very traditional." Now she looked back at the window and added darkly, "A wayward farm-boy looking for redemption."

"Redemption? Redemption from what?"

She turned, as if startled away from some internal conversation. "Oh, sorry. What I mean is that Hamish still really wanted to please his family. He'd moved away; he was living a different lifestyle, but deep down, he wanted back in. He wanted all the milestones. That's why he got married, I think. That's why he chose me. Unfortunately, there was one pretty big milestone I couldn't provide." Again, she turned to the window. Again, that darkness, that strange tension in her voice. He didn't understand any of it. He chopped celery, irritated, unsure of how to respond.

Now, she sat down across from him at the table. "And how about you? Why didn't it work out between you and your wife?" she asked.

He looked down at the cutting board. Suddenly, Jen and Jacob were right there in his·mind. He could picture them at home in their clean, modern house. It would be bedtime now, he realized. Jen would be in Jacob's room, sitting on the bed in her pyjamas, reading stories with Jacob nestled close beside her; maybe she was explaining how Daddy went away for a few days, but not to worry, he'd be back.

"Why didn't it work out?" he repeated abruptly. His voice came out too loud. Aggressive, somehow. "She had an affair, that's why." He didn't know why he said this, why he felt the need to be brutal, why it somehow felt true. "She and my best friend were hooking up behind my back for three years," he elaborated. "I caught them together in the shower. They were naked. Fucking. Just going at it." Each word felt raw, ragged, pressing down.

Annika looked confused, "That must have been terrible," she said quietly, then put her hand gently on top of his. He slouched and looked away, hating himself yet unable to break out of the angry, sullen role he'd suddenly slid into. All supper, he felt himself going deeper and deeper.

Then, later: her kisses tentative, asking, wondering, and him, taciturn, insensitive, until he felt himself harden, aroused by his own anger, by the possibility that lived in it, the what next? what next? even if what was cruelty, even if what was disaster, the awful daring drawing him on. Soon, they were naked and he was on top, pushing towards something he couldn't quite reach and she, clinging, arching beneath him. Was this making love? Fucking? Just fucking? Each thrust felt frustrated, like a doomed plea for understanding: This. Is. Not. Who. I. Am. Everything about it felt wrong.

Afterwards, he lay awake, the silence around him grown monstrous, like a physical presence crouching in the shadows of the frigid room. He felt horrible. Annika was curled up beside him, sleeping. He ran his hands over her back and shoulders. Her frailty, her isolation, the monstrous quiet . . . was the lie, the thing he didn't understand, really so hidden? Was it really such a mystery? Or was it right here? Were the answers to his questions right here, in the quiet, in the painful thinness of this woman beside him? He shivered, pressing close to her to feel her warmth, to shield her sleeping body from the monsters that were lurking in the corners, in the quiet. He stroked his hand over her sleeping brow and whispered, "Forgive me."

The next morning, he left while she was at the café opening. He didn't tell her he was leaving or leave a number for her to contact him, he simply drove away.

Chapter Fifteen

Months went by and Annika never heard from Michael. She kept telling herself that he wouldn't contact her; yet she still jumped when the bell jingled above the café door and often found herself wandering down roads where there were properties for sale, thinking about him. Forgive me, he'd whispered, stroking her hair. Had she been dreaming? Imagined it? What did it mean? She wanted so badly to see him again, to talk to him. Each night she lay in bed and listened, holding her breath at the top of every inhale, scanning the silence for a car in the drive, for footsteps on the path, for a soft rap on the door, and each exhale was a disappointment and these piled up and up inside.

And somehow, life went on. She worked hard to keep the café going. She went to Healing Journeys once a week and did breathing exercises at Marion's advising. She went for walks. She hosted jam night. At Christmas, she baked a turkey for Barry and Kat and her little cottage was filled with light and laughter for a night.

In January, she caught a cold that lingered for a while and wouldn't go away. It was the weather, people assured her. It was the greyness. A lack of vitamin D. Yet it woke a fear in her and each morning, she scanned her body, breathing deeply, trying to decipher if the hardness had returned. Every ache, every pain, frightened her, yet she never got any worse. It was just a feeling, a nagging sense that something was wrong.

Then, one day, out of the blue, Beverly called the café. Her familiar, dramatic voice seemed to smash through the fog of winter and Annika was glad. She held the phone to her ear and listened in amazement as Beverly launched headlong into a long, convoluted narrative about signing up for a marathon then having to withdraw because of a strange illness, then having her iron levels checked by several different doctors.

Almost immediately, Annika guessed it and she smiled to herself as Beverly circled around the real reason for her call; the way she danced around it reminded Annika of her father's dogs growing up: how they'd slink down the drive to greet her when she came back from school, ears pinned back, their bellies brushing the ground, as if their pre-emptive display of guilt would mitigate her father's rage when he saw they'd left the property.

"And so . . ." Beverly trailed off.

"And so what you're saying is that you're pregnant?" Annika concluded.

"How did you know?"

"You can be excited about it, Beverly!" Annika laughed. "I'm not secretly pining away for a baby."

"No! No! I don't think that at all. I just, you know, I wanted to be sensitive because I know that there was a time when you and Hamish . . ."

"There's a lot of water under that bridge," Annika said and, at the same time, she realized it was true. She hadn't given Hamish so much as a thought in months. It seemed impossible to her that a situation at one time so consuming could eventually become just a fact of your life, that the years could pile on and press out all the pain. "I'm really happy for you," she said and meant it.

"You are?" Beverly asked hopefully then launched in again with her excited chatter. "We'd stopped trying so I didn't expect it, but you should see me now, I'm huge. I just can't stop eating. I used to care but now I don't even bother. I've surrendered to it: that's a term they're always using at these birth classes Al roped me into. Surrender. I quit smoking and I quit coffee so I might as well surrender to ice cream, right? Anyway, Al and I are having a party, I don't want to call it a shower because I hate those things, that degrading needle over the belly thing and whatever else they do, so we're having a kind of pre-baby celebration instead. I wanted to invite you. I'd really love it if you could come. I miss our chats."

Annika looked out at the water and the slow grey day outside. Her throat grew thick with emotion. It surprised her.

"Will you come, Anni?"

"Yes, of course I'll come. I'd love to."

Several weeks later, Annika took the ferry back to Seattle. It was a clear, cold day and she was full of good intentions. She was looking forward to seeing all her old colleagues, even to seeing her old haunts again.

On the ferry, she sat out on the deck despite the bitter cold. She sat wrapped her arms tight around her and watched the blue shapes of the islands glide across one another, blue on blue then paling back to the ghostly solitude of Mount Baker on the Eastern horizon. Such a beautiful, magical place! she thought. What did it matter how she'd ended up there? She was here. She had her life to live.

Halfway across the strait, a school of porpoises appeared alongside the boat and she watched their taut, glistening bodies pop up then dive back down into the black water. The cold staccato puffs of their breath were audible even above the sound of the ferry, and they seemed to her an affirmation of the great gasping effort that life took, the sheer energy that was required. She breathed deeply the cold clean air. She would forget about this Michael, she vowed; she would forget about the cancer and get on with living. What else could she do?

Her sense of purpose did not last long, however. As she drove southbound into the Seattle traffic, her stress levels began to rise almost immediately. Everything around her seemed too bright and too loud, the concrete tentacles of the Interstate too narrow, the cars too fast.

The whole shower/party had become unnecessarily complicated, too, she thought, irritated. First, she'd been asked to bring cinnamon rolls which made sense, seeing as she was Twisted Anni, but then it turned out that Karen really, really wanted to make her grandmother's sweet bread and Ellen and Katie were both on the Atkins diet and didn't even eat bread, so she'd offered to bring a veggie tray instead but Rehab got back to her and said that *she* was bringing veggies and dip so could Annika please bring a fruit plate? That was how things worked now and Annika wanted to be graceful about it, but, as she drove, she felt increasingly annoyed. She clover-leafed around the Northview exit, then turned the car onto the wide expanse of sun-bleached asphalt in front of the Super Value. She felt oppressed and put-upon.

She parked far away from the store and sat for a moment before getting out. There were people walking across the lot from all directions, their angled trajectories converging on the doors as if they were being pulled by some magnetic force: a woman in sweatpants and puffy jacket; a little red-haired boy with the same thick-hipped body as his mother; a lumbering worker with the tongues of his great boots flapping; all pulled towards the door. High above, white puffs of cumulous moved steadily across the arc of the sky.

Annika got out and joined the procession, feeling strange and out place amongst so many cars and people. It had been over three months, she realized, since she'd left the islands. At the entrance, two glass doors hissed open. A sign warned 'Careful! Sliding Door!" She crossed the threshold and the doors hissed closed behind her.

Inside, the air was dead and stale and filled with a dull roar, the ceilings looming high above the tops of the shelves, the vents and the pipes all naked and exposed, as if she was looking upwards into the guts of some great machine.

An elderly man in a red vest was greeting people as they entered. "Nice to finally see the sun," he said. "A little nippy out there today," he said. "Just in time for Valentine's," he said but everyone just ignored him and walked past.

Annika caught his eye. The way everyone ignored him made her feel bad. He reminded her of Marcus Wylie who used to stand outside the Church when he couldn't farm anymore, making comments on the weather, only in Rose Prairie people shook his hand; it would have been considered a disrespect not to shake the hand of an elder. "Windy one out there," Annika said.

The mans tired face crinkled up in delight. "You be careful not to blow away out there dear," he said.

She wondered briefly why he would say it; if, perhaps, she was getting too thin. She'd lost weight in recent weeks. Don't think it, she told herself. Stop. She shook her head and moved into the aisles, clutching the plastic basket while armies of boxes and cans snapped to attention all around her, so neat and orderly she felt feral and out of place with her wild tangle of hair that wouldn't sit flat. She wandered around in a daze.

When she got to the fruit aisle, there were several choices of pre-packaged fruit plates, so brightly coloured they looked fake. She chose one with an arrangement of melon and pineapple and strawberry, a plastic cup of pastel pink dip in the middle, all the while longing for the farm market in Saltery Bay, for the simple joy of slicing slowly through the skin of a spotted pear with her one good knife in the quiet of her kitchen.

At the checkout, she fell in behind a woman and her two teenaged daughters, all three dressed in long-sleeved, pastel dresses and white socks in sturdy shoes. Their long blonde hair was twisted into shiny braids down their backs and their faces were plain and freckled, their eyelashes the colour of the sun. She smiled at them to show them she understood, to show that she too knew how it was to always feel judged, but they looked away and she realized how she must appear now: a slim woman in tight jeans with loose, wild hair just like everyone else. There was nothing in her appearance that would give them any evidence of her past. She was just like the people they warn you about: those other women, all the drinking, crying, needing, fucking people with skin on skin like a Band-Aid ripping, just like all the other people. A caustic bubble of shame rose to her face and she remembered the weight of his body on top of hers, his hands in her hair, his voice in her ear: Annika Annika Annika . . .

Forgive me.

She shook her head. The air was so stale in this terrible place with its terrible roar and the guts all hanging down. She studied the magazines: bail-outs and break-ups and baby bumps. Like love was a glass of wine. Stop. The Christian women moved forward. One of the strawberry blonde girls picked up a divider from the metal runnel alongside the conveyor and set it down. She smiled tentatively at Annika.

Annika's heart surged. "Thanks," she said, relieved that her kindness had been recognized; her sympathy was real; she remembered what it was like coming to the supermarket as a girl; she remembered all the town girls smirking. Maybe there was still something about her appearance after all. She glanced down at the divider, a clear triangular prism with an ad inserted into it. She squinted and looked closer. There was a picture, a photo of a man in a blue sweater standing next to a sold sign.

Michael.

She shook her head then looked again. The text said: Matt Campbell. A name you can trust.

She frowned. She was hallucinating. She must be. Seeing things that weren't there because she was crazy and obsessed and couldn't let things go. That was all that was happening. It was a tiny photo. It was a one-time thing. Hamish had always told her she had a problem letting go.

She looked closer. He'd said he was a real estate agent, and, yes, it was hard to see but there, there was a little white scar on his eyebrow. She remembered it. And the name, she knew the name from somewhere . . .

A drunken hook-up, that's all it was.

Matt Campbell was a common name.

The conveyor moved forward. The girls twisted in their sturdy shoes in front of her.

Then she remembered. Not Matt but Matthew. A bubbly, sloppy signature at the end of the letter. The letter! It had gone to Twisted Anni's, not her house. He had come to Twisted Anni's. He'd wandered in like he was lost, like he was looking for something. He'd asked about her health.

Forgive me.

Sound bled out of the world. The ceiling yawned upwards and the brightness of the lights seemed to increase and swirl and pound.

Her mind raced. It's not true; it's a common name; it's a little picture; it's like ripping a Band-Aid: you just have to move on.

And yet she knew.

You were sweet.

Far off, someone was speaking.

"Would you like a bag for that ma'am? Ma'am? Ma'am? Would you like a bag?"

The police had called her Ma'am once. When she'd parked in front of Hamish's house on Christmas. They'd come and told her to stay away as if she were a criminal; a young officer, so handsome and young, had said "Ma'am? Ma'am, you'll have to leave," and she'd watched Hamish draw the curtain closed.

She walked towards the door in a daze. The sky winked back and forth, the brilliant blue sky hissing back and forth.

"You forgot your fruit . . . Ma'am?"

She went back to the car and sat there with the sound of the world turned off, unable to move or think or do anything but watch dumbly as the great beasts of the clouds continued their endless migration across the sky.

She did not go to Beverly's party.

Matt Campbell was easy to find online. She went to the café and sat in the dark on the computer in the back room and found him. He had a web page. He was wearing the same blue sweater as on the divider, standing in front of a sold sign with a happy family. There were listings and blog posts and testimonials. She read it all, then read it again.

"Matt Campbell guided us through the entire process, providing expert advice every step of the way. We're so happy with our new home. Matt Campbell thought of everything. There's even a playground for Mackenzie."

Annika began to tremble. You don't know for certain, she reminded herself. You don't know, and yet it all made sense: the strange letter, unanswered for several weeks, and then this strange man, just showing up out of the blue at jam night. And the way he'd acted at the end . . .

"This stunning gem on the water excels at entertainment and recreational living."

Stunning.

There were pictures. Here he was pounding a for sale sign into a lawn. His teeth. His hair. The endearing unsureness she'd seen at the café hadn't made it into the photos; in the photos he radiated confidence. His teeth glistened.

A stunning gem.

She started to shake.

"Matt Campbell has that wonderful mix of professionalism, business savvy and down to Earth charm that makes working with him a pleasure, not a chore. Highly recommended."

The way he'd waltzed in with his chest out and sat there at the crowded table with his legs spread wide underneath while the rest of them made room, folded themselves in half to accommodate him. She reached out and turned off the computer. Forgive me. She sat there in the dark.

When she got home she didn't bother eat. She just sat on the floor in front of the fire as her mind replayed it over and over. The cottage, her beautiful cottage, was full of him: where he'd stood, where he'd kissed her, the way he'd stroked her hair.

It was naïve, she thought bitterly, naïve to think you could outrun the past when sin stayed in the walls and in the air and all the choices after.

Behold the sower went out to sow . . .

And suddenly she thought of her father; she thought of her father and the men, the Rose Prairie men in their scratchy wool pants standing outside in the Church parking lot; those priggish uptight men with their tight-lipped judgment and medieval beliefs; those self-righteous controlling old men who would never, ever, not in a million years do such a thing as this.

"What have I done?" she whispered. She started to cry but even in the crying Michael was there: his hands on her forehead, brushing her hair back when the emotion had come, when the floodgates had broken and the loneliness had burst forth, he was there in the crying now, his shhhhh shhhh shhh it's okay and the fact that she'd wanted his comfort, and even worse, that she wanted it now.

Later, she lay in bed and listened to the waves and the pitter patter of heat in the pipe getting further and further apart as the fire died and she found herself holding her breath as her heart counted out the silence, listening for footsteps on the gravel, for a car in the lane; each night she waited and no one came and that was worst of all.

Part Three

Chapter Sixteen

Matt sat on the bed, watching his wife toy with her scarf in front of the mirror. He caught his breath. Something was different about her. Something had changed. What was it? The colour of her shirt that brought out the highlights in her hair? The way the light fell? A smell? A whiff of an old perfume she'd resurrected? Matt couldn't say exactly what it was, only that Jen looked beautiful; she looked suddenly, impossibly beautiful.

He came up behind her, wrapped his arms around her waist and buried his face in the back of her neck. "Jen. My poor, beautiful Jen," he whispered and there was a delicious coolness at her neckline, an undertone of something clean and earthy and cool.

She turned into him and let herself be held, then she pressed the palms of her hands flat against his chest and pushed back so she could see into his eyes. "What's gotten into you lately?"

"Nothing's gotten into me. You look good that's all. I think you look beautiful."

Her eyes narrowed as if she didn't quite believe him, then she turned back to the mirror and fiddled with her earrings. He sat back down on the bed. He wanted to grab her and shake her, to hold her tight and make her understand how much, how very much he wanted to make things better; instead he sat watching, saying nothing. She ignored him.

She was going out without him for the first time in years. Some friends she'd met at her yoga class were doing a girl's night at a local bar and he supposed he was happy for her. He supposed it was a good thing, yet he felt abandoned somehow, uneasy.

"Do you remember that day we went out to Point Roberts Beach?" he asked.

She held a pair of gold dangly earrings up to her ears, then put them down. "What about it?"

"You had on that green swim suit and you just dove right in. None of the other girls went in but you went right in and swam."

"I grew up near the ocean, remember." She was playing with the lipstick now, doing that smacking thing.

"And that cook, what was his name? The creepy one? He tried to follow you out to the raft and practically drown."

"Jason. Jason Dupuis," she said matter of factly. She had a memory for details. Names. Dates. She turned around. "Why are you bringing this up?" It was not an attack, but a question, as if she found it strange he would bother revive such ancient history.

"I don't know. It was fun, that's all."

She picked up her purse, straightened her skirt and smiled at him quickly. "It was fun. It was a fun day." She kissed him airily on the cheek. Again, he was filled with the urge to grasp her, to hold her against him and explain how he felt, to make her understand, but then she turned and went downstairs. "I'm going to be late."

He followed her down. She went into the den and said goodbye to Jacob who was watching TV, then she was out the door. He watched her walk down the steps. He watched her get into the car.

A fun day. It hurt that she would be so dismissive of it, that day their life had changed. He remembered it so clearly:

He'd been working nights at that time and partying a lot, maybe drinking too much; the majority of his days had been spent in a state of hungover exhaustion. He'd wake at noon to find the day half gone, the sun too bright, its unforgiving glare hunting out the squalor of his dirty little bachelor pad: the tangled sheets and take-out containers, the inside of his mouth tasting like his father's house used to taste: sour and smoky. Somehow, life had gone stale. Everything felt dull and unhealthy, and then Jen had arrived. She'd been hired to work on the patio for the summer: a smart, beautiful girl in her first year of University. She'd been so different from the other waitresses: whispery and cool and healthy; she'd swum in the ocean; she'd simply jumped right into the frigid water, just like that. He'd felt something wake up inside him when he was around her, the desire to be better, cleaner, smarter; he couldn't explain what it was. He'd known she was much younger than him but hadn't thought it would be a problem. He'd actually imagined them being together, making a life together, despite her accusations that all he'd wanted was to fuck.

That day at the beach, he'd felt alive, truly alive. He'd been funny and daring and full of energy, playing football and splashing with her in the ocean. He'd had so much fun that he hadn't wanted it to end so he'd taken her out for a drink and then another and then the next morning they both woke at noon in his bed, in that hard light, with that stale breath he'd wanted so badly to get clean of. Shortly after this, there'd been a terrible crying scene in his bathroom, her voice behind his bathroom door saying: my life is over my life is over my life is over and that whispery coolness, that dark humor he'd been so attracted to, slowly disappeared. She was so different now, it sometimes felt to him like he'd killed her.

He stood in the doorway and watched the red taillights of her car recede down the quiet street. The night air was cold on his face and he felt the wind pick up as he stood, then he heard the rain come sizzling across the pavement, running towards him on tiny prickling feet, closer and closer as if it might leap up out of the blackness at any second. He slammed the door and stood against it, his heart pounding.

Jacob was standing in the hall, watching him. "What's wrong, Daddy?"

"There's nothing. Nothing's wrong." He forced a smile. "Come on, you dirty beast. Time for your bath."

He brought his son upstairs then sat on the toilet with his elbows on his knees and his hands clasped in front of him; the warm, lemon-scented steam wrapping itself around him as his son splashed about in the great white tub. The white tiles, the white floors, the glistening white boy.

Jacob held a green, plastic dinosaur under the water then let it go so it jumped up above the waterline and splashed down.

"Pop!" Matt supplied and Jacob laughed then did it again and Matt said it again and Jacob laughed again and on and on it went. He must have said "Pop!" a thousand times and yet he didn't tire of it as he sometimes did for each time it was beautiful and new and precious. Pop! Pop! Pop! He could sit and say Pop for all eternity he realized, just to stay here, to be here, and he ached for the moment even though he was in it, he ached for his own life even though it was right before his eyes. If only, he thought. If only and then, in the ache, he felt a cold pressing in; he felt a fog and a silence and then Annika, Annika . . . His mind rushed away.

He clapped his hands. He stood suddenly. "Okay mister. You're turning into a prune. Time for bed."

Jacob stood, his smooth, white belly extended over his dangling, pinky-finger of a penis, his limbs loose at his sides. So unashamed, so completely and utterly unashamed it seemed a goddamn miracle. Matt swooped in with a great, white plush towel and wrapped it around him and lifted him up and carried him; the warm, firm, living weight in his hands; the glistening, white, magical boy in his hands. He dipped his head down and kissed the top of Jacob's head as they walked down the hall to the room, the warm, clean room. The lamp was on, the stuffed animals on the shelves standing guard. Jacob's jammies were neatly folded in the top drawer, sitting there like a gift at Christmas. Again, Matt was struck with a sense of wonder at their lives, at the fact that this moment should belong to him. He read a story about a boy who could fly then stood in the door as the light slanted in across his son's little blonde head and he was filled with a terrible ache inside. He closed the door and was alone.

He went back downstairs and sat on the couch. He flipped through the channels then turned the TV off. When he looked up, his own reflection in the window startled him. He didn't like how the rain blocked out the other sounds, how you couldn't hear anything but the rain pounding down. It was stupid, he thought, for a grown man to feel afraid in his own house, and yet he did feel afraid. He didn't know why.

He went to the liquor cabinet. Since the incident in Saltery Bay, he'd made a concerted effort to cut back. He'd made new rules for himself: only the hard stuff now, in small doses, like medicine. But tonight, he felt lonely; tonight, he needed the burn to take him away for it was close now, what he'd done. He perused his selection, then took out the bottle of Chartreuse, poured a couple ounces into a brandy snifter over ice, then closed his eyes and tried to let the burn take him back to another, less complicated time. Chartreuse. He'd bought the bottle in France, as a souvenir. Thinking back, he tried to picture the monk across the wall. The monk and the gem-bright leaves and the silence.

Jen hated it whenever he told people the story about the monk. She sensed a resistance in him, something unrelated to her or Jacob or their life together and she resented it: if she had to give up everything; so too, would he. Whenever he started to tell people about the trips he used to take when he was still single and working at the bar, she would cut him off. "It was a Contiki tour," she'd say, "All they did was go around Europe and get drunk. They drove around in a bus, went to pubs and screwed each other. That's all they did."

She wasn't entirely wrong, either. He'd gone on a few tours that were like that. The tour where he'd seen the monk had an insane itinerary of five countries in ten days. They'd seen a few castles and museums but it was mostly pubs and nightclubs, the whole trip steeped in sex. At the beginning, he'd been on the front lines of the debauchery but quickly grew tired of it. By the end of the trip, he'd felt harried and annoyed. When they'd visit old castles and estates, he'd stop to read the information on the plaques, but only ever get halfway through before being rushed on by the tour guide or pulled away by one of the girls. He'd wanted to slow down, to stay in one spot and just breathe the air, to press his forehead against the ancient stones, but was not allowed to do so.

His irritation had come to a head at the Grand Chartreuse monastery in the hill country outside Grenoble. It was the ninth day of their tour.

The monastery stood alone in a forest of leafy trees, a large compound of old buildings surrounded by a great stone wall. Inside the wall, the monks still lived a traditional existence and visitors weren't allowed inside, but there was a museum and a gift shop where you could buy Chartreuse and, after a long, winding bus ride, their sorely hungover little group had trooped across the parking lot and filed into the museum like a herd of well-trained, slightly onerous cattle.

As a bartender, Matt had been genuinely interested in how the liquor was made. The story had fascinated him: a secret recipe handed down through the centuries, through wars and exile and political strife, an elixir of life made from 130 different herbs, this quiet castle in the forest . . . Afterwards, the guide had handed around tiny samples of yellowish green liquor that shone like budding leaves.

"It has the funny side-effect of making everyone look like a woman," one of his companions had snickered and then there was a flurry of Catholic molester jokes. Matt had felt so annoyed he'd taken off by himself for the time remaining.

While the rest of the group nursed their hangovers in the shade by the bus, he'd walked around the stone wall. At first, he'd stayed on a trail overhung by trees, a kind of green tunnel along one side of the monastery, then he'd cut up into the forest and walked along a small rise at the far end.

Above him, new leaves shimmered and danced in the sunlight, and, as he walked, he became aware of a profound silence, the whispering of the leaves just tickling its surface, drawing his awareness to something deep and powerful underneath. After spending so much time in noisy pubs and busy tourist attractions, he'd been almost overwhelmed by the desire to stop and sit for a while in that quiet forest.

Eventually, he'd come to a place where he could see down inside the monastery wall to a small stone courtyard. At its center was a garden of raised beds with many flowers and fan-like trellises draped with vines. The monastery's interior buildings looked down into this garden from three sides; its near end butted up against the outer wall.

As Matt stood, looking down into the garden, a monk had appeared in the doorway of one of the interior buildings. Unlike the hooded old priests of Matt's imagination, this monk's head was bare and he was relatively young. His blonde hair shone in the sun. He began moving about with a graceful, unhurried athleticism: crouching, kneeling, standing. Maybe he was able to sense Matt's gaze because, after several minutes, he'd looked up and scanned the edge of the forest, his eyes coming to rest on Matt. Matt's first impulse was to turn away but the young monk had regarded him with such a peaceful expression, he remained where he was.

They'd stood, each on one side of the wall, looking at each other for some time. A strange sensation had come over Matt then; he'd never felt so powerfully towards anyone in his life as he did this young man. He felt as if they were almost the same person, differing only in their wildly different circumstances. He'd raised his hand slowly in greeting and the monk had raised his, then a profound feeling of calm had come over him. They were the same. He'd felt it with utter certainty. They were different; but they were the same. He couldn't describe it, only that, for a moment, he'd felt less alone in the world. The feeling lasted only a minute, then he'd hurried back, excited to share what had happened, but when he told the group they laughed and called him Matty the Carthusian Brother Fucker. They kept teasing him about his spiritual awakening.

Much later, when he'd tried to explain it to Jen, she'd scoffed and said, "You? You wouldn't last a day in solitude." And it had hurt him because he felt like he could live that way, or that he would like to try, but that no one had ever given him the chance.

His face began to burn, even now, so many years later, when he thought about how he'd been ridiculed: Matty the Carthusian Brotherfucker. A Contiki Tour. All they did was fuck. He lay his head back and rested it on the sofa. He closed his eyes and sipped his Chartreuse, listening to the rain. Suddenly, he was back there again, in that cold, lonely cottage. In the greyness. In the quiet. It was never far from his mind now, all shames seemed to lead him there, no matter how unrelated: how he'd lied and gone down there, how he'd stayed, how, at the end, she'd fucked him like she was drowning and now these cold fingers clawing upwards from the dark whenever he was alone, groping at the bright spot of the burning on the roof of his mouth. Annika, he thought, what the fuck did I do?

He got up suddenly, unable to sit with his thoughts any longer. He wandered the house like someone lost, then lay in bed but didn't fall asleep until he felt Jen crawl in beside him, and even then it was a fitful sleep, fraught with the sense of falling.

Then there was an alarm. A sound. Something. He felt himself clawing towards it like a man trapped underwater, fighting up. Ringing. There. His phone. A glow in the fabric of his pants at the foot of the bed.

Who?

Jen was already going for it, her spidery shadow spanning across.

He snapped to and grabbed her arm. "Don't."

"Who is calling you at three in the morning?" There was a straining in her muscle but he held firm.

"Well whoever it is can wait," he said. The ringing stopped. She was above him. He could see the glisten on her eyes, black as stones.

"Who would call you right now?"

"I don't know." He lay flat on his back, heart hammering.

"What if it's your parents though? What if something happened?" she wheedled and began to move for it again and he snapped to again and pulled her down. Maybe it was rough, he thought later. Maybe it was too rough. Then he went to get it himself but it was a number he didn't recognize.

"Who was it?"

"I don't know."

"Matt! Who was it?" she insisted.

He said nothing.

"I want to know who it was."

A few nights later, he received a call from the same number and this time he answered. No one spoke but he could sense someone on the other end; he thought, maybe, he could hear waves sighing gently in the background. After that he turned his phone off at night.

But Jen suspected him now. He'd barely managed to convince her that his lost three days were business, and now she was on high alert. The youthful beauty he'd marveled at retreated and she became hard and brittle, her voice like broken glass. He insisted he had no idea who'd call him late at night, but she could sense there was a lie somewhere; she could sense his fear of who it might have been and began rooting around during the days when he was gone, going through his pockets and his drawers. He felt under siege. He drank a lot. Things began to spiral quickly. Her snooping made him aware of other secrets, things he'd put off and downplayed but that were now coming to a head, secrets that were accruing interest by the minute.

When he finally mustered the courage to go to the bank, they escorted him to a back room behind the lines of tellers. The room was divided into sections by frosted glass partitions under which he could see the feet of the other penitents like himself, tapping nervously in the gap. All around him was a low murmur of voices. He felt sick as he sat there waiting. He didn't know what he was going to say.

Soon, he saw the top of a head glide along the frosted wall, then a giant man entered the room. The man was tall with broad shoulders, narrow hips and a great handlebar mustache. He had tired, world-weary eyes like someone who could kick your ass but would really prefer not to. Matt stared. He'd met this man before, he was sure of it.

He racked his brain but couldn't place him. Was it Kato's? Did he sell this guy a house? There were so many faces, so many years, his memories slipping and sliding on top of one another, it was impossible to say. Saltery Bay? Jesus, he hoped not. The man's eyes seemed to twinkle with recognition, yet he said nothing. He stuck out his hand and introduced himself, "I'm Ron. I've been assigned to your file."

"Matt Campbell."

There was a pause, a twinkle of expectation before the man's face dulled over again by the business at hand.

Ron laid it out in plain English, just how bad the situation was. Matt had known it was bad, yet somehow, he'd deluded himself. Somehow, he'd convinced himself he still had more time. The blood rose to his face as he heard it spoken out loud. What had he been doing to let it get so bad? Yet he knew that too. He'd been waiting for something to save him. The big sale. The viatical settlement. Something. He stared down at the desk.

Ron laid out his options and they were also bad. "You could consider bankruptcy," he said. "There's less stigma now than there used to be. If you were to file now, you could apply for a loan again in seven years."

Matt rubbed his head, his mind scrabbling. His brain hurt. "Okay. Okay. I hear what you're saying but just say, let's just say I could make the next two mortgage payments and then make the minimum payment on the line of credit, would that work?"

The man sat there, unearthly still, regarding him with sad, tired eyes as if Matt were an injured animal. "I mean, the market's going to turn sometime," Matt went on. "I mean, things can't get any worse." He laughed and it sounded wild, unhinged, even to his own ears. His every whisky tainted word befouled the air. The Jesus-goddamn fresh-breath strips he'd taken from Jen's drawer did absolutely nothing, he thought. What was the fucking point of fresh breath strips if they didn't work? Ron watched him, all calm and collected like he was the financial horse whisperer and Matt a crazed rodeo bronc.

"Because there's a possibility I can pull something together," Matt heard himself say, "I might be able to borrow some money from my parents and I've got a friend out in the oil patch who said he could get me a job . . . I used to be a bartender and I could go back, working nights, then the real estate during the day . . ."

Still, the man was quiet. Finally, he spoke. "Mr. Campbell, you've been a good customer up until now, so I'm willing to give you another month here to get your affairs sorted."

"Thank-you. Thank-you. I'll get it sorted. I promise."

"But this can't go on indefinitely. You owe a huge amount of money, on your mortgage, on your visa, on this other loan, not to mention your line of credit. It's going to take a major, major turnaround to pull out of this. Are you sure you're not just delaying the inevitable?"

Matt was sweating despite the cool; he could feel sweat prickling up into his face, "I'll get it fixed. I swear. I've got some irons in the fire and I just need a bit of time."

The man regarded him. "One more month, but that's all that I can do. After that, you're looking at foreclosure."

"Awesome. Super-good. One month is all I need." As he stood to leave, he banged his knee on Ron's desk and pretended it didn't hurt but tears came up in his eyes. Ron stood over him, towering behind the desk and watching him with those sad, steady eyes.

"Mr. Campbell?"

Matt turned.

"You take care of yourself now." One of those giant hands found Matt's shoulder and rested there, its warm gentle weight pressing down. The fact of it shocked him! People didn't touch one another anymore and certainly not in banks. Matt looked into the man's eyes then it dawned on him where he knew him from: Ron had been a bouncer at Kato's for a couple of seasons and they'd gone to Vancouver Island together on a road trip. Matt could picture it now, this huge man crammed into the backseat of his car. Surely Ron knew who he was. Matt looked down at the ground. Somewhere along the line, he'd become a person you pretend not to know.

He walked out of the bank, trying not to cry.

I'm okay, I'm okay, he kept repeating as he walked to the car but he wasn't okay. He was all torn up inside. It was as if that one sympathetic hand on his shoulder had invited all his troubles to it and now they were pushing forward, scrambling over one another for a bit of recognition, a bit of sympathy. He sat in the car and now the tears came. Everything he did was stupid, everything was wrong and a complete and total fuck-up. He thought about Annika and remembered her kindness, then he cracked his head against the window to make the thoughts go away, then he did it again, then again, until a crack appeared on the glass.

The rest of the day, he drove around aimlessly, his mind a mess. There was still a month, he reassured himself. A lot could happen in a month. His parents might loan him some money; his mother had squirrelled a bit away and was always keen to help him, although even the thought of asking made his insides squirm. He could call Leo, he thought. Get set up with a job. And the contract: he would contact a lawyer and maybe he could at least get his initial investment back. Ken could go fuck himself that underhanded little fucker.

When he arrived home the house was quiet. The lights were off and it smelled of fresh paint. The furniture in the living room was covered with plastic sheets, the couches hulking strangely in the dim light.

"Jen?"

"I'm here," came her voice from the shadows.

She was right there in front of him but he'd missed her. She was sitting on one of the covered sofas, staring out at the darkening street. Her voice was flat and her face was grey in the murky twilight. He felt a chill. "Is everything alright?"

"No," she said flatly. "It's not alright. Nothing is alright, Matt."

He felt the blood drain from his face.

She stared out at the grey street and the grey sky and the rows of houses and the driveways and the cars. "Jacob had another appointment at the dentist today," she said.

Matt sat down. The plastic crinkled underneath him. He perched gingerly on the edge, unsure of what to say. There was a resignation, a tiredness in her that he'd never seen before, as if she'd grown old in his absence. He would have preferred her anger then to see her looking so old. "How did it go?" he asked when she didn't elaborate.

"Shitty. He has three new cavities. They're in his baby teeth, but still."

"Rotten," Matt said, and he shifted uncomfortably, unsure if this was the reason for her upset, or if there was something else.

"I had to suffer through some condescending hygienist lecturing me about fruit juice," she said.

Matt put his arm around her. "It's okay," he said but she didn't relax or look at him. The tone of her voice frightened him. There was a deadness to it that wouldn't let him near, a flatness that didn't acknowledge him at all. He had a horrible feeling that she'd outgrown him somehow, that she had moved on and he could no longer reach her.

He stood suddenly.

"Where are you going?" she asked sharply.

"I need a beer. Do you want a beer?" he asked as he opened the fridge. He held the cans, the clean, cold, uncomplicated cans in his hands and it calmed him slightly, then her voice came again from the living room. It was quiet and deadly but he heard every word.

"A woman came by the house this afternoon. She was looking for you."

He opened the tab and the hiss slithered away into the silence but he felt no relief at all.

"I told her you'd be back soon but she didn't wait."

He gulped at the beer. He closed his eyes and tried to focus on the cold prickling in his throat.

"She said her name was Annika. She said you'd remember who she was."

He stared out the window. It was a long time before he was able to speak.

CHAPTER SEVENTEEN

Annika lay on the floor of the cottage with her hands on her belly, trying to do the breathing the way Sasha had shown her. In and out. In and out. Her stomach went up and down; yet there was something halting and labored about the motion that she couldn't quite pinpoint, as if her lungs had dried out inside, like a leather bellows cracked and stiffened with age. She stared at the ceiling. She was afraid.

She'd gone and done something. She didn't quite know how to feel about it. It was not an altogether bad thing, it was just . . . it was just that she couldn't remember deciding to do it. Lately, all her thoughts seemed to snowball and run into each other so they were hard to pick apart, hard to understand. Most of them were bad thoughts, made up conversations, fantasy encounters, what she'd say, what she'd do if she ever saw him again. Whole hours, whole days were lost to it. She understood how this could happen; she'd been through a similar thing when Hamish had left her, yet somehow this was different. Back then, even on her worst days, she'd felt she could control the bad thoughts if she needed to; now, it felt as if the stops were pulled; what used to work didn't work anymore. It scared her.

She didn't even remember the ferry ride.

She didn't remember driving. She'd just ended up there, in this warren of streets and cookie-cutter houses that were all empty in the afternoon. She'd found the address he'd listed on his contact page, then driven around the cul-de-sac. There was a house with a foreclosed sign near his house so she'd parked in the driveway, slouched down in the driver's seat, and watched Matt Campbell's house. She didn't remember deciding to do any of this; she was suddenly just there, watching.

She'd sat for hours in her cold, damp car. Her body had ached and she'd been hungry but she'd sat there watching and there'd been something terrible and satisfying about the discomfort, the way calamity, when it finally comes, can be satisfying, for there is a neatness, a rightness when outer circumstances come to match the ugly things inside. Like pressing on a bruise. Like there. *There.*

When Hamish had left her, he'd told her she needed to get over it. He'd said it was unhealthy the way she kept calling and showing up. He'd said she needed to move on and that moving on was like ripping a band aid; that the pain would be short-lived, she just had to do it and get it over with. He'd told her this and then he'd gone back to be with his family and friends for Christmas but she hadn't had anywhere to go so she'd sat in her car outside his family's house, watching. She'd seen the lights come on; she'd seen the warm orange lights spill onto the side-walk and the Christmas tree wink in the window and she'd seen all his friends and relatives go in and out; she'd seen the family she used to be part of in the window of his parent's house and then he'd closed the curtain and still she'd sat in the car until the police had come and said, "Ma'am? Ma'am, you can't be here anymore." And it had felt like there. *There.*

And so she'd driven to Matt Campbell's neighbourhood and sat in her car and had watched his house, Michael's house, for she still thought of him that way, and she'd had a sense that history was repeating itself, like sitting in cars, this outside looking in, was who she'd always been.

She'd watched the house until a woman and a little boy came home and seeing them, her bad thoughts had started up again: that he should go about his respectable life being a respectable man after coming down there, after waltzing in and lying and being charming and funny, making love like it meant something . . . She'd wanted to tell this woman that her husband was a cheating prick; she'd wanted to ruin his life and make a giant mess and her anger had propelled her to the door but when the woman answered, Annika hadn't been able to say it. The woman was so young and wore her jealousy on the surface; it was so refreshing to see, the way she'd tossed her head like an angry colt, her young eyes flashing with warning. She'd been so proud and jealous and mean and flashing that Annika had liked her right away and couldn't do it. She hadn't been able to hurt the only living thing in that deadened neighbourhood. So she'd simply left a message and went back to her car.

She'd watched the house until he came home. He'd been wearing the same coat, had the same walk, there was no question in her mind anymore, and she'd wanted to get out and scream at him, but then the energy seemed to leave her and she'd felt sick and tired and saddened by all of it. Forgive me. She'd thought then that maybe she would just go home and forget it all but couldn't find the strength, so she'd sat in the car and watched some more. Towards evening, there'd been yelling from the house; it was the woman's voice mostly. She'd been unable to hear the words but it went on for some time, then it had stopped and the lights went out and she'd curled up in the front seat and slept.

In the morning, she'd been so stiff and aching that she'd been barely able to move. She'd seen the woman and the little boy come out of the house, the woman carrying a suitcase with her chin held high, her green eyes flashing and they'd left in a shiny green car.

After that, Annika had felt like maybe that was the end of it, that maybe this was enough punishment, and she'd turned on the heat with the intention of leaving, but she'd been unable to warm up. She'd barely had enough strength to turn the key in the ignition. When she looked in the rearview mirror there'd been a line, a small red line of blood coming from her nose. And now she was scared.

She lay on the floor and tried to do the breathing. It's not that, she told herself. It's not that, don't think about that. But there was another voice that seemed to say, there. *There*. This is what you get.

She decided to go to Marion's. She was almost desperate to go and see them all again. She hadn't been for a while. Healing was about intention, Sasha had told her. You had to want to get

better. And she wanted to; she wanted to see her friends, wanted
to be there, surrounded by people she knew, away from her own
thoughts if only for an hour. She jumped up from the floor and
ran out the door without taking a coat, then she sprinted through
the streets under a sullen grey sky, sprinting so fast that the shocks
came up into her shins. When she arrived on Marion's doorstep,
she was gasping and wild.

"Welcome," Marion said in that long, dramatic way she had.
She was wearing a white robe with golden earrings the shapes of
leaves. Her skin glowed as if it had been anointed with oil.

"Hello," Annika breathed, aware, suddenly, of her own tangled hair and sour clothes. She hadn't changed, she realized.
She'd forgotten to change her clothes after sleeping in the car.

Small, vertical lines appeared between Marion's manicured
brows. "How are you? Annika?"

Over Marion's shoulder, Annika could see the rest of them
already gathered in the great room. She could hear them chatting
and laughing as they drank their tea. Marion placed a hand on her
arm. "Annika? Are you alright?"

"I'm fine," she said and smiled, yet she knew it wasn't true.
Her sweat was already beginning to cool and she felt hot and cold
at the same time. She was unwell.

She went into the room. They were standing in the murky
confluence where the slate grey day met the rosy glow of the
lamps, chatting to one another as they fixed their tea. Annika!
they greeted her. Annika! We're so glad you came! We didn't
know if you were coming anymore! Annika! She poured herself
tea. Her hands were shaking badly. Barry came up and slapped
her on the back. "Hey girl! Where'd you go last night? I stopped
by to see if you wanted to go for a walk. Susan and I are on a
new walking kick."

"I was . . ." she began. "I had to . . ." Her heart began to
pound and she was almost overwhelmed with the desire to throw
herself in his arms. To tell! To tell! To say help me Barry, I don't
know what is happening anymore; she wanted to melt into him
as if they were dancing. "I had to do something," she replied
vaguely, then trailed off.

Now it was Barry's turn to frown, but then Marion rang the bell and they took their seats around the table. The usual suspects were there: Velma, Doug, Barry, Kat, Susan and Marion. Annika could feel their eyes on her and she knew she must look awful. She knew she must smell bad. She sipped her tea and despair rose up inside her. How could she ever explain it to them? That she'd gone to Seattle to spy on a man whom she'd invited into her bed, the same man who happened to have a bond on her life? It was crazy. She felt crazy. What could they know about sleeping in cars and skin on skin and the sower and the sown and all the rest of it, all of it, yet she wanted to tell them: that was how it always was, how it had always been, a life torn apart by hiding and wanting to be seen. They looked at her with baffled, wide-eyed concern.

Then Helmut walked into the room.

"Hello. I will be joining you."

All eyes darted to Marion who appeared tight-lipped but not surprised. "I've finally convinced Helmut to give Healing Journeys a try," she said, her voice curiously neutral.

Velma smiled warmly, her wizened face like an old apple at Halloween. "We're so glad you've come."

The others followed Velma's lead though Susan's welcome remained a bit perfunctory. She and Marion exchanged knowing glances.

Helmut sat down and placed his notebook on the table. He squared the edges then arranged the pen in parallel with the edge of the book. "Thank-you. I am interested and open to learning," he said. He folded his hands on top of the notebook, his back perfectly straight. Something about his keen masculine presence made everyone sit a bit straighter. They forgot about Annika. They shifted their pens and papers; they straightened their tea cups.

The session began with a series of chants. "Ohm," they said in unison. The sound was round and full, Helmut's low voice filling out the baritone, blending with the others, with Susan's shrillness, with Velma's sandpapery mezzo. Ohm they said. Ohm. Annika tried to say it too but her voice was so strangled and weak that she stopped, remaining outside the circle of sound, in a cold car outside the circle of sound. Ohm. She opened her eyes and looked at Helmut, but he was far away.

Soon Marion sounded the chime. Kat and Susan kept stealing glances at Helmut as if expecting a sociopathic meltdown, but he appeared completely at ease. They did a round of four and one breathing after which he told them, "We did similar training in the army. To help focus the attention."

Marion frowned.

Annika still had the strange hot and cold feeling. The room seemed to sway and part of her hoped it would take her with it, that she'd lose consciousness so they would know there was something seriously wrong, so that they would help her, but she didn't and there she was again, hiding and wanting to be seen.

"Okay, so the next exercise is something I learned at the Creative Therapies Conference in Boulder last year," Marion said brightly. "I did it with a workshop group and it was amazing what came up. So much incredible sharing came up." She reached behind her and brought a small, pink silk box onto the table. She handed it around the table. Inside were folded pieces of paper.

"On each paper is a poem or a quote by the mystic poet Rumi," she explained. The box came to Annika and she took a paper, then passed it on to Helmut. "I want you to read the poem and to think about its meaning. We'll think about the meaning, then do a five minute free write. Remember: there are no rules. Write whatever comes to mind and don't censor yourself. The idea is to keep the pen moving forward on the page and not go back. It may be complete gibberish but that's okay, just keep writing. Whatever's there, let it out. It's amazing what comes up."

Annika unfolded her piece of paper. She held it in her trembling hands. There was a cold sweat on her brow.

Marion rang the bell. "Begin."

It wasn't difficult. The words were already there, fully formed in Annika's mind, and the poem she'd chosen seemed to fit perfectly. All she had to do was transcribe what was already there, her hand pressing the words down, carving them into the page.

After what seemed a short time, the bell rang and everyone put their pens and pencils down and looked at one another, hands guarding their notebooks and papers. Annika's heart quickened with excitement: here was the chance to say it. To be known.

"Now, you don't have to share if you don't want to but I encourage you to do so. It can be an incredibly validating experience. My only rule is no criticism."

Annika's heart was pounding. She was about to volunteer then Helmut said, "I would like to share."

There was a collective intake of breath. Annika leaned forward over her own paper, her hair falling round her face on either side.

Helmut cleared his throat and began: "The poem is this: *The sky was lit by the splendor of the moon so powerful, your love has made me sure I am ready to forsake this worldly life and surrender to your being.*"

Kat and Susan glanced at one another. There was something pious and greedy in the way they were acting; it made Annika angry. They would be upset to be judged that way themselves. Helmut took no notice. He continued, "The exercise, my response, is this: The moon comes to a soldier parched and shaken, blue and gentle it comes; the hills shine like the shoulders of a sleeping wife. Anything, anything, in this moment anything for you. Was there ever such a love as a faraway soldier? Is this why we go to war?" His voice was deep and resonant, as if he'd been reading poetry all his life.

Kat looked down at the table. Susan's eyes were wide and unsure.

Barry punched Helmut in the arm. "Holy shit! The man's a goddamn natural! That was awesome. You make me look bad."

"Barry. We're not here to compare. This exercise is not about comparison," Marion said.

Velma put her old, wrinkled hand over Helmut's brown leathery one. "Thank-you for that. I get so angry at politics sometimes I forget about the sacrifice of individual soldiers. Thank-you for reminding me."

Marion, however, did not appear gentle or moonlit or impressed as her husband took his praise with becoming, straight-backed humbleness. Finally, she jumped in. "Would anyone else like to share? Anyone? Annika?" Her mouth was a thin hard line.

Annika looked down at the dark scrawl on her page. Her heart beat wildly. "Okay. Okay. I'll read it." Her breath came in short excited puffs. "The poem: *We are pain and what cures pain both. We are the sweet cold water and the jug that pours. I want to hold you close like a lute so that we can cry out with loving. Would you rather throw stones at a mirror? I am your mirror and here are your stones.*" Already there was a thickness in her throat, a shake in her hands. "And then I wrote: Coloured stones glisten under the river's skin; they wink and glisten like gemstones underwater; but pick them up and find they are but rocks in the hand. Not the cool round gems placed in the mouths of the dead, not pearls for the underworld, but gravel sharp and broken, shoved roughly, this cruelest viaticum. Now tell me: whose boots, whose boots are these?" Her voice came so thick it was like speaking through water. Her hair fell in her face.

No one said a word. Not a single word. When she looked up, she didn't see a single glimmer of understanding or recognition, only wide-eyed, baffled concern. No one touched her. No one thanked her for her beautiful words.

"Thank-you, Annika," Marion said perfunctorily. Her mouth was still hard and thin.

"Those are some powerful images," Doug tried then petered off.

Annika stared back down at her notebook. Tears welled up in her eyes. Her aching body, the confusion in her mind, the loneliness rushing: it was more than she could take. A single tear escaped and landed on her notebook.

Still, they sat frozen, unsure of what to do. Annika wanted someone to be sure. She desperately needed someone to be sure. The moment stretched on then she pushed her chair back from the table. "I can't do this anymore. I'm sorry. I really have to go."

Now they came to life, protesting. Annika! Annika! Wait! Annika! She saw Barry struggle to rise, saw him stumble up after her but she was already on her way out. She was half walking, half running, out the foyer, then down the steps and out into the yard, past the great room windows, their confused and baffled faces looking out after her.

She walked along the road under the slate grey sky.

Several minutes later she heard a vehicle behind her but she didn't turn. It slowed alongside then Helmut rolled down the window. "Get in," he said. It wasn't a question.

She got in.

The pickup was an old, rusted Mazda resurrected from the dump. The rear window had been smashed out but Helmut had replaced it with clear plastic, the duct-tape applied just so. He drove slowly past the cottages with their long, rambling drives. He didn't look at her. "I liked this poem that you read," he said. "The rawness of it."

She leaned her head against the glass. "You're about the only one."

"Life can be like this sometimes. Brutal. Like rocks in the mouth. Some people do not want to see it," he said mildly. She looked over at his profile. He had a square jawline and tired eyes. She'd never noticed before how awfully tired and sad they were.

He looked over at her now. "Marion is dishonest," he said. "She is just as narrow in her views as those she would criticize."

They left the pavement. The gravel crunched. Helmut pursed his lips and continued. "She says she wants to help people heal but refuses to be honest about the ways in which they're injured. She wants pain to just go away, like a magic trick. It is not a realistic view. I have told her this but she won't listen."

He turned into the lane and they drove in silence. The small whips of poplar scratched the underside of the truck. He parked in front of the cottage and they sat, staring out at the sea for a moment. Neither said anything. Then he said, "You are unwell again."

She closed her eyes. "I don't know."

They sat a while longer. She listened to the waves. "Yes. Yes, I'm unwell."

He nodded. "What will you do?"

"I don't know. I don't have much money left."

He nodded. They sat.

"I guess I should decide pretty soon. Things are happening."

"Will you go to the doctor?"

"No. I can't expect the doctor to help me now."

"There are difficult choices to make."

"I thought about the hospital. But the doctors, the tests . . . I opted out of chemo, you know. My doctor was upset, but I . . . I'm just tired, Helmut. I'm very, very tired."

He nodded. "And your family?"

She shook her head. "Not anymore."

He nodded again then looked at her with his grey eyes. "If you need anything, please ask me. Whatever you decide, Annika. I'm not a man to judge."

Chapter Eighteen

Matt wandered around his empty house in a daze. Without Jen and Jacob, the house seemed cavernous and bare. There was nothing, really, aside from a few toys and random junk lying around, that made the house theirs; nothing that said anything particular about them at all. The stainless-steel appliances, the bone-white walls . . . One sweep of the countertops and he might have been standing in someone else's kitchen; he might have been standing in a magazine. In a dream home! That's how he sold it to his clients: buy a house; own a dream. But who's dream? Was it a good dream? No one ever said what kind of dream it was. Maybe it was a bad dream; maybe it was a fucking nightmare, a cuckoo dream that the world foisted on you, a dream that sucked you dry, left you bankrupt and alone, staring at your bone-white walls.

He closed his eyes. Jen was gone. She'd taken Jacob and gone to stay with her parents and he couldn't tell from what she'd said whether she was taking a break or if she'd meant forever. He'd called her parents' phone but Crystal had answered wouldn't let him talk to her. Crystal kept saying give it time. She needs time. When he'd asked to talk to Jacob, Crystal had said he was asleep.

Matt didn't know what to do. What was he supposed to do? Let it all fall apart? Let his son be fucked up and the past five years be a total fucking failure? But if he went up there, if he showed up, he knew how they'd see it: that he wasn't respecting her boundaries; that he was some kind of life-ruining prick and out of control drunk like she'd said before she left.

He went to the liquor cabinet and opened a bottle of vodka. To take the edge off. To calm him down. It was eight am and he didn't bother with a glass. He walked around the living room, then back to the kitchen where he stood and looked out the window. Greyness. Rain. Thinking to fix himself a coffee, he turned and came face to face with the generic print of red peppers that was mounted above the counter. He remembered buying it. He remembered standing in Ikea and wondering if he was making the right choice. Red peppers! What did it even mean? It meant nothing, that's what it meant! It meant a pointless waste of money by someone so fucking guilt-ridden and afraid to offend he couldn't even make a simple decision! And now, after feeling bad and changing his life around and saying he was sorry for five fucking years, they wouldn't even let him talk to his own son! Suddenly, the red pepper print was in his hands and he was ripping it off the wall, taking a great chunk of drywall with it, then he raised it above his head and smashed it down against the countertop so that the shitty composite board it was mounted on snapped in two except that some of these tenacious particleboard fibers didn't rip so the two pieces still hung loosely together which made him even angrier so he kicked it and stomped on it until it was in pieces. Then his phone rang. He answered it. "Hello?" he practically hollered.

Silence. He could hear someone breathing. "Jen!" he cried, "Thank God! Thank God! I need to talk to you; I want to talk . . ."

"It's not Jen."

At first he didn't recognize the voice. He stood amidst the red pepper carnage, confused.

"I just need to know why," said a quiet, female voice. "Did it mean anything at all, what happened between us?"

He didn't understand, then, suddenly, he did. He felt his blood go cold. "How did you get this number?"

"Why did you stay with me like that? Why bother act like you care? You could have just asked me about the money; I would have told you."

Hearing her voice, something started to build inside him, a kind of tidal wave, a too-muchness, too much guilt-remorse-loneliness-the-memory-of-her-kindness he couldn't really say, just that it was building up and up, threatening to overwhelm him. "My wife told me that you came here," he retaliated, shoring up his anger against the oncoming flood. "You can't just show up here, spying on me, scaring my family." My family! The words came out thick, full of sentiment, power; they put him in the right—my family! my family!—even when he knew he was wrong.

"Look, you're the one that tracked me down. You're the one that . . ."

"I'm the one! I'm the one!" he bellowed, allowing his rage to take over. "That what? Took $50,000 of someone else's money?"

"What are you even . . ."

"That opened a café on a fucking *island* with stolen funds?"

"You can't possibly . . ."

"That faked my medical records because I was divorced and wanted to start over? You know, I'm fucked now because of your little scheme, I hope you know that!"

There was silence. It went on for a long time. Then, finally, she replied in a voice that sounded flat and dead and completely different from the one she'd used before, "Well. Maybe I should just go ahead and die then."

"Maybe you should!" he hollered back and as soon as he said it the blood-rage-torrent stopped. Everything went cold. Everything went still.

Now she said quietly, pointedly: "If I ever see you again, if you ever even think of contacting me again, I'll call the police. In fact, you're really fucking lucky I haven't done so already." Then she hung up the phone.

There are thoughts that should not be spoken, thoughts that come forward despite their wrongness, maybe because of their wrongness, thoughts that rise like a bubble in the mind despite everything we do and all the busyness we use to guard against them. Matt had one of these now.

He stood in his empty house and thought: it *would* solve my problems if she died.

Immediately, he wished he hadn't thought it. Immediately, he wished he could put it back, but he couldn't. It stayed there,

alone in his mind. Clear. Polished. Fully formed. It didn't feel
like his own thought; it felt like someone had put it there, trans-
planted it into his brain.

A wave of despair rose up inside him. He didn't know why
he'd stayed with her at the cottage but it certainly hadn't been mal-
ice, it hadn't been . . . this. But it *would* solve things, wouldn't it?
He felt the cold pull of its logic like a current all around him. Help
me, he whispered. Please, please, please, but no one answered.

I have to get out of here, he thought.

Later that day, he got in his car and headed South. He'd rallied what remained of his optimism and faith in the world and
made a plan. He would give Jen one week to calm down, then
he'd go and see her. In the meantime, he'd go to Sedona and ask
his mother to borrow enough money to stave off the bank, then
see if he could get a job out in the oil patch to claw himself out
of debt. He knew it was desperate, but at least it was something.
At least it was not this other thing.

He drove, his mind so full of thoughts and fantasies, he barely noticed the landscapes through which he passed. In the suburbs
outside Seattle, he imagined that his mother would loan him
enough money to pay down his line of credit and get back on
track with the mortgage. The thought of actually asking her for
money made him almost sick with guilt; he knew how little control she had over her own finances now that she was re-married,
but, at this point, it seemed like his best option. His mother
would help him if she could.

He kept driving. As he crossed the Columbia River and
drove through Portland, he imagined that Jen forgave him and
that they sold the house, that he got a job working at a small-
town bar in the evenings and helped her with Jacob during the
days while she went back to school. Through the rolling farm-
lands of Oregon, he imagined going out to the oil patch, bringing
back a pay cheque every two weeks, and slowly, slowly digging
himself out of this hole. He did not think this other thought, the
one he'd had before. Whenever he felt that it was close, too
close, he'd think something else: loud, bright thoughts on the
surface of his mind.

By the time he crossed over the Sierra Nevada, he was worn out by his own anxiety. It was late and the air was cool and blue, the moon so bright he could see the shadows of the trees on the road ahead and the granite boulders that were scattered like tombs amongst the heather glowed white in the shadows of the pines.

Here, his thoughts drifted from his own life to the land around him, to the Gold Rush and dreamers and fortune seekers heading west, all these stories he'd learned in high school: the Donner Party and the Mormons and characters from Steinbeck novels, all crossing over the Sierra Nevada. He imagined how they must have felt at the end of winter when the snows broke, when they were finally able to make their descent; he imagined how it must have felt when they finally lay their eyes on the glittering bowl of the sea. In his tired, half-crazed state, he felt a kinship with them, as if they were one and the same only that he was late, a Century too late because where was left to go once you'd already made it to the sea? Where did you go when there was no West left? Back East? Back to your parents? Back to beg forgiveness from the life you'd left behind?

Eventually, the road descended onto a wide, moonlit plain that stretched away from the mountains and he started across, intent on driving all night, but soon his eyes grew heavy. After another hour, he had to pull over.

He stopped at an Interstate rest station and bought a bag of chips from a vending machine inside the concrete bunker of the restrooms, then he got back in his car and curled up in the front seat, aching for Jen. He wished that she could see him now, contorted around the steering wheel, stuffing his face with junk. He wanted her to know, to understand how badly he felt, but no one was there to witness his wretchedness. He twisted about miserably, then, after a few hours of fitful sleep, he was on his way again.

Sunrise found him in the desert proper. It seemed almost impossible that he was in the same country as the day before, the coastal rainforest having given way to miles on miles of emptiness, to sharp rocks and white skies with the thin line of the road cutting across. Alongside the road were telephone wires strung between forlorn wooden crosses, miles on miles of wire stringing small, dirty towns together like dusty beads of civilization with this roar of nothingness pressing in . . . It made him think about the game they'd played at Jacob's birthday. What was it? Telephone. Madness, pass it on, he thought. Madness and aliens, pass it on. Weird military shit and surreal psycho acid trip, pass it on, I'm going fucking mental in the desert pass it on.

Every once in a while, he'd pass a dusty old trailer tucked away in a ravine or a small house in the lee of a blackened hillside and think why? Why would someone choose to live out here? What kind of person would go to such extremes for solitude? Then he'd find himself thinking about Annika in her lonely cottage by the sea, Annika who'd seemed so normal and beautiful at first and then he'd think of her thin body arcing upwards towards him on that last night and his mind would go rushing, rushing away along the telephone wires pass it on.

The night before she'd left him, Jen had looked at him with utter contempt and said, "Doesn't it bother you? That you're waiting for someone to die?" and he'd felt terrible, he'd felt like the worst person in the world, even worse because she didn't know the half of it. He'd come clean about the viatical settlement and most of the financial stuff but had lied about who Annika actually was. His face began to burn just thinking . . . don't think don't think don't Annika Annika he'd slept with her he'd loved her told her to die he was sorry pass it on. He drank coffee and smoked cigarettes and ate candy for the rest of the way.

When he arrived in Sedona, his mother greeted him outside the yellow stucco villa she shared with Al. She looked good, he thought, fit and streamlined in bright athletic clothes, her white hair cut into a sleek, stylish bob; the frizzy curls he remembered from his youth long gone. He hugged her tiny birdlike body next to his and felt bad about all the time gone by.

"Oooooo it's so good to see you," she said. She kept repeating that he was welcome to stay as long as he wanted. "This is your home too," she said but of course it wasn't.

It was Al's unit in a retirement complex in Sedona and it was nothing at all like the townhouse where Matt had grown up with its wood paneling and rust-coloured carpets and yellow light in all the windows. After the divorce, his mother had always kept the lights on and that's how he remembered her house: looking back from the school bus window before dawn to see all the windows filled with yellow light. Al's unit couldn't be more different. Al's unit had cool blue carpets and vague watery artwork and Al was fighting a war against brightness, the modern white shades drawn down against the day.

Matt took his things into the dainty spare room. His mother had laid out the towels for him on the bed, as if it were a hotel.

When Al got back from the golf course, he announced that it was happy hour and poured them all drinks. Al put his hand on Matt's mother's back and guided her out through the screen door and Matt followed, watching Al's papery hand on his mother's back. Al's forearm was still wiry and strong despite his age and there was a glimpse of blue ink peeking out the old man's shirt sleeve.

Al was ex-military and still lived his life as if the enemy might swoop in at any moment. When Matt had first met Al, he'd figured it would never last between Al and his mother. He'd figured his mother would never stand for it: this hawkish presence hovering over her, controlling her every move, checking her tire pressure before he'd even let her drive to the store. And yet, to Matt's surprise, his mother had not only stood for it, she even seemed to like it, submitting to Al's authority with a kind of peaceful acquiescence. It always made Matt embarrassed to be around. It made him feel like he didn't know her at all, like he'd never really known her as a person.

They sat out on the concrete slab behind Al's unit and watched the sun on the red hills in the distance. Matt asked his mother how she was doing and Al answered for her.

Al said that Matt's mother was going to an exercise class. He said they were planning a vacation to Panama City with friends and that he'd taken her up in a hot air balloon for her birthday and they'd seen the Grand Canyon from the air. He said that she'd enjoyed it.

"It was beautiful," his mother added and Al put his hand on her thigh.

Matt looked away. He gulped the watery gin and tonic and watched the shadow creep up the hill. He hadn't remembered her birthday in years.

The following day he came out of the spare room to find they'd already been up for hours. Al was out with his cycling group and his mother was just getting back from Pilates. There were several varieties of cereal laid out for him on the counter and coffee in the pot.

"Sorry I slept in."

"Don't be silly. You young folks need to rest. Working so hard all the time. Take it easy. Why don't you go out to the pool?"

He slouched over his bran flakes. The coffee cups were too small and the coffee was weak and his mother already annoyed him, the way she flit about tidying the already tidy kitchen. He felt like a horrible person for being annoyed.

"The pool gets the afternoon sun," she said.

He took a shower and shaved his face then came back out to find her reading the paper. She looked up and tilted her head to see overtop her fashionable, pink rimmed reading glasses. "It's so great to have the pool. Why don't you go out and have a swim? Go and relax by the pool."

So he went.

He put on his bathing suit then went out to an inner court-yard surrounded by more yellow villas and concrete slabs and boxwood hedges. A small, liver-shaped pool glimmered in the middle of a white concrete deck ringed with empty lawn chairs. There was no one else around.

When she'd first moved in with Al, Matt's mother had used the pool as a way to entice them to visit: Jacob could swim in the pool, she'd said. Then, the week they'd come down, Jacob had practically grown fins. He'd barely left the pool at all while his grandmother sat out on the deck in her tilly hat, proudly watching his every move.

Now, Matt jumped in the water and lolled about. He did a handstand in case his mother was watching from the window. It used to be his father that took him to pools, he thought, not his mother. His father used to take him to hotels with waterslides and ice machines and long pink twilights. Now it was his mother who had the pool. He went underwater and opened his eyes, staring up at the shimmering interface where the water met the air, the sky and the red hills just visible beyond the tumbling glass.

When he thought he'd been in long enough to satisfy her, he hauled himself up and installed himself in one of the lawn chairs. He put on his sunglasses, lathered his chest with sunscreen then lay back. He felt restless, like he was wasting precious time there by the pool, yet somehow, he felt like he owed it to her after not coming down here for over a year, before he could ask her for money.

He tried to relax but couldn't.

Then movement behind one of the hedges caught his eye. Something quick and dry and rustling. He sat upright. Annika, he thought, his heart pounding. It was stupid to think it, he knew, yet that was the first thing that popped into his head: that Annika might have followed him down here. You're going mental, he chided himself, and had just settled back when he saw it again. Someone really was there, hiding behind the hedge. He was about to get out of his chair and go investigate when a tall, thin old woman appeared between two hedges. She was covered completely in white and tan cotton. A large sunhat and what appeared to be glacier goggles obscured her face. She looked at him, then loped away carrying a small bucket and pruning shears. He shook his head. He felt like he'd landed in outer space.

He sat back and stared at the water, wondering how much time would be appropriate to sit by the pool. The sun was high now and it bounced off his slimy chest, making it glisten as if he were some giant, newly hatched pupae. Jesus. What was it they called them now? The adult children? The adult children that came back to stay in your basement and eat your food and drink your beer? Isn't that what the big problem was these days? The adult children coming back and tanning their greasy guts by the pool, doing underwater handstands so they wouldn't feel so fucking guilty?

That night they sat out on the concrete slab again with their watery gin and tonics. The hills were bright but they were in the shade. High above, hot air balloons drifted lazily. Al said, "Have you talked to a lawyer, Matt? Your mother and I were talking. We think you should talk to a lawyer."

Matt watched the balloons as they drifted higher and higher. "We're not getting divorced, though. It's time away. A break. That's all. We've been under a lot of stress."

His mother shifted in the plastic chair. She crossed one leg, then the other. "It wouldn't hurt though, Matt, to talk to a lawyer. As someone who's been through a divorce, I look back and wish I'd been more practical instead of just assuming your father would be fair. I could have gotten a much better deal if I'd acted sooner."

Al took her hand and massaged it with his papery fingers. He looked at Matt with fatherly concern. "You know, I have a friend that used to specialize in family law. Why don't you go and talk to him? He's retired now but I'm sure he wouldn't mind helping you out."

Matt closed his eyes. You'd think someone who used to kill people in the jungle would mix a stronger fucking drink. "We're not getting a divorce," he repeated. "We're going through a rough patch, that's all. Everyone goes through a rough patch on occasion."

"They're not as hard on fathers as they used to be," Al continued as if he hadn't heard. "Back in my day the mother was always awarded full custody, no matter what. Now a man's got at least a fighting chance. I've seen a lot of men go through it. Friends. Colleagues." Al himself was a widower. Al's own adult children were doctors and lawyers and paid for a yearly gathering in the Dominican. Al's adult children remembered his birthday every year.

"Look, I know it looks bad, but really, I'm not about to let that happen. I would never, not in a million years, leave my family." Matt's voice grew thick and he looked with pleading eyes at his mother but she sat in the shadow with her legs crossed and her mouth in a hard set line.

In River City, she'd always been a person who seemed slightly surprised, her lips parted, her hair in disarray; he remembered a charming unsureness, a gentle shyness in how she used to move and speak but now she was different. She was like a different person. "You should start keeping a journal of your interactions with her," she said. "Times. Dates. Conversations. If she's harsh with Jacob, write it down. If she's late. Anything that might help you in a custody battle. Just in case."

Matt felt as if he'd been slapped. "Mom. We're talking about Jen here. Jen. Not some abusive crack addict. You can't be serious."

"Of course I'm serious," she said. "Why wouldn't I be serious? The lawyer will tell you the exact same thing. It helps to have everything in writing, just in case. I always thought she was too young for you anyway."

He looked down at the concrete between his feet because he couldn't stand to look at her. There was an ugly, shrill note hiding behind her attempt to seem casual; he recognized it from growing up, in the years after the divorce; he did not want it to be there but it was.

They were silent for a moment then she said, "I'm not about to give up my grandson!" Her voice rose in pitch and intensity with every word. "I'm not about to let her take Jacob away!"

Take him away? She only ever saw him once a year! Matt looked up unbelieving to find that his mother was actually serious and he recoiled to see her face so pinched. Looking at her, he had a terrible, blasted feeling, as if the entirety of the desert were passing before his eyes, as if all of life were drying out, shrinking down to this one week a year, to a sapphire pond in the midst of a vast dryness, to this one thing, this one precious thing: the beautiful, the beautiful, the opalescent boy.

He gulped at his drink to make the feeling go away but he couldn't drink fast enough. Eventually, he went back to the dainty spare room for the night and lay awake, aware that he didn't have the gall to ask for money.

He stayed another three days because he felt too guilty to leave, and then, as he was going, she stuffed some bills into his hand when Al wasn't looking. "To help with the stress," she whispered and he thanked her. It was $500.

Chapter Nineteen

After her conversation with Matt, Annika went to find Helmut.

She knocked on his door but it was Marion who answered. Helmut wasn't home, Marion said, then tried to entice Annika to stay for tea. Annika refused. She got back in her car and drove out to the dump, hoping to find him there.

Annika had never been to the Saltery Bay Transfer Station before and assumed, wrongly, that a person would be able to drive right in. Instead, she found that the dump was under tight security. It was situated in an old quarry, tucked away as far as possible from the rich people's summer homes and surrounded by an eight-foot chain fence with barbed wire at the top. The entrance was guarded by a surly little woman who sat in a trailer alongside the scale.

Annika pulled up beside the trailer and rolled down her window. "I'm not taking anything in," she explained. "I'm looking for someone."

The woman glared at her. "He's here," she said then rolled her eyes. "He's always here. I'll let you through this once, but I'm getting awfully tired of you treasure hunters." She made Annika weigh in anyway.

Annika drove overtop the scale and waited for the light to turn green. She'd been shaken, physically rattled after talking to Michael but now she just felt strange, light-headed and faraway. The day around her seemed impossibly bright; the sky was too tall and pulling upwards, expanding up into the darker blue of the stratosphere. It was the illness, she realized. The sickness was starting to take her.

When the light turned green, she eased her car onto a compacted old road that wound through a series of tiered excavations and old mounds that were covered with wildflowers and grasses. She passed various piles of waste: a great heap of appliances, a metal container labelled e-waste, mountains of brush and grass, the bright deadheads from someone's flower bed scattered amongst them. Above her the sky kept pulling up and up while the gulls wheeled and screamed and hovered on the wind.

She spotted Helmut. He was out on the main face, combing a pit of miscellaneous refuse peppered with the white heads of the gulls. His truck was parked at the edge. She pulled up beside it.

He didn't notice her at first, and she watched him for a while as he clambered about in the pit, stooping, bending, considering. He wore rubber boots and a bandana over half his face.

Eventually, she got out of her car and climbed down. The wind stung her face and whipped her hair up around her as she made her way towards him, stumbling occasionally as the garbage shifted underneath her. There were buckets, a broken lamp, great heaps of clothes and plastic, lots of plastic.

Helmut looked up, then stood with his hands on his hips, waiting. She couldn't see his mouth but could tell by his eyes he was smiling.

"I thought you'd be here," she said as she approached.

"Welcome to the Saltery Bay Thrift Store," he said. He pulled the bandana down over his mouth so she could hear him better, then his face changed as he looked her over. "You've lost weight."

"I'm not feeling very well."

He nodded. A gull landed near his foot, then came at him with its neck extended and its wings in a wide V behind it. He flicked his hand at it and made a hissing noise. "They are more aggressive each time. I would like to bring my gun one day but this dump lady is very strict with me."

"Yes. I was worried she wasn't going to let me in."

"She is *very* strict with me," he repeated, raising his eyebrows mischievously. Annika laughed. She wasn't even sure what the joke was meant to be: the dump lady's outrageous aversion to firearms? Helmut and the dump lady in an elaborate bondage scenario in the little trailer? And why not? Nothing seemed impossible to her anymore.

His face brightened as he watched her laugh. "Come. I've found an amazing score," he said, taking her hand in such a princely manner she giggled even more. "I'd like you to have it."

Hand in hand, they walked back out of the pit. She allowed Helmut to help her. She leaned against him. She felt like she was floating. Tendrils of her hair lifted and danced around her face. The sky kept pulling upwards, the clouds racing along.

When they got back to the vehicles, Helmut helped her back onto the gravel, then walked over to his truck and reached down into the bed. When his hands came up he was holding some kind of animal. She took a step back but it didn't move. Its tawny fur glittered in his hands. It was a coyote. A taxidermed coyote.

"You're crazy," she laughed and he smiled. He could tell she liked it.

The strange, rigid little creature was in a standing pose, its matchlike legs sticking straight out, its head cocked to one side as if it were intensely interested.

"Here, you have it," he said, handing it over.

She turned it over in her hands, caressing the thick, glossy fur. In the course of her life she'd received many gifts yet somehow, she'd never felt any of them belonged to her. Most of the time they'd seemed more like hints than gifts, hints of what she should want, how she should be, and now here was this useless, bizarre thing; here was this odd broken man standing in the dump with a bandana around his face, giving her a coyote and somehow it felt perfect; it felt final. It felt like what life was actually like. The wind whipped her clothes against her. Yellow dust devils lifted and swirled along the road. Yes, she thought. This is how life is.

"Thank-you, Helmut. I love it." She could see her own shadow on the bright gravel in front of her. Her thin silhouette with her hair blowing all around, the coyote in her arms with its legs jutting out, looked just like the shadow of a young girl whose boyfriend had won her a prize at the county fair. She smiled. When she was a child, she'd imagined that love looked something like this: boys winning prizes for girls at fairs. In her Spartan room, in her secret fantasies, she'd imagined going to the fair herself; she'd imagined wearing jeans and lip-gloss with her hair untied and a handsome boy handing her a prize. She closed her eyes and felt the wind ripping at her clothes and pulling at her hair and she imagined that pieces of herself were sloughing off and pulling away, memories and dreams and desires, and she wondered if death happened all at once or a little at a time.

When she opened her eyes again, Helmut was eyeing her curiously. "You have come to ask me something," he said.

She straightened her shoulders and met his eyes. "I have."

He nodded but said nothing.

"Things are happening quickly now. I don't know . . . how long I have."

He leaned against the tailgate and looked down at the ground, nodding slowly all the while.

"I've been thinking that, after a certain point, there is really no sense prolonging things. After a certain point, it benefits no one."

He kept nodding slowly and looking at the ground. He said, "These are difficult choices to make."

She took a deep breath. She was thinking of herself, but also of Matt Campbell. Of Michael. "I've thought of a way that you could help me. Something you could help me get."

When Annika returned to the cottage, she went upstairs and sat down on the bed. She placed the coyote beside her then took out the gun that Helmut had given her. She turned it over and over in her hands.

Its cold, grey weight felt foreign to her. Each time she turned it over, it seemed as if someone had handed it to her anew and she was surprised and surprised again by its smallness, its gravitas; it might have been a child's toy but for the weight of it.

Annika was no stranger to guns. She'd used her father's shotgun and the rifle on the farm, just never one like this. She shivered and placed it on the bed beside her. It lay heavy on the quilt, pressing down. Already, its presence cast a pall over the room: the sound of the waves seemed muffled; the light seemed strangely dull even though the sun was still shining outside. Even the cat would not come near. She called to him: Zebedee,

Zebedee, but he would not come. He stood in the doorway, watching.

It made sense, did it not? she asked herself again. She was dying anyway. Was it a sin if she was dying anyway? She didn't know but the idea of Michael, or Matt Campbell or whoever he was congratulating himself when the payment came in, taking his wife out to dinner, maybe; buying himself a new coat, maybe; it was too much; it made her sick to even think about it. She would end it, she thought; she would end it in such a way that Matt Campbell wouldn't see a cent. She remembered that about the contract: that she could void the whole thing with one final act, by making one final choice, and she was dying anyway.

He'd made it come back, she thought bitterly, working herself into a rage. If illness had spiritual roots the way Marion said then it meant that anger could cause it, that stress could cause it; and he'd come down here and lied and made love to her like he meant it then hollered like a maniac on the phone and now the cancer had come back. Suddenly she felt sick. The world narrowed then widened. She hated being angry all the time. She was so, so tired of being angry.

She picked up the gun again, and thought, for the first time in decades, about Jesus. Gentle Jesus whom she'd loved as a child. She remembered how she used to imagine that Jesus was secretly on her side, even when her parents condemned her, even when they said God was angry with her decisions, she'd always imagined that Jesus, with his soft expression, with a lamb on his lap, would forgive her. Would He forgive this? Could He? The anger she felt towards Matt Campbell was unlike other angers she'd felt before: it was colder, foreign somehow; there was a metallic taste to it, like blood or the air before it rains, as if the cold metal of the gun were already in her mouth.

She closed her eyes. When she'd left home, her parents had told her she was choosing a life of sin; yet she'd never really believed them. Even when she'd proclaimed to be an atheist, as she had for many years, she'd secretly held to the belief that the spark she felt inside was sacred somehow, that the voice in her heart, the voice that wanted to run and live and see and love was not the voice of sin but of life itself; she'd once felt so very sure of this.

But her life had only gotten lonelier; one choice had led to another to another, and now here she was with this final choice; here she was alone with this ugly task, alone with this cold metallic anger. She looked at the gun: its short blunt muzzle, its lack of ceremony, the extremes of its logic seemed an insult to everything she'd been through. Was this the consequence, then, of her rebellion? This ugly, final act? It's your choice, Anni, they'd said. You've chosen. You chose. And what if all her life she'd chosen wrong?

She stood, suddenly. She wasn't ready. She needed to think. She held the gun away from her at arm's length, then walked slowly over to her dresser and placed it carefully in the top drawer. After shutting the drawer, she backed away and stood in the middle of the room, aware of the pain in her stomach, the lightness in her head, the storms of anger and confusion that were tearing her up inside. She was dying and did not know who to turn to; she was dying and did not know what to do.

CHAPTER TWENTY

M att lied to his mother about where he was going next. She looked so tiny and hopeful standing there on Al's doorstep that he couldn't bear to tell her the truth. Instead, he hugged her to his chest and told her that he planned to go straight home, that he was going to sort things out with Jen right away and she didn't need to worry: Jacob would always be a part of her life. He shook Al's hand, then climbed into his car and headed for Las Vegas. He was going to see his father.

He drove through the desert, annoyed at himself. Here he was almost forty and he still didn't have the guts to be up front about his Dad. Somehow, even after so many years, visiting his father still felt like he was betraying his mother. It had been like that growing up, every second weekend this impossible choice: choose one and betray the other; there was no right or wrong, just guilt on either side.

Still, it had been a long time since he'd seen his father and the fact that his old man was parked relatively close by seemed gratuitous. There was a chance that his father would help him out. While the state of the old man's finances was unpredictable at best, when he had money, he tended to be generous. Of all people, his father would understand what it was like to screw up your life, he thought.

Matt drove all day then, towards evening, he crested a rise and there it was: Las Vegas sprawled in all its glory across the desert floor below.

Las Vegas. He'd been to the city several times for stag parties and once for a wedding, but he'd always flown; he'd always been whisked through the glittering airport half-cut from high balls on the plane, shuttled from one air-conditioned venue to the next in a blur of casinos and hotel bars surrounded by his friends.

Driving in alone felt different. It felt strange, frightening some-how. He could feel all this space around him, the dryness, the improbability of the place. There was no river, no farmland or obvious organic reason for it being there, just a city plopped into the middle of the desert like a dream turned inside out and pinned down at the corners; its inner wants, its deep desires bulging skywards; the roads from a distance like silver veins, puls-ing beads of mercury like the vivisection of a dream.

Arizona Charlie's was off the main strip, out on the Boulder Highway where the city fanned out into the desert. His father and his father's lady-friend, Ginger, were staying in the RV park, waiting for the weather to warm so they could continue their trek up to Alaska. The RV park was a huge flat area with small patches of lawn interspersed between the rows of hulking, white RV's. Each site had a picnic table on its mini-lawn; there were a few ash trees peppered about for shade. In the center of the lot was an office building with a concrete swimming pool surround-ed by struggling palm trees.

A high, chain-link fence separated the park from the sur-rounding neighbourhood of low, ranch-style stucco houses. When Matt pulled in, the first thing Ginger did was warn him not to go outside the fence. "It's right dangerous. Drugs. Gangs," she said. "You'll get yourself shot at." She was younger than his father by a couple of decades and she had a kind of sloppy attractiveness: large breasts that always found a way to brush against you, big heavy-lidded eyes with black mascara clumping in her lashes, wide hips and skinny legs and a splay-foot way of walking.

"I'll be careful, Ginger," Matt said and smiled. Ginger was easy to get along with. She was not a complicated person. He always felt bad for liking her as much as he did. She squeezed his shoulder. "Glad you're here, kid," she said, then toddled back inside to watch her programs, leaving him and his father out on the patch of lawn as the air cooled.

His father sat in a lawn chair in a pair of swim trunks with his hard, round belly like a ball in his lap, his gnarled feet in flip flops held out in the same splay foot way that Ginger had. He held his glass out to the side, the ice cubes clicking softly as he waxed philosophical: "If there's one thing I can tell you after being around the block a few times, it's this: when it's over, it's over."

"It's not over," Matt said. He held the rum in his mouth. At the very least, his father mixed a decent drink.

"There's no sense in prolonging the drama. It only makes it worse for everyone. Especially the kid." Matt's anger flashed in a kind of reflexive allegiance to his mother, but then he sighed and let it pass. Who was he to throw stones? He sipped his drink and sat in the long twilight while the blue light flickered in the pop-out section of the RV where Ginger was watching her shows. They were both proud of the pop-out, how much extra room it gave.

He watched his father's little white dog snuffle around in circles. It was pegged to the patch of lawn with a tent peg. His father patted his lap and it popped up and sat there, leaning against his father's hard belly and looking at Matt with a ridiculous smug expression on its pointy little face. "Montmorency here has been enjoying Las Vegas. Ginger took him to have his hair done."

"Great," Matt said. "I'm glad to hear that Montmorency is having such a grand old time."

His father chuckled and stroked his thick grey mustache. The ice cubes clicked. The sun went down and the bleached pavement turned a pale purple. Matt sat out in the cooling air while his father went in to fix more drinks, then came out wearing a Broncos sweatshirt. "So, shoot straight with me here son," he said, handing Matt a glass. "Is there someone else in the picture?"

"No." He held the glass to his forehead to let the cold seep into his brain.

"Oh come on. You're saying she just up and left you? She's got no job and a little kid to look after and you're saying that she just wakes up one morning and bang! She decides she'd be better off on her own? I don't know, Matty. I've seen enough of these things to know, there's always someone else."

"I told you already. The stress. The house."

His father chuckled. In the distance the strip had begun to glitter on the paling sky and it was beautiful in a lonely way.

"So, was it you or was it her?"

"Jesus Christ, Dad."

His father stroked Montmorency, then bent and kissed him on the head. Sirens rose up in the clear, cool air. Matt sighed. "I made a mistake, okay? It was a onetime thing."

"Ahhhh . . ." his father nodded and looked away at the glittering skyline. "And Ms. Mistake, what's her story?"

"She's a fucking nutjob is what her story is," he spat vehemently. "She keeps calling me. She just showed up at the house. Jen doesn't know anything for sure but she suspects. Jen's always been crazy jealous, right from the start. I even look at another woman and she's mad."

His father nodded. "Ahhh."

"It was rough at home," he elaborated. "I mean, we hadn't had sex in a long time, maybe even a year, so I was on edge, you know how it is, and then I went out of town for a couple of days to look into this investment because I needed to figure stuff out, and maybe I had a few too many and I got talking to this woman . . . She was attractive and had all these great stories..." he trailed off. He'd pushed it away, those three dream-like days in the fog. He didn't like to think about it, couldn't think about it without this tidal wave building, threatening his very existence. "But it was a mistake," he added quickly. "I got back to her place and I knew it was a mistake right away. Her place was this crazy hovel in the middle of nowhere. She had a cat named Zebedee for Christ sakes," he was speaking quickly, loudly, he didn't know why. "And it's not a habit, you know what I mean? I mean, I guess I could have confessed to Jen but it didn't make sense. What makes more sense: ruin my marriage for a onetime mistake or just vow never to do it again? Anyway, I thought that was the end of it, and then this woman showed up at the house."

"Well," the old man said, "There's no sense in getting all tied up about it. You figure out what you need to do and go from there. Can't change the past." He took a sip of his drink then held it in his mouth and nodded slowly. "Can't change the past, even when you want to." They were quiet for some time then he said, "Gotta keep the wife and mistress separate. Never involve the family."

They sat in the dark. The ice cubes clicked and the strip sparkled and winked and the cars went by and the stars came out and there were long silences and more drinks and then it was time for bed. His father patted him on the shoulder and said quietly: "If there's one thing I learned it's this: you gotta keep the sex dirty and the fights clean."

Matt woke to find Ginger watching TV in the pop-out and his father making eggs. "I thought we could go out for a little fun," his father said. "Hit up a buffet. Play a game or two. A father-son thing, you know." He was already dressed for the occasion in a yellow golf shirt and khaki pants, his grey hair slicked back.

Matt had planned to ask him for a loan that morning then get back to Seattle right away and deal with his own life, yet it didn't seem to be an option with the old man standing over the frying pan, looking at Matt with his hopeful face. "Sure," Matt said. "That sounds like fun." They dropped Ginger off at a mall with a wad of cash and she waddled off uncomplaining, then they drove the rest of the way to the strip and parked the car.

His father hustled him along the crowded sidewalk, holding onto his elbow. "In here. In here," he'd say as they allowed themselves to be funneled into the casinos with their flashing lights and glitter and sound. They'd get drinks and his father would stuff bills into Matt's hand and say let's play and let's drink and let's eat and Matt drank the drinks and ate the food and dutifully lost money at the slots.

After several such stops, he wandered into a gift store to look for souvenirs for Jen and Jacob, remembering how he used to like it when his father brought back souvenirs for him, T-shirts from all the places he'd been to. He'd always been so proud to wear them at school. He found two T-shirts with glittery letters on the front. I HEART LAS VEGAS they said. His father came over and whistled, "Tighty whitey. Nice one."

They continued along under the awnings, the giant signs reeling above them in the blue. They were arm in arm now, leaning into one another. There were a lot of families with kids, Matt noticed and he wished Jen could see it. One time, when he'd come down to Vegas for a stag, he'd asked Jen and Jacob to come along with him and she'd gotten angry and said, "It's no place for a child," but if she could see it, he thought, if she could see it, then she'd change her mind. So many families. Him and his old Dad.

They sat and drank martinis and watched the roller coaster at the New York, New York do the loop de loop over the sidewalk. They watched the people screaming as they twisted and roared on the track above them.

"Want to try?" his old Dad asked eagerly.

"Try what?"

"Let's go on the roller coaster. What do you say?"

"I don't think so."

"Oh come on. It will be fun. You used to love roller coasters."

"Jesus, Dad."

But they went. They stood in line and his father struck up a conversation with a couple of ageing RVers who were staying out of town. "I'm here with my son," he told them. "Father and son day on the town."

When they got to the ticket window, his father put the money down and said, "Two adults. Me and my son here."

They were herded through the turnstiles and into a loading bay where they waited on a platform next to the track. The train pulled in and the bars released and people climbed out on the other side, then an attendant opened the gate and let them on. Matt and his father were in a car near the front.

The tiny seats were hard and rickety and when the bar came down Matt felt like he couldn't breathe. The discomfort seemed to cut into his drunken haze and he had a moment of clear and painful sobriety: what the fuck am I doing here? he thought. I have my own family. I have my own problems to attend to and here I am on a fucking roller coaster that I don't want to be on.

His father elbowed him and grinned. "Here we go," he said.

The little train began to tick slowly upwards towards some critical point that would give it enough momentum to get it through the loops. This is ridiculous, Matt thought as the train clicked inexorably upwards to where the narrow rails crested and the fake Manhattan skyline ended in the impossible brightness of the day beyond it; yet still the tension in him rose as the fake train approached the fake crest. His heart thudded in anticipation even as he reminded himself how ridiculous, how totally and utterly ridiculous it all was.

Then they were up and over and the G-forces pushed him back and he was screaming, he was screaming and up and down and whipping around, streaks of red and green and glass and the streaking red rails ahead.

When they got off the old man elbowed him again. "Hey, hey. Fun, no?" Then he toddled off to buy the photo. There was a camera that took your photo at the exact moment you were upside down and you could purchase it for an exorbitant sum of money. Matt wondered briefly how his father could afford to live like this, then it occurred to him that he probably couldn't.

Matt sat at a table and ordered another drink and one for his father and soon the old man came back and slapped the photo on the table. He was red-faced from laughing and he slapped Matt on the back. "Look at you!" he wheezed. "You look like you're about to shit your pants. Bahahahahaha!"

Matt slid the photo closer so he could get a better look. He shook his head. His father could be so . . . so ridiculous sometimes and yet a smile played at his mouth. The old drunk. Carrying on like that.

His smile froze when he saw the photo. It was not his own face which was the typical wide-eyed, open mouthed grimace you'd expect, but his father's that made him catch his breath. His father didn't have his hands up and he wasn't screaming like the rest of the people. In that moment, with the world upside down, his father was perfectly composed, upright, erect, beaming with pride.

The old man was coughing now, wheezing and laughing and ridiculous. Matt put his hand on his father's shoulder. He said, "You keep that Dad. I'll be right back." Then he went to the washroom and locked himself in a stall. He took out the little T-shirts and held them next to his face and began to cry. It was over, he realized. He was through.

Chapter Twenty-One

There were no lights on at Matt Campbell's house, no cars in the driveway. Annika didn't know whether to be disappointed or relieved. She sat in her darkened car staring out at his darkened house, wondering what to do. Most of the houses around the cul-de-sac had their lights on and she caught glimpses of people inside: people laughing, talking, sitting down to dinner. Seeing them made her feel lonely. It made her hate Matt Campbell even more.

She was parked in the driveway of the foreclosed house, the same spot where she'd parked before. She'd turned the headlights off almost immediately when she pulled in and was pretty sure no one had seen her. She waited for a while, then, taking a deep breath, she picked up the gun from where it sat on the passenger seat and tucked it into her coat. Quietly now, she climbed out of the car, then gently pressed the door shut behind her. The night air was cold and still. Somewhere far-off, she could hear the roar of the highway.

She cut swiftly across the lawn of the foreclosed house to avoid the glare from the streetlamps, then skirted along the edge of an empty lot adjacent to the Campbell residence. Here, the ground was rough and stony. It was so dark she could barely see and she had to step carefully, feeling for the ground with her feet.

Suddenly, she stopped. She had a sense of an empty space in front of her. There was a slight change in temperature, in the quality of the darkness. She peered ahead, squinting. When her eyes finally adjusted, she realized that she was standing at the edge of some kind of pit, a foundation most likely, eight feet down, a little deeper than a grave. She shivered. One more step and it might have been over; one more step and he might have found her there, broken, covered in mud . . .

She shook herself free of the bad thoughts—she was always shaking free of the bad thoughts these days—then continued to the back of the Campbell house. Here, light from across the narrow alleyway illuminated a small, fenced backyard. She stopped and listened. She could hear music, voices. She looked around. There. She could see several people laughing and drinking wine through a patio door in one of the houses across the alley. For a moment she was afraid; they seemed so close, so near that surely they'd see her, then she remembered: she was the one in darkness; they were still in light. If they were to look outside their warm, well-lit circle, they wouldn't be able to see her at all; they would see only the reflections of themselves.

Reaching over the Campbell's fence, she found the latch and let herself into the yard. Compared to the stately front of the house, the backyard was small and shabby. The paint on the fence was flaking; the cedar shrubs along the fence line half-dead. A child's Hot Wheels lay overturned in the middle of the yard and there were boxes of empties stacked under the porch.

She climbed the steps up to the patio, then peered between cupped hands through the sliding glass door. She could see into the kitchen, the microwave clock casting an eerie glow over the room. She tried to open the door but it was locked.

She walked back down the porch steps, pausing as loud laughter erupted from the house next door. She wasn't sure what to do next and thought, maybe, she should abandon this craziness and just go home. She wasn't entirely sure why she'd come in the first place, just that she needed some resolution before the end and the end was close now. She could feel it in her body, in her mind.

She was about to turn and go back to the car when she noticed a window low down, almost at ground level, half-hidden by the dying shrubs. She knelt, tried to open it and was surprised to find that the glass slid easily to the side. She looked over her shoulder. Her heart was pounding wildly. She'd never done anything like this before, never even imagined that she would. She pushed the screen aside, then slipped through the window after it.

She had to jump down and landed heavy. It took her a moment to catch her breath. She was in the basement of the Campbell house. It was dark and smelled like paint. From the little light available, she sensed that it was bare, unfinished, as if they were in the middle of a renovation. Not daring to turn on any lights, she ran her hand along the walls, searching until she found the stairs leading up.

On the main floor, more light was filtering through the open concept living room from the streetlamps in front of the house. She wandered around. The house was relatively new and had all the modern comforts: leather couches, dark minimalist furniture, a big area rug with a geometric pattern on the floor; yet something about it felt strangely empty, strangely bland, more like a way station than a home, like people pretending at marriage, pretending at family . . . She frowned. She thought about Michael, how strung out he'd seemed to her at first and her anger towards him softened a bit. Being in his house made her sad.

She wandered into the kitchen then stopped short. There was a gaping hole in the wall and a mess of something—wood or boards or fibers—all over the floor. On the counter was an open bottle of vodka, half-empty. What had happened here? She'd been so angry, so upset after their phone conversation, she'd thought only of how horrible he was, but now, remembering, she thought that he'd sounded truly crazy, unhinged, like there was something seriously wrong with him. She frowned again. She didn't know how to feel.

She climbed the stairs into a hallway and entered the first door she came to. It was the little boy's room. Here, a plug-in night light shaped like a boat lent the room a soft glow. She touched the stuffed animals on the shelves and ran her hands over the space-ship blankets on the bed. She opened the dresser. Inside, the clothes were neatly folded. They smelled clean, like lemon scented detergent. Is this what her life would have been like, she wondered, if the treatments had worked for her and Hamish? A clean, neat world with pyjamas and tiny socks and stuffed animals? Would she have been happy in it? She didn't know. There were times when she envied other women who were swept up in the busyness of children and the tasks of caring; she envied the way time seemed to carry them; and yet she liked her solitude; she liked the quiet. Who could say how it might have been, who she might have become had the treatments worked? It was too late now to ever know. This didn't make her particularly sad; it just was. It had become a fact, time moving on, the pain and drama had bled out of it.

Next, she went into the master bedroom. This was the first room in the house that seemed truly occupied. The bed was unmade and there were clothes scattered over the floor as if someone had left in a rush. She sat down on the bed. Wasn't it strange, she thought, how all couple's rooms looked the same? Here were his things. Here were her things. The digital clock. The marital bed. It reminded her of the space she'd once shared with Hamish. She smiled sadly in the dark. This is what Hamish had wanted. Exactly this. Maybe he would even get it one day with his new partner. The house, the car, the kids. Would it make him happy? She thought of the half-empty bottle downstairs. The hole in the wall. Was anyone really happy?

She sat there thinking about people and their lives and their paths and their choices, her mind wandering, wandering until a light swept suddenly across the room. She froze. There was the sound of a car in the driveway. Now it turned off. A door slammed, then another. She heard a key in the lock. He was home! She looked around wildly for a hiding place.

Downstairs, the front door opened and light from the foyer spilled into the open bedroom door. Annika darted into the bathroom and climbed into the shower. She drew the curtain closed.

"I'm just going to take our clothes and some of Jakey's toys," said a female voice. "We'll get the rest of the stuff later, when we come back with the truck."

Then a male voice, one Annika didn't recognize, said, "When is he coming home?"

"Who knows? He went to visit his Mommy in Arizona. I don't really care if he ever comes back, to be honest," the female voice answered. She sounded young, flippant and terribly, terribly angry.

Annika's heart was thundering in her chest. She could barely breathe. The shower was a stupid hiding place, she realized. The curtain was flimsy and half transparent and if anyone came in to use the washroom, they would see her. She climbed out of the tub and went back into the bedroom. She stood at the door. She could hear them walking around downstairs. If I'm quick, I might slip past them and out the front, she thought. She held the gun tight to her chest, getting ready to bolt.

"Nice," came the woman's sarcastic voice from the kitchen. Annika heard the clink of a bottle on the counter. "What did I tell you?"

"I never thought I'd feel sorry for the guy, but don't you think you're being a bit harsh?" said the male voice. There was a bored, nasal quality to it that made everything sound ironic.

"Jesus, Jeremy. I told you what he did didn't I? His idea of an investment? And look at this shit!"

"I know, but it seems like he's really upset. If he has a legitimate drinking problem, then maybe . . ."

"Oh, he *definitely* has a problem. He's a total fucking drunk."

Michael, a drunk? He hadn't seemed like that to her. He hadn't seemed like that at all. Annika caught her breath. They were starting up the stairs! She had to do something fast, but where? What? The closet? The woman was coming up here to pack clothes! The boys room? No, they'd go in there, too. She peered out into the hall. There was another door at the end, passed the boy's room. It was open. She had to be quick. Just as their heads crested the top of the stair, she dashed out of the bedroom and slipped into the open door. She held her breath.

"Take everything from Jacob's closet and dresser. Don't forget his shoes," the woman said. Annika let her breath out. They hadn't seen her.

Annika was in a room with a computer and little else. There were some boxes against the wall. The walls were bare. She stood very still. Once both of them were busy packing, she reasoned, she would sneak past them and down the stairs. If they saw her she would run; she would wave the gun around and act like a crazy person.

She heard the woman say: "Look at this mess! What a pig."

They were both quiet for a while, then the woman called, "Bring his toys too. He misses his stuffies. And his books."

Then the male voice, closer now. They were both in the master bedroom. "Does he even know that you're doing this?"

"I don't care what he knows."

"Maybe you should wait though. Maybe you should talk to him first."

"I told you, I'm done talking."

"I know, Jen, but he doesn't know. He thinks this is just a marital squabble and that you're coming back. He was practically begging Mom to talk to you on the phone last night. You could at least tell him you plan on filing before you clean the place out."

"Why do you keep defending him?"

"I don't know, I just feel bad doing this. I mean, I've known the guy for the last four years and he is still Jacob's father. Maybe he's a bit of a dolt, but he did marry you; he could have fucked off but he didn't . . . And he loves Jacob, you have to give him that . . ."

"You know what he is to me? He's some guy I fucked because I was 19 and drunk. That's all he is to me," she said in a voice so filled with resentment that Annika felt a wave of sadness for Michael. The feeling was unexpected. Powerful. Forgive me, he'd whispered, stroking her hair. Forgive me forgive me forgive me. For a long time, she thought she must have dreamt it but now she wondered if it had been real. Poor Michael, she thought, he was almost as screwed up as she was.

Suddenly, she felt impossibly tired. Tired and sad for herself and the world and all the people in it. Lately there were times when she felt her perspective pull back, become wider, as if she were already starting to see things from outside her body, from somewhere up above. It happened most often when she was tired, fatigued from her own thoughts. It happened now. What was she even doing here? she wondered. Was this really how she wanted her life to end? Creeping around with a loaded gun? Her own anger suddenly felt small, childish somehow. What did it matter what Matt Campbell had done? Now she remembered something that Sasha had told her, one of Sasha's hippie insights about dying that she'd dismissed but which she was starting to understand. Death can be an opportunity, Sasha had said. An opportunity to show people who you really are in the face of adversity and suffering. Annika thought about this. She stood in the darkened room thinking about her life, about the kind of person she wanted to be.

Quietly, she slipped out into the hall, a figure so frail and silent, they may not have even noticed her had they looked. She stole out the front door, then ran back to her car. She drove though the darkness, unsure of the road ahead.

Chapter Twenty-Two

Matt sat in the frosted room and waited. There were murmurings and shuffling all around him; he could see nervous feet tapping under the gap but he remained slouched in the chair, utterly motionless. He was finished. Done. Everything he'd tried to do in the past five years, all his plans and ideas to make life better had only ended up making it worse. The big house, the shot-gun wedding, his career change, the viatical settlement . . . none of it had made a lick of difference. Jen still hated him. Now Annika hated him. One day, his own son would probably hate him too. He waited for what came next.

After a while, three bankers in crisp blacks and greys filed into the room, their faces set in a look of practiced serenity. Ron was there, his great towering frame between the two diminutive female bankers a reprise to his old role as bouncer, the bank's version of a heavy lest one of the financially beholden grow unruly and try to take matters into their own hands. Matt supposed it happened. He could imagine it happening. A younger version of himself might have mustered his outrage at the whole humiliating process, the frosted rooms, the terrible solemnity; but as it was, he was beyond outrage. He simply wanted it to be over.

"Mr. Campbell," Ron said. "Thank-you for coming."

Matt nodded and waited for them to say what they had come here to say.

It wasn't nearly as bad as he'd anticipated. One of the female advisers took the lead and explained how it would work. Her language was cool and polished and skirted around the swampy pit, avoiding altogether the muck of wanting and fucking and lying that was at the core of it. Instead, she presented him with the facts of his life as coolly and as neatly as if she were handing him a set of polished stones. There was his current position. His assets. His investments. There were his options. His credit. His file. He sat and nodded, grateful for her calm, methodical delivery. She had a generic prettiness that required nothing of him.

Ron slid the papers in front of him. "Do you have any questions, Mr. Campbell?"

"Let's just get it over with."

Ron handed him a pen, frowning slightly as he did so. "You are aware that once you sign, the bank will take over all of your investments?"

Matt thought of Annika and the lonely cottage by the sea. His face began to burn. He couldn't be free of it fast enough. "I just want out." He signed his name.

He'd read on websites that it would make him feel lighter. He'd read stories about people who, after declaring bankruptcy, had literally danced out of the bank but he didn't feel that way. Instead, he felt hollowed out inside. The bright, busy world of the street came at him in high relief; every detail, every sound, every smell so sharp and clean and real that he knew the fault, the trembling weakness he felt inside was entirely his own. His failure. His weakness. All he wanted was to be alone.

When he got back to the house, he closed the blinds on the bright, quick world with all the bright, keen people and their busy, successful lives. He sat on the couch and watched TV and waited for the eviction notice, the divorce papers, whatever came next. Jen wasn't coming back, he knew. She'd cleared out all her stuff and wouldn't return his calls, and, if he was being honest with himself, she was probably better off with her parents anyway. She'd never wanted to be his wife, never wanted to be pregnant at 19, to be a young suburban mom at 23. It had been a mistake. He was her big mistake. Nothing he could do now would change that.

He drank beer and watched a show called Interventions, reflecting that rock bottom was bullshit for it seemed that each time you came to a place where you thought, this is the absolute worst, the lowest of the low, you simply crashed through to another layer of bad that made your former self seem like a naïve asshole, and then, just when you thought, okay, now this, *this* is suffering, you crashed through again and life was just a series of rotten layers with a man-shaped hole torn through.

When the beer was gone he drank tequila, the last of a bottle he'd purchased in Mexico. With whom had he gone there? He couldn't remember. Maybe even Ron, the cowboy banker. How was it that one ended up with a head full of memories and no friends to call? He held the dregs up to the blue light of the television and watched the shriveled worm rock back and forth. The worm with John Stewart behind it. The worm with Obama behind it. The worm with Stephen Colbert. It was like one of those things from the Little Mermaid, the skleem, once proud mermen and mermaids reduced to wormlike creatures by an evil witch. He brought the bottle to his mouth. The worm with Matt Campbell behind it.

He kept drinking. He got very drunk. The empty house felt like a dare: how far would he slide? How drunk could he get? To what new level of depravity would he sink? He opened a bottle of scotch he'd been saving for a special occasion and with every sip, he found himself wishing for someone to stop him, to come to the house and find him here in this state and tell him to stop. He wished for Jen. For Ron. For Ken. For Annika. But no one came. He pissed in a houseplant because he could, then started to cry.

When he woke the next morning, he was on the living room floor in his clothes. The sun was streaming in the windows and he felt curiously coherent and alive considering how much he'd drank. Part of him knew the feeling wouldn't last, that it was only a short window before the horrendous hangover; still he allowed himself to hope. Maybe it wouldn't be so bad. Maybe he'd be okay. He struggled up from the couch, then he put on shoes and went outside.

It was so bright out that he had to squint to see. He could smell the wet Earth warming, the grass on the lawns coming up. In the flowerbeds, daffodils and tulips were beginning to unfold, tight and pale, just on the cusp of revealing themselves. He blinked, then started walking. He walked passed the houses on his street. There were cars in most of the driveways and people were out in the yards, gardening. A man said hello to him as he passed. There were women with baby strollers and people out walking their dogs, their faces flushed with exercise and fresh air. He continued on, passed the playground where Jen took Jacob in the afternoons; there were children playing on the monkey bars, laughing and shouting; a toddler being coaxed down the slide. Little birds twittered in the green space behind the park. He kept walking. How was it that the neighbourhood seemed so different today, so friendly?

Eventually, he left Sandy Hills and walked through an older more established neighbourhood with smaller houses and larger trees, their swollen buds glowing in the sun, their over-hanging branches throwing a delicate lace of shadow onto the pavement. He kept walking to a set of lights. Traffic was heavier here. He passed a diner and a convenience store, then he came to a Church where he stopped and stared longingly at the people in the parking lot.

The People's Pentecostal Assembly was a great, octagonal structure with a sprawling asphalt roof and a steeple that ramped up at one end like a launch pad into heaven. Jen always called it the mothership whenever they drove passed. She called the Pentecostals zealots and holy rollers but they looked like normal people to him.

A service must have just been ending because the parking lot was full of cars and there were families walking back to their vehicles. A crowd was gathered near the front doors, talking and laughing with one another. He kept staring, envying their belonging, their togetherness. They all looked so clean and fresh in their suits and dresses; he could see the preacher in his robes with everyone clustering around him . . . and he thought that he would like to be part of it, that he would like to join something like that, something wholesome and good, then quickly he remembered the monk in France and how everyone had made fun of him. Matty the Carthusian Brotherfucker, they'd said like this feeling he'd felt had been nothing at all, as if a guy like him wasn't even capable of having that kind of experience. It was all just drinking and fucking, Jen had said about his trips and the things that he had seen and experienced, that was what she said about their marriage too, about his love and their struggles and all that it had created; she said that it had just been about fucking, that all he'd wanted was to fuck her like it was the only thing a man could feel.

A woman with two small children was walking towards him on the way back to her car and he smiled at them, tentatively, with the corners of his mouth as they passed him on the sidewalk. "Nice day," he offered, but the woman pulled the children close and hurried away, the children looking back over their shoulders with worried blueberry eyes. He must smell bad, he realized. He must look terrible.

Despair rose in him. "Doesn't it bother you," Jen had snarled before she left, "that you're waiting for someone to die?" and yes!yes!yes! it bothered him, all of it bothered him, it was all so fucked up and he was sorry but how? How did you get back? How did you make it okay? You ruined my life, she'd said when she found out she was pregnant. My life is fucking ruined and he'd said I'm sorry I'm sorry I'm sorry but she'd said that sorry wasn't good enough. She'd said sorry doesn't change things. His head began to pound. He turned away from the Church and started walking. He'd go back to the house, he decided. He'd go back and finish it all off, all of it, he'd draw the blinds and clear the liquor cabinet of everything because what was the point? What was the point of trying if you've already been condemned?

Then his phone rang. He fished it out of his pants pocket. Annika.

"Hello?"

"Matt. Michael," she said. Her voice sounded small and muffled, like she was talking through water.

"Annika? Is that you, Annika?"

"Yes, it's me. How are you?"

He felt confused. Why was she calling him? She'd been so angry before. He'd yelled at her, insinuated that she should die. He stood on the sunny sidewalk with his head pounding. "Good. I'm super-good," he heard himself say. "And you? How are you?"

There was a long silence. He thought he could hear the sea in the background, then there were strange muffled noises. "Hey, are you alright? What's going on?" She was crying, he realized. Crying and struggling to speak.

"I'm sick," she managed. "I don't feel well. Ooooo I really don't feel well at all." Her voice rose with every word in such a way that there was no mistaking the realness, the deadly seriousness of her panic. He felt his scalp crawl, the ceiling of the world pulling upwards. He remembered her kindness, how terribly vulnerable she'd been. "What's going on? Do you need a doctor? I can call a doctor for you." He hadn't meant to harm her.

"No, I can't . . . I screwed up. I made the wrong choice. I made all the wrong choices. I can't go back to the doctor . . ."

He wanted to help her; he could feel her panic through the phone. He wracked his brain. "Barry. What about Barry? I could call him; he could come over."

"No. no." She was sobbing now. "Why did you come here? Why did you pretend to like me? You didn't have to pretend to like me."

"Annika," he said. His heart was bursting, overflowing, the tidal wave crashing, crashing down. "Look, I've been wanting to talk to you. I feel terrible about what I did. I did like you, very much, I do like you, that part of it was real, you have to know that. I didn't mean for it to . . . happen like that. I just . . ." He was crying too now, tears falling down his face.

"I'm dying. I think I'm dying."

"Oh no. No no no."

There was a long pause. "I guess you'll get your money after all," she said with a short laugh, like she was trying to make light.

"I don't care about the money. The money doesn't matter to me anymore."

"It's over anyways. There's no point in keeping on. Some things are better quick, you know. Hamish used to say that pain is better quick, like ripping a Band-Aid."

He felt cold. Her voice was different now, strange and hard. "Hey, Annika? Don't do anything crazy, okay? I can . . . Look,

I'm going to come down there and we can talk. Annika? Annika? I'm going to come and see you, okay?"

She was gone. He stood there with the phone in his hand. What did she mean ripping a Band-Aid? Then he knew. He started to run. All his life, all his stupid dumb life he'd just let things happen; he'd just sort of slid along, afraid of choosing, of being guilty, but this was too much, this was too far: he would not, he could not let this happen. He sprinted through the streets like a wild man and was surprised by how strong he felt, how suddenly alive.

CHAPTER TWENTY-THREE

Why had she called why had she called why had she called? She had called Matt Campbell. Matt Campbell was coming. She wanted him to come and did not want him to come and was full of hatred and hopeful all at once. Her insides hurt badly now and she lay for a while curled up on the couch. Her thoughts drifted in and out. I'm dying dying dying she thought death is on its way but she couldn't die yet because there was something she still had to do. What was it? She didn't know. She couldn't remember. She managed to stand and went to the window where she stared out at the flat grey sea and then the sea seemed to blur, the shoreline blended together with the sky and it was all a palette of grey light and she let her mind go into it and she wandered over fields and firescapes and city streets and thought she might rest, she felt an overwhelming urge to rest and then D'Arcy, her foreman when she'd been firefighting, was there clapping his hands with a whistle around his neck, egging her on: Up! Up! Up! You're a fighter, Anni! and she was a fighter even though no one wanted her to be and D'Arcy winked and disappeared in a hole in the ground and she clenched her guts like she knew how and pried herself from the window.

He was coming here. Matt Campbell was coming here to get the money after causing the cancer to come back. He was coming down here to protect his big payout because he was afraid that she would do it, afraid that she would make the final choice. That was the only way out of the contract, she remembered, to make the final choice like a bullet to the brain. If Matt Campbell wanted the money than the viator had to go naturally, the viator had to drift away like sea ice, docile, like a little lamb; the viator couldn't choose, no, the viator couldn't go out with a bang and she was sick of all these pricks running around making life complicated and miserable when all she'd ever wanted was peace.

She labored up the stairs. Her footsteps on the floor were hollow, decisive. Yes. Decisive. A decision had been made, she thought. A choice had been made and she remembered her brother Jonathan full of righteous fire in the parking lot of the forest service compound trying to get her to come home. A choice, Anni! Your choice! he'd hissed and her whole life was a scattering of choices like genes like seeds and Sasha had said there was peace but she didn't feel it because Matt Campbell had come here and ruined it and now she was trapped in the momentum of the choices like someone in a current is trapped, she was in the river of the choices now and in the river one must stay the course.

She shook her head. Focus, she told herself. Matt Campbell was coming. Michael was on his way. This was what was happening. She had to be ready.

She went into the bedroom and went to the drawer where the gun was. She took it out and held it like a toy a deadly serious toy. He wouldn't get the money; she wouldn't let him get it. She remembered the man with the quick blue eyes and the way the air had quickened right before she'd signed and how she'd known he was a crook by the quickening and the heartbeat in her fingers on the pen and his sharp little intake of breath right before she'd signed.

He would get nothing. Not a cent. She would make sure of it.

She took the sheets from the bed and stood before the mirror. The person there was yellow. The skin, the whites of the eyes all yellow and sunken and sexless with the ghost of a beautiful woman in the cut of the cheeks. She hung the sheet over the mirror and the image went away. There, she thought. *There.* Her mother would be happy. She wished she had gone back to see her mother; she wished she'd gone back and told her parents that she loved them and seen her brother and his children she'd heard he had children but had never met them and she wished there'd been catharsis and atonement and a rightness and the people in her life all around her and her lying in bed in the clean bright air lying in the clean bright sheets but she was out of time and she'd chosen wrong and they could not forgive it and this was the consequence and one had to live with the consequences of one's actions like seeds in the poison ground. Matt Campbell needed to be made to understand, one way or another to understand, but she wasn't about to damn anyone because the last thing the world needed was another soul flapping about like a crazed bird. There, mother. *There.* This is for you. She thought of purple fireweed blowing on a burned-out hillside and her mother in the yard with her skirts whipping up around her and her father, tight-lipped and angry, turning away and Michael, sweet Michael, she remembered, stroking her hair saying forgive me forgive me forgive me.

Matt Campbell would be here soon if he was coming at all and there were still choices to be made and she didn't want to be caught inside the cottage before she could make them so she took the gun and went back downstairs where she covered the mirror in the bathroom with a blanket from the couch, then she poured dried cat food for Zebedee and placed multiple bowls around the cottage. She did the same for water. Zebedee placed a paw on her shin and meowed. "I'm sorry little friend," she said, "Barry will be a good Dad." She bent though it hurt her and kissed him on the head.

She went outside and locked the door behind her. Leaving the cat wrenched her guts and she sobbed so hard her vision tunneled and she had to sit down on the porch and she sat there sobbing.

Sasha had said there would be peace and that it came for everyone but it wasn't coming because he'd ruined it, because Matt Campbell had come down here and ruined it just waltzing in pretending he cared and then expecting her to just let go, just let go like ripping a Band-Aid, Hamish said: just! just! just! Always just as if life were just so easy and he would be made to see it wasn't just anything, it wasn't just go out and make some friends and it wasn't just be positive and it wasn't just get over it and it wasn't just accept that a little poking and prodding was necessary because she was a fighter a FIGHTER and God had spoken in her heart she swore it was true and when her head was on his chest his voice had rumbled like thunder and the words didn't matter only his arms around her and he had called it letting go.

She struggled to her feet. Focus. Focus, she said out loud. There was something she had to do. She took the gun and walked into the woods near the drive where the arbutus trees stretched and twisted above her in surreal arches spanning grey light. Their old leaves littered the forest floor, the yellows and browns scattering like genes or choices or seeds. Salal scraped against her legs, then she lay down behind a log. From here she could see the cottage and the beach. He would be a while still, but she didn't want to get caught at the cottage and then have him arrive. Barry and Susan had been snooping lately because they were worried about her. Even Helmut was snooping, Helmut who said he'd never judge kept coming around and asking if she needed anything. They might come here and stop her before she had a chance to choose, before she could make the right choice and then it would be over.

Cold came up from the ground and went into her body. She lay on her back and stared up at the light through the branches and her eyelids grew heavy and the edges of the world began to blur then she shook her head. A fighter. Boo-yah. She'd done the hose carry in under five minutes, she remembered.

Time passed.

Then there was the sound of a car creeping up the gravel. She tensed. She clicked the safety off the gun as Helmut had shown her; Helmut hadn't asked her what it was for only made sure the serial number was filed off so no one could blame him and she liked that about him, that he would think to file the serial number. He was a practical man, sentimentality was dead to him and she understood what that was like.

The vehicle came into view. It was Cosmo and Sasha's minivan. Animal Matters Therapy it said in white letters on the side. Sasha was gone to India for palliative yoga but she had put her partner Cosmo on the snooping trail like everyone else, snooping for the chance to round her up and poke her and prod her in the dead and airless space and talk to her like a plastic surgery robot about how it would all be okay. She wouldn't let them do it. The van stopped next to the cottage and Cosmo got out. He opened the back door to let Max and Kia out. Dogs! Annika sucked in her breath. If they were to find her here . . . The dogs bounded off towards the beach. Cosmo went to the door. He knocked then tried the handle. He cupped his hands to the glass and peered inside.

"Annika? Annika?"

Go home, Cosmo, she thought. You don't need to be here. Even from a distance she could see the concern on his elvish face.

He walked around the cottage, peering into the windows along the side, then he came back around to the driveway. He stooped and peered into the car, then stood and frowned. He looked out to the beach, then down the lane. She flattened herself even lower to the ground.

Finally, he whistled for the dogs and they came sprinting back across the grass, then another vehicle pulled in and parked next to the van. A man jumped out. He seemed desperate and out of breath.

The dogs came up to him but he ignored him. "Is Annika around? Is she here?" the man yelled at Cosmo.

It took her a moment to realize it was him. It was Matt Campbell. He'd transformed into a wild man with a silver beard and dirty clothes and hair standing on end. "Is Annika here?" he demanded again.

"I knocked but no one answered. Her car's still here though so she can't be too far. Is something wrong?"

"Jesus!" Matt Campbell exclaimed and just like that he kicked the door in. He literally broke it off the hinges. "Annika? Annika?" he hollered, "Are you alright?" His urgency startled her. He was like a super hero in a movie, the way he broke down the door. Maybe he . . . Focus now. The river of choices could not go back.

The two men were inside the cottage yelling her name but the dogs were now in the drive. Max, the black lab, stood still and sniffed the air. He turned to stare at where she was hidden then wagged his tail. She held her breath. They would find her. It was done. She wasn't ready yet for the final choice, she wasn't ready to do it.

Then a flash of silver streaked out of the cottage. Zebedee! Max and Kia went racing after him. Zebedee her savior.

Now Matt Campbell and Cosmo came out in the drive again, talking to one another with serious expressions. She couldn't hear what they were saying. Cosmo nodded several times then whistled for the dogs, got back into the van and peeled out of the drive.

Matt Campbell stayed. He looked around then went down to the beach. She saw him crane his neck in both directions then he sat down on a log and faced the sea.

He seemed so alone as he sat there, completely motionless and staring out at the grey that she almost felt sorry for him. She was filled with despair. She wanted to scream at him, talk to him, kill him, hold him, she didn't know what she wanted just that he needed to understand and that no one understood or had ever understood and she was hiding and wanting to be seen and she rose in the forest with the gun in her hand and held it out in front of her and it pulled her towards his silhouette the way a divining rod will lead you to water. You, you, you, she thought.

She came to the place where the grass stopped. She stepped onto the small round stones. He turned. She came around in front of him. He didn't understand at first then he did. He stood up from where he was sitting.

She raised the gun. "You," she said. Her arms were shaking terribly.

He held his hands out to the side with the palms up like he was saying the Lord's prayer. He didn't raise them in front to protect himself, he raised them to the sides. He said, "I'm sorry."

She blinked. She pointed the gun towards him then she put it to her temple.

"No, no," he said, "please no."

Then she pointed it at him again, then at herself again. "I'm sick," she said, then the world seemed to spin and she slumped to the ground and everything went grey then white then grey again and she didn't know where she was or if she had died. There was the sky white and reeling above her and cold stones against the side of her face and she was afraid because she didn't understand what was happening and she started to cry.

Then she felt herself being lifted up by a pair of hands. She felt herself being lifted and carried across a wide, open space and she heard a man's voice rumbling through his chest, it's okay, you're okay, I'm with you and for a moment the confusion left her for his hands on her body were steady and strong.

When she woke again she was in her bed and Matt Campbell was there, in her room. She told him she hated him. She told him not to leave. He made phone calls; she could hear him on the phone and then a nurse came, one of Sasha's friends, and the pain went away for a while. She heard the nurse talking quietly to Matt Campbell downstairs then he came up and sat in the corner of her room and just sat there.

People came and went. There was a nurse. A doctor from the hospice. Matt Campbell slept on her couch and did not leave. There was such sadness in his face, such pleading when he looked at her that she felt sorry for him, in spite of everything he'd done. She went to sleep and woke up and he was still there.

Sometimes, he sat by her bedside and moistened her lips with a towel. Sometimes, he brushed her hair back from her face. Sometimes she was angry and told him to go away and he did go, but never far. She'd hear him downstairs, talking to the nurse, puttering around, making tea. Sometimes, she remembered how they'd made love and she missed him even though he was there.

Days went by. Sometimes she thought about the contract and the creepy stuff he'd done, but somehow her old hurts, her old angers didn't seem to matter anymore, only the moment, the people, the warm caring hands. Matt Campbell sat in her room on the hard boards day after day, looking so much like a castaway in his dirty clothes and unshaved face that she was filled with a softness, a desire to help him. She remembered him stroking her hair. She remembered he whispered forgive me. She held out her hand and he came over and took it and she said, "It's okay. I'm not mad anymore," and she saw his face utterly transformed in that moment and it gave her peace to see it, as if in this one small act of forgiveness lived the forgiveness of all things: of self, of world, of others, and she thought about the strange journey of her life, how it had narrowed down, funneled her towards this one final choice and she was no longer afraid; she felt grateful that she could do this one last thing. She said to Matt Campbell, "I forgive you," and she knew by the look on his face that she had chosen well.

And in the end, the peace that Sasha had talked about did come. It did. Sometimes she slept and sometimes she woke, always in the safe, warm bed with the quilt overtop of her. When she ran her fingers over it she thought of her mother and her family and the farm. She drifted in and out and there was the crackling of the fire at night and the sound of the waves and slow, steady breathing in the room.

Sometimes there were faces that she recognized: a trembling man with long white hair, a fat woman with a beautiful voice, a fairy goddess in a white dress, a sharp faced man with silver hair and there were others too and though she couldn't find the names she was glad they were there.

Sometimes there were animals that came and pressed their warm bodies against her and she touched their fur and smiled and there was the gentle weight of a sleeping cat that sat atop her feet and kept them warm and the sound of the heat in the pipe tat tat tat like a small creature climbing.

And there was a man also who was often in the room and sometimes she thought he was her father and sometimes she thought he was Hamish and other times she knew him to be Michael and she was glad that he was there.

Then one day there was a pain inside her and when she cried out the man's hands were there, warm and dry and steady. They stroked her forehead, pulling gently, smoothing her hair back from her brow the way a breeze does when you turn to face it. Shhh . . . Shhh . . . he said and it was a whispering sound like wind through the trees shhh it was a soft and streaming sound like water rushing over stones shhh like grass that bends silver and tosses and shifts and is restless and beautiful shhh and she found there were spaces in the sound, bright white spaces between the threads of the sound shhh shhh and that she could part them, she could part them like curtains to reveal an extraordinary brightness and she found that she wanted to go towards it, she wanted to go, she was ready to go and there was nothing holding her back anymore.

CHAPTER TWENTY-FOUR

After Annika died, Matt let his life fall apart. The bank took his house and Jen filed for divorce; he didn't fight any of it.

With no job, no family and no house to go back to, he decided to stay in Saltery Bay. It seemed like the right thing to do. It was just a short ferry ride to his in-laws so he was able to see Jacob more often and he liked it there: the smallness of the town, the slower pace. He took a job as a bartender at the hotel and rented a basement suite from an elderly lady in exchange for maintenance on her property. The transition happened quite naturally; there was no fighting or striving or anxiety; the pieces simply slid into place. He liked working at the bar; he was good at it and quickly established himself as a quiet, competent worker, someone that did his job and wouldn't judge if you happened to find yourself alone with a pint and your problems on a Sunday afternoon.

When the off-season rolled around, he took other odd jobs to help pay for his rent and child support payments. Cosmo, the man he'd met in Annika's driveway, and his partner Sasha were converting an old estate property they'd purchased into a private hospice and they needed someone to help with the renovations. He made himself available whenever he could. The location was beautiful and they paid him well. They said that any friend of Annika's was a friend of theirs. What little extra money he managed to save, he sent to Jen and Jacob.

Jen and Jacob! It was bittersweet, in a way, to see how much they were thriving without him; yet, even though his heart was broken, Matt kept his rule: he would not let his own son be torn in two. He allowed Jen to make whatever arrangements suited her best and, after a few months had gone by, he found that she was more than fair. The darkness that had hung over her since

Jacob's birth finally seemed to be lifting. She was back at school part-time finishing her degree and helping her father build cabinets on the side. While reluctant at first, she eventually encouraged Matt to visit and even joked with him about being a resentful teenaged Mom one time when he came to pick Jacob up and he thought, maybe, that he heard a bit of softness in her tone, so he joked back about being a bankrupt alcoholic, and, without warning, they both burst out laughing. It felt good, even if it didn't change anything. Jacob was thriving too, spending lots of time outdoors with his uncle and his grandparents.

Time passed. A kind of quiet crept into Matt's life then, a kind of greyness. It was not a bad thing. There was some peace to it, like a grey and colourless day when the air is still, the kind of day that passes quietly without event, waiting for tomorrow. His life was simple, spare. When he wasn't working, he spent his time walking and thinking and reading. He'd never been much of a reader but, since he no longer owned a television and couldn't afford cable, he picked it up and read anything and everything he found at the thrift store: crime novels and history books, but mostly, he liked reading about religion. He liked how it calmed his mind.

And yet, despite this newfound peace, Matt wasn't entirely at ease. A sense of unfinished business still hung over him; the liquor still called to him late at night. He managed to stay sober, but barely. It was because of the lie, he knew. To everyone on the island, he was still Michael and he worried constantly that someone who knew him as Matt would show up and then he didn't know how he would explain it. He didn't know if he had the strength. All the people he'd met at Annika's bedside, except for Cosmo and Sasha, he avoided whenever he saw them in town. They were always friendly and never failed to tell him how thankful they were, yet he couldn't quite face them, couldn't quite look them in the eye.

Then one day, about a year and a half after Annika's death, Barry, the Trembler, came into the bar. Matt barely recognized him; his decline had been so rapid. Barry looked like an old man now, stooped and shaking, leaning heavily on his cane.

Matt came around to help him when he saw him struggling with the door. He took Barry by the arm and walked him over to a stool, surprised at how small and frail the old man felt under his hands; it made him think of Annika, how tiny she'd been at the end, how vulnerable. "Barry! It's good to see you," he said brightly, trying to disguise his sadness at the old man's decline. "What can I get for you today?"

"A b-b-beer," came the halting response as Barry settled himself down.

It was late afternoon and the bar was empty. The light from the windows was gold and warm where it lay on the floor. It was odd for the old man to be here, Matt thought as he poured: Barry wasn't a drinker and it was early yet for dinner.

He slid the pint across. "How've you been?" he asked, trying not to cringe as the glass teetered and tottered on its excruciating journey from the bar to Barry's lips. "I don't see you around very often."

Barry brought the glass down, rivulets of beer running down the sides where they'd spilled over the rim. His trembling lips were covered in foam. Matt pretended not to see; he picked up a rag and started wiping down the bottles on the bar behind him.

"I kn-kn-know who y-y-you are."

Matt froze. He felt cold, unable to move or speak. "I'm not sure what you're talking about," he managed after a few long seconds, then he turned and began to polish the glasses that were drying on top of the dishwasher. He didn't look up.

"Th-the l-letter. Th-the viatical s-s-s-settlement," Barry said.

Matt kept shining the glasses. He could feel a blush creeping up the back of his neck.

"I f-f-figured it out. I d-d-did some snooping, M-m-matt C-c-campbell."

"She knew who I was, you know," he blurted out. "I wasn't lying to her, at the end." His hands were busy, moving quickly, running the rag expertly around the rims faster and faster. "I never saw that money. I didn't make any money off it." He was speaking quickly, the words loud, desperate, his face on fire.

"Sh-sh-she w-w-was a-a good friend."

He wanted to die, to run away, to be anywhere but here. "You probably won't believe me, but I did care about her. That part was real."

There was a long silence. Matt ran out of glasses and started wiping down the sink, the tabasco sauce, the taps, the bar, anything. "I'll leave," he said, not looking up. Leaving, at this point, seemed easier than facing it. "I'll get out of here and you'll never have to look at my face again. None of you will ever have to . . ."

"D-d-don't," Barry interrupted.

Now, Matt did look up to find that the old man was staring at him with a kind of sad smile on his lopsided face. Despite his trembling, his eyes were steady and clear. "M-m-maybe I b-b-believe you. A-a-annika w-w-was a smart p-p-person."

Matt put down the rag. He hung his head and leaned against the bar.

"We h-h-have a group," Barry said. His speech was getting slower, more broken, as if it were an enormous physical effort for him to continue at all. "It h-h-h-helps t-t-to talk s-s-sometimes."

"I can't. I couldn't do that."

"I kn-kn-know it h-h-helps b-b-because I w-w-wasn't always a g-g-good p-p-person myself."

Matt shook his head. "I couldn't do it. I don't think any of those people could forgive me."

Now Barry motioned for Matt to come closer and Matt was suddenly terrified, afraid of what he might say. The old man reached out and grabbed his arm, holding him there, his grip surprisingly strong. "N-n-not th-them," Barry stuttered, staring into Matt's eyes. Now he let go and poked a trembling finger deep into Matt's chest. "N-n-not th-them. Y-y-you."

ACKNOWLEDGEMENTS

Viaticum has taken me seven years to write, edit and publish. Carving out the time to do so has been no small task and one that I never would have accomplished without the help of many people. I would like to extend my warmest thanks to the following: my husband Pierre Hungr for his unwavering support and belief; my parents James and Lucille Fitzgerald for their faith in me and for giving me such a start in life; my good friends Melanie DiQuinzio and Sarah Fuller for taking the time in this busy world to read a work in progress; Chris Needham of Now Or Never Publishing for taking a chance on an unknown; author John Metcalf for his mentorship and advice; the many volunteers at Vancouver Writer's Fest and Salmon Arm Word on the Lake, two festivals that have provided me with a much-needed sense of community as I've wrestled with this solitary pursuit; and all the people over the years who've expressed interest and enthusiasm in my work: to be able to share it with you now is an honour and a privilege.